PENG...

THE RUNAWA...

Paul Davies is lecturer in applied mathematics at King's College, London, and was formerly visiting fellow at the Institute of Astronomy, Cambridge. He is cosmology correspondent of *Nature* and author of *The Physics of Time Asymmetry* and *Space and Time in the Modern Universe*.

THE RUNAWAY UNIVERSE

Paul Davies

PENGUIN BOOKS

Penguin Books Ltd, Harmondsworth,
Middlesex, England
Penguin Books, 625 Madison Avenue,
New York, New York 10022, U.S.A.
Penguin Books Australia Ltd, Ringwood,
Victoria, Australia
Penguin Books Canada Limited, 2801 John Street,
Markham, Ontario, Canada L3R 1B4
Penguin Books (N.Z.) Ltd, 182–190 Wairau Road,
Auckland 10, New Zealand

First published in the United States of America by
Harper & Row, Publishers, Inc., 1978
Published in Penguin Books by arrangement with
Harper & Row, Publishers, Inc., 1980

LIBRARY OF CONGRESS CATALOGING IN PUBLICATION DATA
Davies, P. C. W.
The runaway universe.
Reprint of the 1978 ed. published by Harper & Row,
New York.
Includes index.
1. Cosmology. I. Title.
[QB981.D27 1980]   523.1'01   79-21716
ISBN 0 14 00.5366 2

Printed in the United States of America by
Offset Paperback Mfrs., Inc., Dallas, Pennsylvania
Set in Sabon

Contents

Illustrations

Preface

Modern science advances so rapidly that the gulf in understanding between the specialist and the ordinary person can seem unbridgeable. Yet recent discoveries in fundamental research have such profound implications for all people that some effort at communication must be made. Never has this been more true than in the subject of cosmology — the study of the structure and evolution of the universe as a whole. We are all products of the universe, and our future is inextricably bound up with the forces of nature that shape our environment, near and far. Questions concerning the creation of the cosmos, the development and disintegration of order in the universe and the end of the world, have long dominated the thinking of philosophers and theologians. Now, with the tremendous technological advances of the twentieth century, scientists too can contribute much to our understanding of these fundamental issues. Discoveries made in the last few years have cast new light on the nature of space, time and matter, and for the first time enable a fairly detailed outline of the birth, life and death of the universe to be given with some confidence.

I have intended this book to be more than just a description of developments in modern physics and astronomy. Instead I have tried to show how all physical systems, from a man to a galaxy, share the common, and somewhat enigmatic, quality of organization. The laws of nature which govern the appearance and disappearance of organized structure and activity are known in great generality and are very basic to modern physics. Using this general framework, a picture of the

Preface

future of the universe can be given. Much of this picture is based on conventional astrophysics: the processes which bring about star and planetary formation, the behaviour of the sun, the explosion of super-novae, the implosion of burnt out stars to form neutron stars and black holes. These topics I have described in some detail, because many are well understood and uncontentious. However, our future contains more than just astrophysics, and a book which purports to indulge in cosmic futurology would be incomplete without some speculation about the role of life, mankind and other possible intelligent communities. In particular, the arrival of technology in the universe promises new epochs of intelligent control over our destiny, which transcends ordinary astrophysics. In these sections of the book I have gone beyond established science and given a personal view of what I feel may be the impact of technology on the structure of the world around us. This is intended to be entertaining, educational and, above all, thought-provoking.

I should like to thank Dr D. C. Robinson and Professor I. W. Roxburgh for making valuable comments about the subject matter of the book, and for many fruitful discussions; the Royal Observatory, Edinburgh, and the Royal Astronomical Society, Burlington House, for their help in supplying photographs; and Mrs M. Woodcock for typing the manuscript.

Paul Davies
King's College London

Note on technical terms

In preparing the text I wanted to avoid being too abstract in dealing with subtle and abstruse scientific concepts which are vital for an understanding of the subject. Where possible I have attempted to use analogies of more familiar things, but the reader should be careful about extending these analogies too far. I have also been mindful of difficulties over technical terminology. The use of the word 'mass' may be misleading: as a physicist I have used it in the sense of, roughly, quantity of matter — the condition of the matter (such as its degree of compression, or its density) is unimportant.

The unit 'billion' often occurs, and is used as the U.S. billion, i.e. one thousand million.

Finally, when temperatures are discussed, the Celsius (centigrade) scale is implied, except in the discussion of very low temperatures, for which degrees absolute are more appropriate. When this is the case it will be mentioned explicitly; zero absolute is about $-273°$ C.

1.   The emerging universe

Modern science has shown that the elaborate organization and activity of the world around us cannot always have existed, nor can it continue for ever. The universe may appear to be unchanging over a human lifetime. but it is in reality slowly and inexorably degenerating. The nature of its fate can be predicted from astronomical observation, which may soon be able to determine whether all cosmic activity will eventually run down and cease, or whether the whole universe will be overtaken by a holocaust which will cause it to collapse out of existence.

Perhaps the most fascinating feature of the physical world is the way in which matter and energy are not arranged randomly, but in a hierarchy of complex organization. Wherever we look, from the deepest recesses of the atomic nucleus to the far-flung galaxies, we encounter order. Even on Earth, biological systems, human society and technology, animate and inanimate matter are examples of the highly structured and organized activity which make the world we inhabit so interesting and exciting. The universe is indeed a very special place, but where did all this organization come from? This question must be answered before the impending disintegration of the world order, and the fate of the universe, can be understood.

In the coming chapters we shall explore in detail how the universe began and evolved its present arrangement, and examine the physical principles which regulate order and disorder in nature. It emerges from this analysis that the inevitable demise of cosmic order is written into the laws of physics, and could only be averted by assuming bizarre departures from accepted theory.

For centuries, questions of this sort have been tackled within the framework of religion and philosophy. Now, increasingly, science is playing an important part in these conjectures and speculations, revolutionizing thinking about the really fundamental aspects of existence. The science of the universe as a whole is called cosmology. Astronomy is the study of systems beyond the Earth — planets, stars, galaxies and so forth — but cosmology deals with the overall patterns and systematic properties of the universe. Cosmologists make use of astronomical techniques and discoveries to gain information about remote regions of the cosmos, and so build up a comprehensive picture of its large-scale structure and evolution. Actual observation and measurement, being the cornerstone of all science, is especially important in cosmology where opinions are strongly held and emotional prejudices abound. In tackling these challenging concepts about the universe, it is difficult to separate fact from assumption, or to remove religious and philosophical bias. In spite of this, very great progress in our understanding of the nature of the cosmos has been made in recent years, so that the basic framework for a cosmic life cycle is now available.

When science is turned to the subject of cosmology, it makes three important contributions. Firstly, it brings concrete information about the world from careful experiment and observation. Secondly, it injects precision into what may otherwise be a rather vague collection of ideas, by demanding definite numerical values for measured quantities and insisting that these measurements make sense when interpreted according to the mathematical theory in use. Thirdly, and perhaps most importantly in cosmology, the theory furnishes the conceptual foundation for the study and understanding of the observations. This is important because many scientific advances are made, not by science giving an answer to a question, but by determining what is the appropriate question to ask. Many modern theories in physics have shown that the old way of looking at things is misguided or even meaningless. The whole framework of scientific cosmology is constructed on a conceptual basis provided by modern physics, and the modern cosmologist's view of the nature of the universe is very different from the traditional religious perspective.

The word 'universe' or 'cosmos' means different things to different people. In science, the universe is supposed to mean the totality of physical things; not only all matter, in the form of planets, stars, nebulae, black holes, and all radiations, such as light, heat, X-rays, gravity waves and so on, but all of space and time as well — in short, everything that is physically relevant. When we talk of the fate of the universe, ultimately this refers to the fate of all these things, including space and time. The universe, however, possesses a quality which does not come within its definition, yet is the key element in our emotional attitude to the nature of the cosmos; it is the fundamental feature about which we really care. This quality is best described as *organization*. The world we inhabit is not merely a jumble of entities, a collection of physical components interacting in a haphazard fashion, but rather a systematically structured, highly ordered arrangement of matter and energy at several levels of size and complexity. The universe as such is sterile, but the orderly universe we observe is full of interesting activity and evolution. This is what is meant by the world order, and one of the great questions of science has been the problem of where this order has come from, how it is sustained, and whether it will collapse.

Order is the linking theme of this book. It encompasses systems as diverse as galaxies, crystals and human civilization. The scientific study of order as an abstract concept has made great progress in the last century, and the laws and principles controlling the growth and disintegration of order are now well understood. When these principles are combined with modern knowledge of astronomy and cosmology, a comprehensive account can be given of the creation, evolution and end of the organized cosmos that we now observe. It turns out that the collapse of world order is tightly interwoven with the creation of the universe and the processes which characterized its early moments. The foundations for the structures which we observe in the universe around us now were laid in the first seconds after the beginning, and much of the rest of this book will deal with the details of this primeval phase, in particular the way in which the orderly arrangement of the present epoch has arisen from primeval chaos.

The pinnacle of world order in our experience is human society and technology. Man fits into the cosmic organization not just as an observer, but as an integral part in a hierarchy of complexity in the arrangement of matter and energy. In the later chapters we shall see that intelligent organisms, technology and machine intelligence may well become a force for controlling and restructuring the universe comparable in power with gravity or nuclear physics. Being subject to the laws of physics, intelligent communities, human or otherwise, must eventually succumb to the fate which awaits all order. Human history is a story of struggle to preserve order against the natural tendency to collapse into disorder, and in a sense this is the history of the cosmos. Our own fate is inextricably bound up with that of the universe to which the same laws apply.

In everyday life the supreme example of order is human society. It is usual to distinguish the products of human intelligence from the products of nature — we even call human products 'artificial' to separate them from 'natural' things — but from a scientific point of view human behaviour and industry is only another example of the organized activity found throughout the animate and inanimate world. A super-advanced civilization might regard our intelligence as so low that our achievements in modifying the planet we live on would be seen as little different from the changes which occurred in the atmosphere when green plants first appeared on Earth and began to make oxygen as a byproduct of photosynthesis.

For many people cosmic organization ends a few miles above the ground. The universe beyond has very little impact on the conscious-ness of modern industrial society, and although people are vaguely aware of the stars and realize that the Earth is supposed to be insignifi-cant and diminutive in the vastness of space, they have little conception of the hierarchy of order as it extends in scale beyond the narrow confines of our planet.

The Earth belongs to a collection of nine planets which orbit a star that we call the sun. The whole group is called the solar system, and even though it is the smallest astronomical unit to which we belong, its size is still too large to visualize. To help in gauging the immense distances involved in astronomy, it is usual to employ a large unit of some sort such as the distance travelled by light in a certain time, usually a second or a year. Light travels very fast, about 186,000 miles every second, and so one light second is 186,000 miles and one light year is about six million million miles. In these units the solar system measures several light hours across, and the Earth orbits about eight light minutes (93 million miles) from the sun.

The stars which are visible in the night sky are other suns, their apparent dimness being due to their extreme remoteness. The nearest star, in the constellation of Centaurus, is over four light years away. In spite of the superficially haphazard way in which the visible stars are distributed across the sky, they are in fact organized into a gigantic disc-shaped system. Early observers of the sky were familiar with the wide luminous band which may be seen on a clear night, stretching from horizon to horizon. The ancient Greeks used the name 'galaxias' to describe its milky appearance, and supposed that it was a road to heaven. In the seventeenth century the Italian scientist Galileo Galilei turned a telescope on the sky and among the many astronomical objects he scrutinized was this milky band of light. Even with the modest power of this early instrument, Galileo was able to see that the galaxias of the Greeks consisted of myriads of stars, too numerous and too faint to be distinguished with the naked eye. Astonomers soon came to realize that the sun, and all the stars visible in the night sky to the naked eye, are just a small local group among an enormous whirlpool of a hundred billion stars. This great system, now called the Milky Way galaxy, is a cosmic colossus of huge dimensions, measuring about one hundred thousand light years (nearly a billion billion miles) in diameter.

With the invention of telescopes astronomers soon discovered that stars are not the only luminous objects in space. There are also some strange-looking patches of light. One of these, in the constellation of Andromeda, named after the beautiful maiden of Greek mythology who was chained to a rock by her parents as a sacrifice to the sea dragon, can just be discerned on a clear night by people with keen eyesight. The same feature appears on star charts constructed several centuries ago by Arabian astronomers. In 1611 a German astronomer called Simon Marius turned a small telescope on the object and observed the delicate tracery of a wispy, luminous cloud 'like a candle at night seen through a horn'. In the following years many more fuzzy objects were discovered with telescopes, though none are so bright and large as the one in Andromeda. These new objects were a mystery to early astronomers: they are clearly not stars, although some of them seem to have stars imbedded in them. Nor are they obviously distributed in any particular arrangement relative to the Milky Way.

The name 'nebula' was invented to describe the fuzzy patches, and in the early nineteenth century the French astronomer Charles Messier set about cataloguing them. The reason for this interest was somewhat negative. In those days great attention was being directed towards discovering and observing comets — tenuous bodies consisting of rock, gas and dust which orbit the solar system on erratic trajectories and sometimes, when close to the sun, sprout a spectacular luminous tail which may stretch conspicuously across the morning or evening sky. Comet-hunting has long been a favourite activity of astronomers, and in the previous centuries it was taken very seriously. The purpose of cataloguing the nebulae was to enable the comet-seekers to distinguish these stationary bodies from similar looking, but rapidly moving comets. In spite of the methodical cataloguing of nebulae, astronomers were quite unclear about their nature even as recently as 1920, and opinions differed over whether these large clouds of gas are on the edge of the Milky Way or whether they lie outside the galaxy altogether.

The first reliable information about the constitution of the nebulae came in 1924, after the construction of what was then the world's largest scientific instrument — the 100-inch diameter telescope installed at Mount Wilson in California. This new facility, combined with improved photographic technology, enabled the American astronomer Edwin Hubble to scrutinize the Andromeda nebula in the sort of detail that had never been seen before, enabling the tenuous filaments of this mysterious object to be resolved into individual stars. Mankind's perspective on the universe was increased a millionfold, for the fact that the Andromeda nebula was seen to consist of ordinary stars proved that it lies far outside our galaxy. In fact it is an entire galaxy in its own right, equally as big as the whole Milky Way galaxy, but so far away that only very large telescopes can reveal the individual stars that it contains.

Soon it was realized that many more of the nebulae are actually very distant galaxies, Andromeda being among those nearest to us. Any doubts about the extra-galactic location of Andromeda were dispelled when Hubble succeeded in measuring its distance from us by using information about the known brightness of certain types of stars which are recognizable in the nebula. It is no less than one-and-a-half million light years away – dozens of times farther than the distance to the edge of our own galaxy. Then the distances to other galaxies were measured or inferred: the distinctively shaped 'Whirlpool' galaxy in the constellation of Cannes Venatici turned out to be fourteen million light years away, while the huge cluster of galaxies in Virgo, containing more than one thousand members, is at least fifty million light years away, but even these are merely among the nearest. Not all the nebulae, however, turned out to be extragalactic, for some consist of gas clouds and stars situated in our own galaxy. The Andromeda nebula is of great interest because it is almost a twin of the Milky Way. These two, and many other galaxies like them, present a fascinating and beautiful spiral structure, compared by some to a Catherine wheel.

It is now known that the galaxies, and not the stars, are the basic building blocks of the universe. The stars themselves are grouped into these higher structural units representing the fundamental level of cosmological organization. The Milky Way and the Andromeda nebula are merely two typical elements in this hierarchy of orders; modern telescopes can detect billions upon billions of other galaxies, each containing typically hundreds of billions of stars. Some galaxies are known which are billions of light years away and only faintly visible even in the world's largest telescopes. The universe is evidently a very big place, much bigger than the early astronomers ever conceived.

A few years after his discovery of other galaxies, Hubble produced some further results which revealed that there is an even larger scale cosmic organization than the galaxies. The first clue that there is a systematic arrangement of the galaxies themselves comes from the fact that in whichever direction of the sky a telescope is pointed, on average the same density of galaxies of any given brightness is observed. On this very large scale the material in the universe is apparently distributed uniformly around us. The origin of this remarkable uniformity is still something of a mystery in cosmology, and one possible explanation will be described in the next chapter. The second and more significant clue to a supergalactic cosmic order emerged from a study by Hubble of the quality of light from a large sample of distant galaxies.

Light arriving on Earth from astronomical objects contains waves of many different frequencies scrambled together. An instrument called a spectroscope is used to unscramble the light and direct each frequency to a different place on a photographic plate. Light frequency is related to colour perception, red light having a lower frequency (or longer wavelength) than blue. All the colours separated out like a rainbow constitute what is called a spectrum, and the information it carries can reveal a surprisingly large amount about the source, such as chemical composition, temperature, magnetic fields, velocity and gravitational arrangement. The reason for this is that the light emitted by each atom has a characteristic pattern of colours which depends both on its internal structure and its physical situation. A study of light from terrestrial sources, together with mathematical computation in atomic physics, enable astronomers to recognize familiar patterns of lines in the spectra corresponding to known types of atoms, and a more detailed examination of the positioning, width and fine structure of the lines can reveal such things as the presence of a magnetic field or how hot an emitting gas might be. However, from the point of view of cosmology, the most important property of the spectra turned out to be the positioning of the spectral lines in relation to wavelength. In the late 1920s Hubble noticed that the light from faint galaxies is systematically more red than that from bright galaxies, a discovery whose implications soon overturned centuries of misconception about the nature of the universe.

The significance of the galactic red shift, as it is now known, is easily understood by analogy with sound waves. It is a familiar phenomenon that the pitch of a whistle or horn from a rapidly moving train or motor car is distinctly higher when the vehicle is approaching than when it is receding; the sudden drop in pitch when it passes can be very noticeable. The explanation for this effect is that the approaching vehicle compresses the sound waves before it, causing the wavelength to contract and the frequency to rise, and when it recedes the opposite occurs, with the waves becoming stretched out. A similar effect can occur with light waves; when a light source such as a star approaches, there is a shift in the colour towards the blue end of the spectrum, whereas a receding light source produces a red shift.

The existence of a red shift in the light from faint galaxies immediately suggested that they are receding from us at great speed. This vital feature already changes the whole perspective of astronomy and cosmology because it implies that on a global scale the universe is dynamic, rather than static as had previously been supposed. Furthermore, Hubble found that the recession was not random and haphazard, but organized in a systematic motion with a definite simple relationship between the faintness of a galaxy and its red shift. Because the faint galaxies are more distant, this relationship can tell us something about the connection between the distance of galaxies from Earth and the speed at which they are receding. Hubble's results showed that these quantities were in direct proportion: galaxies twice as far away recede, on average, at twice the speed. Because of this relationship, known to astronomers as Hubble's law, it is possible to deduce the pattern of motion not only as viewed here on Earth, but as seen from anywhere in the universe. It turns out that the rate at which typical neighbouring galaxies recede from each other is the same throughout the universe, so

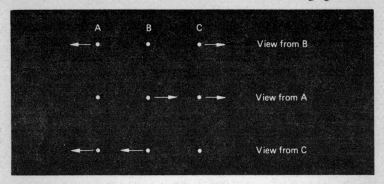

Figure 1   Recession of the galaxies

As the universe expands, so the galaxies move apart from each other. However, they do not move towards, or away from, any special place. This may be understood by imagining a sample of three equispaced galaxies, marked A, B and C, which could be located anywhere in the universe; one might be the Milky Way, perhaps.

The cosmological expansion could be simulated by steadily stretching the page. From B, it would seem that A and C were receding at equal speeds in opposite directions directly away from B, but from A the situation would look different. An observer on A would regard himself as at rest, and B to be receding. Moreover C would seem to be receding twice as fast as B, a fact which illustrates Hubble's law, that the rate of recession of a galaxy is in proportion to its distance: C is twice as far away from A as B is, so it recedes twice as fast as B. Naturally the view from C is that of A receding twice as fast as B. None of these galaxies is at the centre or edge of the pattern of motion, and one should envisage other dots spread uniformly around A, B and C, out through the entire universe, all engaging in the same mutual recession. Moreover the expansion of space is everywhere at the same rate, so that three galaxies anywhere which are spaced out by the same distance as A, B and C will recede from each other equally fast.

In the remote past, this expansion rate was much greater, as it had to be in order to overcome the stronger gravity between the galaxies. When the universe was one half its present age, it was probably expanding 25 per cent faster than now. This means that three galaxies spaced by the same distance as A, B and C are now, were receding 25 per cent faster.

that although the Earth appears to us to be at the centre of the recession, this is not really the case, for the same systematic motion would be visible from any other galaxy. In other words, the universe is expanding everywhere in a uniform way. The earlier, rather sterile concept of the totality of things as passive, inert and unchanging could now, following Hubble's discovery, be replaced by the universe as a coherent whole with a global identity, as something dynamic and evolving, like a living thing with a life history and perhaps a birth and death. The challenging possibility has arisen that scientific investigation can reveal the past structure, general behaviour and ultimate fate of the cosmos, and the fact that it might follow a dynamical evolution subject to laws of physics familiar from the laboratory, enables its future to be predicted from its past behaviour. Only by understanding in detail how the universe has changed in the past can its future evolution be determined. In the coming chapters we shall examine these past changes in order to see how the universe achieved its presently observed ordered structure and arrangement, and thereby discover how this cosmic organization is destined to undergo disintegration and collapse.

If the universe is treated as a dynamic unit, it is important to discover what physical laws determine its motion. Physicists know of four forces in nature which can act between material bodies. Two of these forces operate only at very short range, such as inside atomic nuclei, so could not influence the motions of galaxies. The other two forces are long range, and both are familiar in daily life. The first is electro-magnetism, which is essentially responsible for most everyday experiences of force; the second is gravity, the force which pulls objects towards the ground and, ultimately, the centre of the Earth. Gravity acts not only close to our own planet, but between all bodies in the universe. The moon's gravity acting across the surface of the Earth produces tidal forces which raise and lower the oceans in a daily rhythm, while the gravity between the Earth and the sun causes the Earth to orbit around the sun instead of floating off through interstellar space.

Electromagnetic forces are very well understood and can easily be investigated in the laboratory. They are important in astronomy, for

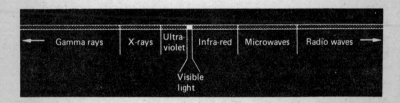

Figure 2 Electromagnetic spectrum
Many physically dissimilar types of radiation are in fact all examples of electromagnetic waves, differing only in size (wavelength). Visible light in fact just occupies a small band in this electromagnetic spectrum, in the wavelength region of about a hundred thousandth of a centimetre. Very long waves (greater than a metre) correspond to radio waves, while very short waves (less than a ten billionth of a centimetre) correspond to energetic gamma rays. In between are found other familiar radiations — X-rays, infra-red (heat), ultra-violet and microwaves.

they have a profound effect on the behaviour of stars and other objects. Indeed we only see stars at all because these forces produce electro-magnetic radiation, which includes light, radio waves, infra-red heat, ultra-violet and X-rays. Electromagnetic forces can be intensely strong and powerful, as the effects of a lightning strike testify. By way of contrast gravity is exceedingly weak: the electric attraction between the constituents of an atom is about one thousand billion billion billion billion times stronger than the corresponding gravitational force. Nevertheless gravity always attracts between bodies, whereas electro-magnetic forces can either attract or repel according to the signs of the electric charges present. For this reason, large bodies, which usu-ally are almost electrically neutral, do not experience large electro-magnetic forces in proportion to the numbers of atoms they contain. On the other hand, gravity is cumulative, so that while it is extremely weak between individual atoms, it can dominate all other forces in bodies of astronomical mass, such as the Earth or the sun. When it comes to galaxies, gravity is the only known force which can control their motion.

The first comprehensive theory of gravity was developed by Isaac Newton. Along with Galileo Galilei, he can be said to have invented science as we know it. Born in the middle of the seventeenth century (1642), Newton lived at a time of great institutional crisis, when the power of Church dogma was crumbling in the face of scientific dis-covery. Already Galileo had been forced under threat of torture to recant his important astronomical discoveries, and Giordano Bruno had been burnt at the stake for daring to suggest that there exist other inhabited worlds. All Europe, which had long been gripped by the intellectual straightjacket of traditional religious thinking, was stirring under the impact of some challenging new ideas. In 1543 the Polish astronomer Nicolas Copernicus, after a careful analysis of the motions of the planets, published a (quite literally) revolutionary proposal about the astronomical arrangement of the solar system. He suggested that the Earth does not lie fixed at the centre of the universe, but revolves around the sun along with the other planets, a revelation that exploded centuries of entrenched belief about the status of mankind in the cosmos.

By his mid-twenties Newton, who had been born in the very year of Galileo's death, had made many far-reaching discoveries in math-ematics, physics and astronomy. Especially important were his theories of space, time and motion, which provided precise mathematical relationships between concepts like force, momentum and acceleration of material bodies. These laws of motion are still used every day, three centuries later. One force which caught Newton's attention was gravity (stimulated, so the story goes, by the fall of an apple). With great insight he postulated that gravity acts not only on Earth, but between the 'heavenly bodies' such as the stars, sun and planets. This hypothesis could be verified by applying his new laws to the motions of the planets around the solar system under the action of gravitational forces. Correctly guessing the mathematical form of the force, realizing that it must diminish with distance between the gravitating bodies, he was able to solve his equations and so find both the shapes and sizes of the planetary and lunar orbits. Success was immediate: the planetary paths were calculated as being elliptical, with the sun located at one focus, exactly as the Austrian astronomer Johannes Kepler had already deduced from observations of the planets made by Tycho Brahe. Moreover, Newton was able to calculate the correct relationship between the speeds of the planetary motions and their distances from the sun, as well as the correct period of the moon. This was a brilliant advance in understanding, for it showed for the first time that laws of science discovered in laboratories on Earth could be successfully applied to heavenly bodies, hitherto regarded as inhabiting a purely celestial domain.

Having applied his laws of motion and gravity to the solar system, Newton went on to investigate the larger structure of the universe using mathematics. Many astronomers of the time believed that the stars were unchanging in nature or location. This posed a severe problem for Newton, because if the stars were arranged in a gigantic distribution surrounded by empty space, then the gravity acting between the stars would cause them to fall together at the centre of the whole mass, thereby destroying the observed cosmic organization.

Accordingly he proposed that the distribution of stars must continue with undiminished density for an infinite distance in space, which implies, among other things, that the number of stars is unlimited. The purpose of supposing an infinite universe is that such an arrangement has no middle or edge, so the stars cannot fall towards any one place in preference to any other; in other words, any given star will be pulled equally in all directions by the gravity of all the others, and so will not experience any net force in any particular direction apart from local disturbances. In this way the universe would remain static.

In the eighteenth century the Swiss astronomer de Cheseaux, and later the German astronomer Olbers, discovered a curious cosmic paradox which puzzled scientists for over a century. The paradox concerns something so simple and basic that at first sight it seems hardly to merit attention at all: why is the sky dark at night? As so often with really simple observations about the nature of the world, a deep truth lies behind the answer. We know that daylight is caused by the sun, which at night is not visible. The sun, however, is only one star among myriads, and de Cheseaux and Olbers calculated the cumulative effect of the light from all the other stars. Superficially these do not appear to contribute much light because they are so far away, but — like Newton before them — these two astronomers assumed that there is an infinite number of stars, scattered throughout space at a more or less uniform density in all directions and at all distances. They went on to argue that the flux of light from all of these stars would be intense, essentially because every line of sight would, if extended far enough into space, intersect the surface of a star. It followed from this that there could be no dark parts in the night sky: every patch of sky would glow with the intensity of the sun, and the Earth would be vaporized. This conclusion is also obvious if we think of the total heat and light emitted by the stars over a long duration, for this radiation would eventually accumulate in the spaces between the stars, heating up the entire universe until it reached the temperature of the stellar surfaces (several thousand degrees). If, on the other hand, the stars were organized in a finite blob surrounded by empty space, then heat and light could escape into the void beyond, and the sky would be dark — but then the stars would fall together under their own gravity. Clearly, therefore, something was fundamentally wrong with these early models of the universe.

With the beginning of modern cosmology and Hubble's discovery of the expansion of the universe, the de Cheseaux-Olbers paradox was resolved. Because the galaxies are receding from us, their light is weakened by the red shift; indeed, very distant galaxies are receding so fast that they are not visible at all, their light being shifted right away from the visible part of the electromagnetic spectrum. It follows that the accumulated light from all the stars in these receding galaxies is relatively small — too small, in fact, to be detected as a background glow even with our most sensitive instruments.

The cosmological expansion has a curious aspect to it: the farther away a galaxy is from us, the faster it appears to recede, and galaxies several billion light years away seem to be increasing their separation from us at nearly the speed of light. As we probe still farther into space the red shift grows without limit, and the galaxies seem to fade out and become black. When the speed of recession reaches the speed of light we cannot see them at all, for no light can reach us from the region beyond which the expansion is faster than light itself. This limit is called our horizon in space, and separates the regions of the universe of which we can know from the regions beyond about which no information is available, however powerful the instruments we use.

Just because we cannot see beyond ten or twenty billion light years, even in principle, does not mean that the horizon is the 'edge' of the universe, as many popular books imply. Like Newton, modern astronomers do not believe that the universe has an edge; instead, following in the tradition of Copernicus, they look upon the Milky Way galaxy as situated in a typical region of the universe. Whether it be the Earth, the solar system or the galaxy, wherever we look around us in space we seem to be sampling just an average picture of the cosmos, similar to the picture which would be obtained from any other galaxy. The galaxies which appear to us to be receding almost at the speed of light, and lie near to our horizon, are really located in a region of the universe much like our own. If we were to travel there we would find that the other galaxies all appeared to be receding from that place also, and that our Milky Way was close to their 'edge' or horizon. The cosmic motion is therefore entirely relative, depending on the position of the observer.

The cosmological expansion resolves the starlight paradox without making reference to whether space is finite or infinite in extent, or whether the number of stars is unlimited. The problem of the stars falling together is sidestepped because the universe is obviously not static anyway. The expansion, however, puts a radically new complexion on the whole basis of cosmology, because if the galaxies are moving farther apart, they must have been closer together in the past. As gravity diminishes with distance, it follows that the gravity between the galaxies was greater in the past than now. But as gravity always attracts it must operate to slow down the recession of the galaxies, so that their speed of recession in the past would have been still greater than at present. Consequently there can never have been a time when the universe was static. On the other hand, the expansion cannot have been continuing for ever or the galaxies would have become completely dispersed by now. If, therefore, the inevitable attraction of gravity is assumed, then there can only be one conclusion from these observations, and it is very profound indeed: the universe cannot have existed for ever — there must have been a creation.

The idea of a creation by divine action is a deep-rooted part of Western culture. Also in 1642 (the year of Newton's birth) John Lightfoot, a Cambridge University scholar, proclaimed that the date of the creation was 17 September 3928 BC, at 9.00 am (though whether or not GMT is not clear). Some years later, James Ussher, Archbishop of Armagh, was able to correct this version and fix the date as 23 October 4004 BC, which became the accepted time of the creation, as taught by the Church, for over a century.

That there was a creation of some sort is never doubted by most Western thinkers. The question is, when? The discovery of fossils in the nineteenth century and the acceptance of Charles Darwin's theory of species evolution indicated that the Earth must be at least millions of years old, a point of view which once again collided with widespread Christian belief. More recent geological dating techniques, especially those which measure the radioactive composition of rocks, are able to provide a fairly precise date for the formation of the Earth at about four-and-a-half billion years ago. The theory of stellar structure can be used to fix the dates of the sun and stars, and this too provides a figure of several billion years.

When Hubble discovered the expansion of the universe he was able to produce from science what Archbishop Ussher had attempted to produce from theology — the date of the creation of the universe. This can be deduced simply by measuring the rate at which the universe is expanding now, and extrapolating back into the past, allowing for the acceleration caused by gravity. The date works out at between ten and twenty billion years ago, and since this is comparable with the ages of the Earth, sun and stars, as calculated by completely independent techniques, we have remarkable confirmation that our understanding of cosmology is along the right lines.

If there really was a creation about fifteen billion years ago, intense curiosity surrounds what actually happened at that time. Hubble's discovery was overtaken by a completely new theory of gravity which pictures the creation and expansion in a novel perspective. Albert Einstein, whose genius was comparable to that of Newton himself,

27

published a new theory of space, time and motion, called the special theory of relativity, in 1906. Later, in 1915, the theory was extended to include gravity, and is known as the general theory of relativity. In these theories, space and time are unified into a single entity called space-time, with properties that lead to curious and unusual effects, some of which will be discussed in the following chapters. Gravity, rather than being regarded as a force is, in the theory of relativity, attributed to the geometrical structure of space-time. The presence of a gravitating body curves the space-time in its vicinity and it is this curvature, rather than any force or action by the body itself, which disturbs the trajectories of other bodies as they move through the surrounding space.

In many ways space-time can be regarded as 'elastic'. Not only can it be bent or curved by a massive body, it can also be twisted and stretched like rubber. Moreover, some physicists believe that if the bending and twisting become too violent, space and time can snap and break apart. Elastic time can lead to bizarre effects such as the possibility of travel into the far future or the apparent cessation of all activity during gravitational collapse. Elastic space can be used to explain the expansion of the universe as a stretching of the fabric of space itself. To assist in visualizing this strange idea it is helpful to think of an analogy where space, instead of being three-dimensional, is pictured as a two-dimensional sheet, or surface, such as the fabric of a spherical balloon. The balloon represents the universe, and is covered in little dots denoting the galaxies. It is important to remember that the volume inside the balloon, or the region outside it, is not supposed to be part of the universe; only the rubber membrane itself represents space. Like real space, the rubber surface is curved and if the balloon is inflated then the membrane stretches or expands in the same way as the universe expands.

It is clear from this model that there is no middle or edge to the universe: it is *not* a ball of galaxies exploding outward from a common centre, with the outer regions racing away into empty space beyond. Instead the galaxies are spread everywhere through space at a uniform density. Moreover the space itself is obviously finite in size, for we could travel right around the 'balloon' and return to our starting point. The real universe may or may not be finite in size; if it is not, then a better analogy than a balloon would be an infinite rubber sheet covered by an infinite number of dots. As the rubber is stretched, so every dot moves away from every other dot, and no dot has the special status of being at the centre of the distribution.

We can use this analogy to understand the nature of the creation event. As we pass backwards in time, the condition of the universe corresponds to the balloon being more shrunken. Unlike rubber, space becomes easier to stretch as it expands; consequently when it was very shrunken it squeezed even more vigorously, which is why the galaxies had to recede still faster in the past to escape this gravity which tried to restrain the expansion. If we imagine the balloon progressively more shrunken, then a point is reached where it simply disappears out of existence altogether. This is the creation as viewed by modern science

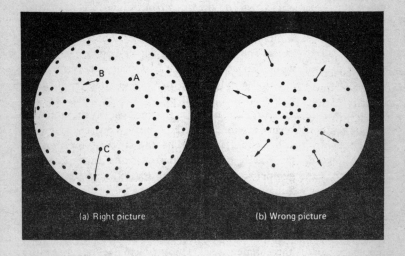

Figure 3   Expanding space
(a)   The meaning of a uniformly expanding universe can be visualized with the help of a balloon analogy. The membrane of the balloon stretches as the balloon is inflated, causing every dot to separate from every other dot. Although the distribution of dots has no special centre or edge, the pattern of motion as viewed from any particular dot, e.g. the one marked A, is that of an outward expansion from that place, the more distant dots, such as C appearing to recede faster than nearby ones, such as B. This systematic behaviour is similar to that discovered by Hubble for the galaxies. Notice that this model of the universe is finite in extent, a feature which may also be true in the real universe.

(b)   This figure depicts a popular but erroneous view of the expanding universe, with galaxies exploding outwards from a concentrated blob into a pre-existing void. This model has a centre and an edge, so the galaxies (dots) are not distributed uniformly throughout space. Astronomical observations show that the arrangement (a) is more accurate.

29

— not the sudden appearance of matter in a pre-existing void, but the creation of space and time as well. According to this picture, space and time could only exist after some moment in the past, about fifteen billion years ago; that is, there is a temporal extremity or boundary to the universe in the finite past. It was not just the material contents of the universe which were created, but the whole thing, including space-time. Existence itself, therefore, began fifteen billion years ago.

Many people are baffled by ideas like expanding space or the appearance of space-time out of nowhere, and they often become sceptical. In ordinary language, space is identified with emptiness or nothingness — the absence of things. The idea of space changing size or shape, let alone shrivelling away into nothing at all, does not seem to make much sense. Scientists, on the other hand, do not regard space in the same way, for they are more aware of the many special properties it possesses: for example, the rules of school geometry provide relationships between distances and angles in space which may or may not be true in the real world. Space can be said to change, because these geometrical properties alter with time. In spite of what is taught at school, geometry is not something that is correct in the absolute sense; it can vary from place to place and time to time. The only reason why school geometry seems to work so well on Earth is because gravity is low enough not to bend the familiar rules too far. Near the creation event, however, the gravity of all the matter in the universe was so intense that the geometrical properties of space-time were, by our standards, very peculiar.

People often have difficulty in understanding the idea of expanding space because there seems to be nothing into which it can expand. The surface of the balloon has all the surrounding volume to move through, but space itself is three-dimensional. This problem does not arise if the expansion is regarded more as a change in scale, or a steady inflation of all distances. Each year the volume of any given region of the universe increases by a tiny fraction. Space is not really spreading out into some higher-dimensional 'superspace', but is simply changing its standard of length. The Earth or the galaxy does not participate in this cosmological stretching, so we may gauge expanding distances through space against these objects for comparison. The stretching of space does, however, stretch light waves that pass through it, causing their wavelength to increase and the colour to redden. This is the red shift discovered by Hubble, and the redness should be seen as a scaling effect rather than as something caused by the motion of the light source. In other words, the galaxies are not rushing away from a common centre; they are at rest in an expanding space.

Passing backwards in time to the creation event, all of the observable universe appears to have been compressed into a smaller and smaller volume until, at the first moment, the density of material was infinite, with the whole universe which we now observe perhaps squeezed into a single point. What was it that caused the universe to burst into existence in rapid expansion and enormous density at some particular moment? Questions of this sort are almost impossible to answer and probably meaningless. If time itself only exists after the creation, notions like cause, effect and 'particular moment' make little or no sense when applied to the creation. The language which is used to convey these ideas already assumes familiar, fundamental concepts of space and time, and it tends to have a strong philosophical or even religious connotation. Perhaps it is expecting too much of science to provide clear answers to them.

The claim that the universe did not exist before a finite time in the past is a provocative one which cannot rest on scientific speculation alone. It raises the alarming prospect that the universe may disappear again at some moment in the future, and it is therefore especially important to obtain evidence that there really was a creation. While we can never expect to verify by observation the first moment itself, we might expect some vestiges of the early primeval phase which followed the creation to be detectable today.

In 1965 two American electronics experts, Arno Penzias and Robert Wilson, were working for the Bell Telephone company on communication systems for artificial satellites, when they accidentally made what may well be the greatest of all scientific discoveries — the primeval heat from the creation. They were attempting to investigate methodically the various sources of radio interference in the very short wavelength range, so that these disturbances could be eliminated. Several sources were identified — radio static from the upper atmosphere, interference in the amplifying equipment and so on — but a further troublesome unknown source of interference persisted — a radio microwave background that could not be accounted for by any familiar source.

Curiously enough, even as Penzias and Wilson were puzzling over this, a group of scientists at Princeton University were busy designing a radio receiver to search for just such a background radiation, but the

The emerging universe

Princeton team knew already what it was: radiation left over from the primeval explosion fifteen billion years ago, coming towards us from very deep space fifteen billion light years away, farther than any galaxy. The simultaneous accidental discovery of this radiation by Penzias and Wilson transformed the idea of a creation from plausible scientific speculation to a full-blown theory of cosmology. It opened up the possiblity of investigating how the universe achieved its present structure and organization, and of calculating whether it started out on a primeval path which is heading for disaster and cosmic catastrophe.

2.   *Primeval fire*

The collapse of cosmic organization can only be understood against a background knowledge of how that organization first arose and how it is sustained. In recent years most scientists have come to accept that the present orderly condition of the universe, with its complex arrangements of matter and energy, its galaxies and star clusters, its planetary bodies and life, cannot have existed for ever. There was a time in the past when the universe was very different from now. As remarked in the previous chapter, many cosmologists believe that the universe did not exist at all before some moment in the remote past. Whether or not this is the case, there is good observational evidence that between ten and twenty billion years ago the universe was in a state of primeval chaos, exploding in a big bang from a highly condensed state. The study of this violent primeval epoch must rank as one of the most exciting intellectual adventures of modern science.

Knowledge of the physical condition of the early universe is gained in two ways: by constructing mathematical models and by searching for cosmological relics. As with all mathematical models, the scientific description of the primeval universe is only a scenario and deserves to be treated with caution. Indeed, some cosmologists reject the standard big bang picture altogether, either on scientific or philosophical grounds, although most accept it as a working hypothesis. It at least provides the basic framework around which to organize the observational data.

The advantage of possessing a detailed mathematical model of the early universe is that a note of precision is injected into what is otherwise a rather speculative subject. Using the model as a practical tool, in-depth calculations can be performed of the detailed processes that occurred in the primeval material, thereby providing precise answers to some fascinating questions about the first few seconds of the universe. Naturally there has to be some input into the model, such as the laws of physics governing matter under the extreme conditions which prevailed during those early epochs. Although some of these laws are not yet fully understood, the big bang scenario is firmly rooted in scientific fact − it is not mere speculation. By checking the answers provided by mathematical computation against astronomical observation, the physical basis of the model can be verified.

The search for relics from the primeval universe provides the second method of investigation. As in history or paleontology, fossil remains are the main source of experimental knowledge of the past. The searcher's task is made easier by an understanding of the physical processes which took place during the big bang. A study of the mathematical model suggests that certain birthmarks may have survived from the creation until the present day. These 'fossil' remains are an important source of information about the detailed physics of the big bang, and will be described in this chapter. Technological limitations currently prevent the observational verification of some of the more exciting relics predicted by the canonical theory, such as those left over from the very early moments. Nevertheless, relics from a time only a few minutes after the creation are known.

The most direct method of finding out about cosmic pre-history is to exploit the finitude of the velocity of light. Although light, which travels at 300,000 kilometres a second, is the swiftest carrier of information, astronomical distances are so great that it may take many millions or even billions of years for light to travel between galaxies. For this reason, we do not see these galaxies as they are now, but as they appeared in the remote past. For example, the nearby Andromeda nebula presents to the human eye the aspect it possessed no less than one-and-a-half million years ago. Objects are now known which are so distant that the light which is received today by our telescopes was emitted before the Earth even existed. Some idea of the scale of distances may be gained by recalling that light takes only about eight minutes to cross the ninety-three million mile gap between the sun and the Earth.

Using a telescope as a 'timescope' enables astronomers to observe directly the condition of the universe in the remote past. Unfortunately the further into the past that the instruments probe, the fainter are the objects to be studied, because of their great distances. This means that only very powerful and expensive equipment can reveal detailed information about very early epochs. Furthermore, the cosmological red shift of light discovered by Hubble is very appreciable from these remote regions. It is actually impossible to see anything at all from the earliest times, because the light radiation is completely shifted out of the visible spectrum. For example, light which was emitted about 100,000 years after the creation has become so red shifted that it is now reduced to infra-red radiation. Unfortunately it is impossible to detect electromagnetic radiation directly from epochs before 100,000 years. The reason for this lies in the physical condition of matter before that moment. Because of the cosmological expansion the density of material in the universe is continually falling by at present about one per cent every hundred million years. About ten or twenty billion years ago the density was so great that the cosmological material was not arranged into galaxies separated by empty space as it is now, but constituted a more or less uniform fluid spread throughout all of space. This fluid was very hot: like all gases, the cosmological material cools as it expands, so it was hotter in the past than now. Calculations indicate that 100,000 years after the big bang the temperature of the fluid was several thousand degrees.

At this temperature matter cannot exist in the usual forms as a solid, liquid or gas. Instead it must be in a state which physicists call a plasma. In a plasma atoms are dissociated into electrically charged particles. This happens because at several thousand degrees, the atoms are moving so fast that random collisions are energetic enough to knock particles out of them, a process known as ionization. Plasmas are readily made and studied in the laboratory, thereby providing important information about the conditions which prevailed during the first 100,000 years of the universe. One important property of plasmas is their high opacity. Whereas ordinary gases are often transparent to light, an ionized gas absorbs and scatters light strongly. The universe during the plasma era is therefore shrouded in a sort of luminous fog, precluding direct visual observation.

It is to the plasma era that we must look to explain the most fundamental feature of cosmic organization — the distribution of matter among the different chemical elements. It turns out that this is the crucial factor which induces the appearance of cosmic organization in its most important and conspicuous forms and which also determines the disintegration of that organization, and with it the end of the universe as we know it.

Scientists have long been faced with the puzzle of where all the different chemical elements (types of atom) have come from, and why they occur with the particular relative abundances that they do. For a long time it was supposed that all substances were composed of four basic elements: earth, air, fire and water. With the appearance of the study of chemistry it was soon realized that the great variety and forms of matter required many more than four elementary constituents. The atomic theory of matter explained the properties of material substances by supposing that all matter is composed of combinations of the same basic atoms. These combinations of atoms are called molecules. The systematic relationships between different chemical substances were gradually discovered, until about one hundred years ago the Russian chemist Dmitri Mendeleev published his famous periodic table, listing all the known elements in an arrangement which displayed qualitative similarities between various types of atoms.

During the early part of the twentieth century the internal structure of atoms came to be understood. The major discovery was that the forces which operate between and inside atoms are electromagnetic in nature. The qualitative differences between the elements, such as their weights and chemical properties, were explained by differences in the number of electric particles which their atoms possess. The internal arrangement of these particles was deduced by the New Zealand physicist Lord Rutherford, on the basis of scattering experiments carried out with radioactive emissions. Rutherford proved that most of the mass of an atom resides in a compact body at the centre, called the nucleus, which contains heavy, positively charged particles known as protons. Later it was realized that the nucleus also contains electrically neutral particles called neutrons, which have about the same mass as protons, but no electric charge. Because atoms in their normal condition are electrically neutral, there must also be negative charges present. These form a cloud of light particles, called electrons, which surround the nucleus, orbiting around it at great speed.

A whole atom is many thousands of times larger than its nucleus. A typical atom is about one hundred millionth of a centimetre across, enclosing a nucleus about one million millionth of a centimetre in size. The simplest atom is that of hydrogen, which contains just one proton and one electron. An ionized hydrogen plasma, therefore, consists of a simple mixture of protons and electrons moving around chaotically. The next element is helium, which contains a nucleus of two protons and two neutrons, with two electrons orbiting around it. As 99.9 per cent of the mass resides in the nucleus, it follows that the helium atom is about four times as heavy as the hydrogen atom. Proceeding in this way all the known types of chemical elements are accounted for: carbon, for example, has six protons, either six or seven neutrons, and six electrons.

An important feature in this scheme is that the heavier atoms are the more complex. The detailed arrangement of the electron cloud in a heavy atom which contains perhaps dozens of electrons is very complicated. Nevertheless, a certain systematic organization is apparent: the electrons tend to stack up around the nucleus in shells which forbid the entry of extraneous electrons from outside. Because of this exclusive property, the interactions between different atoms involve only the residual electrons outside any filled shells. For this reason certain groups of atoms with similar shell structure and numbers of residual electrons have similar properties. Chemical reactions occur when the residual electrons rearrange themselves around two or more atoms. In this way atoms may adhere together to form molecules because of the electric attractions brought about by the redistribution of these charged particles. Clearly the chemical properties of an atom are determined by the number of electrons which it possesses which in turn is fixed by the number of protons in the nucleus. The fact which must be explained is why some types of atoms, for example gold, are very rare whereas others such as iron are extremely abundant.

For some years it was known that about ninety elements occur naturally on Earth. These range from hydrogen, the lightest substance with the simplest atoms, to uranium, each atom of which contains ninety-two protons and from 135 to 148 neutrons. Uranium atoms are therefore very heavy and highly complex. All the elements with more than eighty-two protons are unstable and tend to disintegrate into simpler substances. This is the phenomenon of radioactivity. The absence of many naturally occurring transuranium elements is due to this inherent instability. Many more very heavy atoms have been made in the laboratory, but all of them have half-lives (against radioactive decay) shorter than the age of the Earth, so they would not be expected to appear on Earth in abundance.

It has long been known that the relative abundances of the elements on the Earth is in no way typical of the rest of the universe. Determining the chemical composition of other objects in the universe, especially stars, might seem at first a daunting task. The method used is very simple, as all atoms have such a distinctive structure. Atoms may emit or absorb light by rearranging their electrons, usually by a single electron making a transition to a more, or less, energetic orbital level. Because of very fundamental properties connected with the quantum theory (briefly discussed near the end of this chapter), the energy levels are always at certain characteristic values, which means that when transitions between these energy levels occur, light will be emitted or absorbed in pulses with a particular energy and wavelength (colour), analogous to fingerprints. However far away a luminous object may be, if the particular pattern of colours is detected, the presence of that type of atom in the source is established. In a hot gas, violent collisions are continually exciting the atomic electrons, and when de-excitation occurs, the energy is radiated at these special frequencies. Most people are familiar with this phenomenon from fluorescent lamps: sodium gas emits a greenish-blue light, neon an orange light.

As explained on p. 19, a spectroscope can be used to analyse the colour quality of light in great detail, and this has enabled astronomers to tell what stars are made of. Indeed the element helium, as its name implies, was actually discovered in the sun before it was detected on Earth. Analyses of this sort have revealed that most of the matter in the universe is composed of hydrogen, the simplest substance, while nearly all of the remainder (about 7 per cent) is helium. The Earth, with its great quantities of iron, nickel, oxygen, copper and so on, is really just a speck of contaminant, a concentration of all the rarest substances in one place and quite untypical of the cosmic abundances.

Explaining the relative abundances of the elements, and in particular looking for the reason why so much of the universe is composed of the simplest atoms, hydrogen and helium, has proved a great challenge to scientists. In 1946 the physicist George Gamow published a provocative theory in an attempt to account for these facts. The central idea of this theory is that the big, complex atoms are formed out of synthesis of the lighter ones. For example, an atom of carbon, with six protons, could be formed from three helium nuclei uniting together. This immediately suggests that the universe started with just the simplest substances — protons, neutrons and electrons — in a dissociated form, and the nuclei were manufactured in some way out of this raw material. Wherever this manufacturing process has taken place, it has not proceeded very far, because most of the material has been left in the form of the simplest atoms.

Gamow was faced with two problems, that of explaining why the universe began without any assembled nuclei being present at the outset, and how the genesis of the complex nuclei was initiated. His work, and the later calculations of C. Hyashi, R. V. Wagoner, W. A. Fowler and F. Hoyle, have provided a convincing answer to these questions. Their suggestion is that the universe began intensely hot, so hot that assembled nuclei could not have withstood the enormous temperatures. The image of a hot, highly compressed inferno expanding explosively from a big-bang creation is now a familiar and popular model of the early universe. References to this nascent phase normally use the words 'primeval fireball', although this gives a misleading impression that the cosmological material was concentrated into a ball surrounded by a void. This is not correct. Modern cosmologists assume that the fluid always filled the whole of space. Only the density changed as the universe expanded everywhere.

Computers have been used to calculate the details of the nuclear processes in which the primeval material was involved, and to work out the element abundances which would have resulted. These calculations are extremely complicated because details of many nuclear reactions are fitted together in a mathematical model, and several physical parameters are varied. Nevertheless the results provide a vivid reconstruction of the early stages of the primeval fire and explain in outline how the nucleogenesis occurred.

The crucial phase started about one second after the beginning of the big bang, at which moment the temperature was around ten billion degrees and the density of matter about ten thousand times that of water. At such high temperatures a strange and important phenomenon occurs. According to Einstein's theory of relativity, energy and matter are interconvertible, so heat, being a form of energy, can create matter if the conditions are extreme enough. Whenever matter is created in this fashion, an equal quantity of antimatter appears. Antimatter is, in a crude sense, a mirror image of matter: for example, the anti-proton is a particle with the same mass as a proton, but with a negative instead of a positive electric charge. When a proton and an antiproton meet they annihilate each other in a burst of energy. Antimatter is frequently made and studied in the laboratory, so that the properties of the primeval antimatter are known with great precision. Before about one microsecond (millionth of a second) the universe contained about equal quantities of matter and antimatter, then, as the temperature fell from ten million million degrees down to about ten billion degrees, all the antimatter was annihilated along with most of the matter, leaving only a small residual quantity of matter that we see today. This annihilation resulted in the production of a very large quantity of photons ('particles' of light), so that the universe now contains a billion times more photons than all the particles of matter put together. These photons are the remnants of all the primeval antimatter.

The presence of antimatter before the first few seconds played an important role in determining the abundance of helium in the universe. Calculations show that the abundance ratio of neutrons to protons was determined by various processes involving anti-electrons (or positrons as they are known), and that at around the first few seconds this ratio was about 15 per cent. At that time the positrons suddenly disappeared, leaving this ratio more or less fixed for several minutes. It was during those next few minutes that the vital nucleogenesis took place. Once the temperature had dropped below a billion degrees, the cosmological material was cool enough for the neutrons and protons to start combining together without being immediately disrupted by high energy impacts. According to the mathematical analysis almost all the neutrons were incorporated into helium, the remaining uncombined protons being left, eventually to form hydrogen atoms. The reason why hardly any more complex nuclei were formed is simple: the temperature and density fell so rapidly in the explosive expansion that no time was available for the more complicated synthetic reactions to take place in appreciable quantity.

After some minutes the temperature had fallen to a few million degrees, which is too cold for nuclear processes to take place. At that temperature the primeval nuclear furnace shut down. The results of the computer calculations show that about 7 per cent of atoms end up as helium and nearly all the rest as hydrogen, which is remarkably consistent with the observed cosmic abundances of these elements, and provides a gratifying indication that the essential picture of a hot big bang is correct. Cosmologists regard primeval helium as one of the most important fossil relics from the primeval fire. What primeval nucleo-synthesis does not explain, however, is the existence of nuclei more complex than helium. Their origin involves another important part of astrophysics which will be described later.

If primeval helium were the only relic, the big bang would not have gained such popular support among scientists. Fortunately there is another, more compelling relic left from the plasma era — the primeval heat. The enormous quantity of heat radiation present in the fireball has been slowly cooling as the universe expands. With the nuclear action finished, the plasma temperature gradually faded over thousands of years, until at around 100,000 years, when it had dropped to only a few thousand degrees (about the temperature of the sun's surface), the free electrons in the plasma combined with the hydrogen and helium nuclei to form atoms. When this happened the cosmological 'fog' cleared; the gas became transparent enabling the enormous quantities of light radiation present to pass unhindered through the material. Continued expansion gradually cooled the radiation down to an insignificant glow, filling all of space. This glow is believed to be the radiation discovered by Penzias and Wilson in 1965 when they were experimenting with satellite communication. It is the last fading remnant of the primeval furnace of ten billion years ago. The temperature has now fallen right to the very depths — a mere three degrees above absolute zero — a harmless witness to the fiery birth of the universe.

Impressive though they are, the fossil remnants from the plasma era have not been sufficient to satisfy the curiosity of scientists, and several other eras which precede the plasma era have received wide attention in recent years. If the basic picture of the hot big bang is correct, then there will have been many exotic processes in the first fleeting moments after the creation, some of which could have left traces that would be detectable now. It is important to determine what these traces might be and to try to check them, or at least to verify that they are not inconsistent with known cosmic data. Only by a proper and complete understanding of those early moments can the present structure of the universe be explained, and its future predicted. Furthermore, we shall see that the universe may well return to a fireball condition once again. The fate which then awaits it depends on the very processes which occurred in the earliest moments of the big bang.

Sometimes there is confusion about the terminology used to describe the primeval epochs. Accepting for the moment that there really was a past temporal extremity — a creation event — about ten billion years ago, then as our attention passes backwards in time to that first moment, the rate at which things were happening rises steadily: The cosmological expansion was much faster in the primeval epoch than it is now, the temperature and density of matter were falling much more rapidly. As the initial moment is approached, these quantities apparently change with unlimited rapidity. For example, whenever the distance in time from the beginning is halved the density of matter increases fourfold. Clearly there is no limit to the number of times that we may subdivide the duration following the creation, so that many quantities rise without limit as our attention approaches the first moment. There were greater changes passing from one microsecond to one second, than in the whole hour which followed.

Because the rate of change escalates in the vicinity of the creation event, the different eras occupy successively smaller time intervals: the plasma era lasted from about one second to 100,000 years; the era which preceded this (called the lepton era) lasted from about one microsecond to one second. In duration then, the plasma era is immensely longer than the lepton era, but in terms of *activity* they are comparable, because things happened so much faster during the lepton era. Using activity as a measure, there is no limit to the number of eras which precede the plasma era, which seems paradoxical because the creation is supposed to have occurred just one second before the onset of the plasma era. There is no paradox, however, if it is remembered that the first second is infinitely divisible.

Our knowledge of the relevant physics diminishes as the temperature and density rises. At low temperatures we have to deal with plasma physics; then at the higher temperatures of earlier epochs, nuclear physics. Before that, at higher temperatures still, a more energetic branch of physics comes into play — elementary particle physics. Each era may be classified by the branch of physics which dominates the processes occurring at the time: the earlier the moment, the more energetic the processes, and the more dubious is our knowledge. At the time of writing, most cosmologists accept the standard big-bang model back to about one second, or approaching the end of the lepton era. However, some have pushed on back, through the lepton era into the so-called hadron era (before one microsecond) and even beyond. A brief description of what they have found will be given below.

In order to describe the details of these earlier eras, something about the physics of highly energetic matter must be explained. About seventy years ago, when physicists first suspected the structure of the atom, only two types of subatomic constituents were known: the proton and the electron. Electric currents were known to be caused by streams of electrons. Much heavier electric particles called alpha rays were detected emanating from certain radioactive atoms. Eventually, partly from experiments with alpha rays, it was realized that another, electrically neutral particle, the neutron, was needed to explain how the protons in the atomic nucleus could remain stuck together in spite of their repulsive electric force. The neutron was eventually identified in 1932.

For a time it seemed as though these three particles of matter were the only elementary building blocks of all atoms, but a study of another type of radioactivity, beta rays, led the physicist Wolfgang Pauli to suggest the existence of perhaps the strangest of all microscopic particles — the neutrino. Neutrinos are unlike other particles in that they cannot be brought to rest — in fact, they always move with the speed of light; there is no way to slow them down. Moreover they spin as they move, in an extraordinary way, quite differently from the ordinary spin of a ball, for example. An object like a ball must be rotated through 360 degrees in order to present the same aspect as before but a neutrino needs *two* rotations through 360 degrees to achieve this. It is as though it has a double view of the universe — one for each complete rotation. But most peculiar of all is that matter, even solid lead or concrete, is almost completely transparent to neutrinos: indeed, they may easily pass right through the Earth without being noticed. Not surprisingly, it has been very hard to discover whether Pauli's particle is just a figment of his imagination, or really exists. In spite of the extreme difficulty of actually spotting a neutrino — for instance by absorbing it — sufficiently large fluxes of them have been produced by nuclear reactors in recent years for very occasional absorption of one to take place. Their existence is now beyond doubt.

Another piece of deductive guesswork was performed by the Japanese physicist Hideki Yukawa, before the Second World War. Yukawa reasoned that there must be some form of 'glue' to stick the protons and neutrons of the atomic nucleus together. This glue is best explained in terms of yet another particle, which can be emitted and absorbed by the protons and neutrons, and the glueing effect will operate by the continual exchange of these particles backwards and forwards inside the nucleus. If a proton or neutron receives a sufficiently energetic impact, one of these particles will be knocked out. Yukawa called his particle the meson, because he calculated that it should have a mass somewhere intermediate between the electron and the proton.

Shortly afterwards a meson was discovered in a shower of cosmic rays, which are high-speed particles from space which strike the Earth's atmosphere in a burst of subatomic activity. It turned out not to be Yukawa's meson at all, but a particle rather like a heavy electron and has been called the mu-meson, or muon for short. Muons, like protons and electrons, are electrically charged, and also interact with both light and neutrinos. The main characteristic of the muon is that it only lives for about two millionths of a second, after which it ejects two neutrinos and turns into its close relative, the electron. In fact, Yukawa's meson was not discovered until about ten years later, in 1946, and is called a pi-meson, or pion, which also lives only for a fleeting instant, after which it ejects a neutrino and changes into a muon.

In order to study the new subatomic particles, immensely large and expensive machines called accelerators have been built. Modern accelerators such as the one at CERN in Geneva are too large to fit into a laboratory; instead the laboratories are clustered around the machine, which may be several kilometres in size. Mostly they are built in the shape of a ring, a circular tube, surrounded by powerful magnets, and inside which beams of subatomic particles are whirled around in a vacuum at close to the speed of light and deflected into circular orbits by the magnetic fields. Particle accelerators are technological dinosaurs used for smashing matter apart. The high energy beams of particles are allowed to impact violently against selected targets, and the splinters of matter which burst out are scrutinized in a variety of detecting instruments surrounding the target. The method is crude but effective, for the sudden shock of near-luminal collisions unlocks a whole new world of strange and exotic subatomic particles.

In recent years, progressively bigger and more powerful accelerators have been built, and with each increase in size, new types of particles are discovered. Success has been so spectacular that the number of these now total hundreds — a bewildering array of different species of matter, many existing for only the tiniest fraction of a second before disintegrating. For a while it seemed that the world of microscopic matter was unlimited in complexity and random in arrangement. Then certain systematic relationships were discovered among different groups of particles, similar to Mendeleev's periodic table for the elements. New quantities and labels had to be introduced to systematize the data; mysterious attributes carrying quixotic names like 'strangeness', 'colour', 'isotopic spin' and 'charm' have been given to groups of particles to categorize them and describe their interrelations. Some physicists think that a small number of truly elementary particles exist, buried in the deepest recesses of matter, and that with sufficient energy they could perhaps be liberated, while others have argued that any such fundamental particles will be for ever confined in unbreakable union with each other. With characteristic confidence, these basic constituents have already been given a name: quarks. People hunt for quarks in giant accelerators or in showers of cosmic rays. No one has yet found any. If they exist, it is supposed that they are indestructible.

Machines like accelerators can be used to probe the condition of the primeval furnace inside the first second of the universe, by simulating for a brief moment the colossal energies which temperatures in excess of ten billion degrees can unleash. Each epoch nearer the origin is hotter and more energetic. The violent collisions between particles would have created throughout the cosmological material all the varieties of particles which fly off the production line at CERN and elsewhere. To fully comprehend the big bang and its consequences, an understanding of these particles and their interactions is necessary. The nearer to the first moment that we probe, the higher the energies involved, and the more tentative our knowledge of the particle physics becomes. For this reason, few physicists would have much confidence in speculation about processes before the end of one microsecond. Nevertheless speculation there has been. When studying the physics of the universe on the very threshold of the creation, it is difficult to restrain curiosity and forego some conjecture about ever-earlier moments. Some of this conjecture has led to the prediction of more relics from these earlier epochs.

One example of a relic from the lepton era involves the elusive neutrinos. Calculations show that before about one ten-thousandth of a second, the heat energy of the fireball was great enough to create electrons, positrons and muons, which together with electrons, protons and neutrons, would have been balanced against each other in their abundances by a complex network of interactions, involving mainly neutrinos being continually emitted and absorbed. As soon as the temperature fell below several billion degrees, the muons, and later the positrons, would have suddenly disappeared leaving the neutrinos with 'nowhere to go'. Most of these particles would have just ploughed straight on through the remaining, now transparent, matter, and they have carried on travelling ever since. These neutrinos should be here now, coming at us straight from the first ten thousandth of a second after the creation. This is a strange thought, that every moment, countless billions of these primeval escapees are passing through our bodies. We do not notice this of course, but it is conceivable that some atoms do, and experiments may one day detect their presence.

But this is not all. One ten-thousandth of a second is a long time to an elementary particle and countless species of particles, some we may never know about on Earth, must have been long gone when the muons finally disappeared. What about these others? They undoutedly engaged in many complex processes and interactions before the fireball grew too cold for them to survive. It is curious to wonder whether any relic of their fate has survived to the present day. Undoubtedly the condition of the furnace depended greatly on details of particle physics about which we as yet only have an inkling. If the quarks do exist, then they will have filled all of space during the very brief, early moments of the big bang, before one billionth of a second after the beginning. This instant corresponds to a time so brief that even light could have travelled scarcely a foot since the first moment of the universe. During the era of the quarks the density was colossal, with a mass equivalent to that of the Earth concentrated into a volume the size of a bucket. The energy of the fireball was then great enough to stimulate a most bizarre phenomenon. The quarks, moving chaotically at almost the speed of light and impacting against each other, transferred such enormous quantities of energy that they literally set space ringing. The explanation for this is that space is, in a sense, elastic and like other elastic things it can be set into vibration if shaken violently enough. The violence of the furnace during this first split second is great enough to generate such 'space ripples'. The ripples in space are called gravitons. No one has actually detected any gravitons yet, but if they exist they will be gravity's analogue to the photon of light — pulses of gravitational energy. But these pulses differ from all others in that they constitute a movement of space itself — the very fabric of the universe shaking. If gravitons exist, then these vibrations in space will have come ringing down the epochs from the primeval fireball. This is not all idle speculation; calculations can actually predict the energy of the space vibrations. Like all the relics of the big bang, the echo of the primeval roar is still here, but has now faded to the depths of inaudibility. We could not, for example, feel any tremor as the gravitons pass through us, for even our most delicate scientific equipment is at present totally incapable of detecting them, so feeble have they become. Nevertheless the energy they carry could be nearly as great as the heat energy detected by Penzias and Wilson. Perhaps one day in our technological future we shall have the equipment to *listen* to the distant rumble of the big bang, as well as to feel its warmth.

In addition to the gravitons, some of the quarks themselves might have escaped combination and survived until the present day. This can be expected because the material density was falling so rapidly in the quark era. A few of them may, by fortuitous manoeuvring, have avoided fusion altogether, and soon found themselves in a nearly quark-free environment. It has been estimated on the basis of this theory that quarks may be as abundant as gold atoms in the universe. If that is so it is hard to see why they have not already been detected.

Pushing back to still earlier moments than this leaves us with only a suspicion of what was happening. Remember that as the first split second is divided into ever smaller intervals, the density, and probably the temperature, of the universe continues to rise beyond all comprehension — without any understood limits. But general physical principles can still be applied to give a rough clue as to the condition of the universe inside even the first billionth of a second. Although it is still pure speculation, some cosmologists believe that we can push right back into the first one-hundred thousandth of a billion billionth of a second — the time for light to move only one ten-million millionth of a centimetre, the distance across a single atomic nucleus! Such an infinitesimal duration is quite beyond the imagination, and yet processes which occur over such brief intervals can (and are) studied in the laboratory.

This near to the creation event the density of matter is phenomenally high: the mass equivalent of the material contents of the presently observable universe could have been contained in an average-sized bucket. The entire material content of our galaxy, with its hundred billion suns, would have been squeezed into little more than a tenth of a

47

millimetre. About such an unfamiliar world all intuition deserts us. All that can be done is to try elementary principles of physics and conjecture that they still apply under those extraordinary conditions. This very early stage of the universe has been closely studied in the past few years, and as a consequence of the work some remarkable new results indicate that space was at that time stretching sufficiently rapidly for this motion itself to stimulate the creation of matter.

Some cosmologists have suggested that prior to this moment, the space fabric took on the features of an ocean storm, with turbulent twisting and buckling motions producing large irregularities and geometrical distortions. This turbulence is a scientific version of primeval chaos, only here it is space itself which is churning about. In recent years many very detailed calculations have been made to try and explore what would happen to a universe which started out in a condition of primeval chaos. The calculations indicate that the space motions would create matter straight out of 'empty' space. The effect of this genesis is to smooth out the chaotic motion, leaving only the smooth, regular pattern of expansion which is still observed today. Certainly there is no sign of any space storm in the universe now. The expansion of space as far away as modern telescopes can detect appears to be remarkably, and unexpectedly, smooth and uniform. Either the universe was made that way, or some process back in these first moments, something like matter genesis, damped out the primeval chaos.

This is in fact the point where we obtain the first important clue to the problem of how the universe achieved its present orderly structure and arrangement of matter. It has long been a puzzle to cosmologists why the expansion of the universe is so smooth and uniform in all directions. This is an enigma because the presence of the horizon mentioned on page 26 effectively physically isolated one region of the universe from another. The size of the region inside the horizon grows with time: at present it is ten billion light years, but at the beginning of the lepton era it was only about a kilometre. During the 'space storm' era it was so small that it barely encompassed the size of a single atomic nucleus. The problem is to understand how all these causally disconnected microscopic domains managed to expand at the same rate. One response to this is that they did not. Instead, each little region of the universe could have exploded at random, leading to the primeval chaos discussed above. It is very doubtful if galaxies, stars and planets could have formed in regular abundance if such circumstances continued. However, if the matter creation process managed to smooth out these random irregularities, it would explain the orderly arrangement of the galaxies that we see today, receding from each other in a systematic and uniform pattern of motion.

It might be wondered whether there is any limit to the fractionation of the first brief period of the big bang, or whether the laws of physics break down somewhere and forbid scientists to probe arbitrarily close to the creation event. The ultimate limit of currently known physics does in fact suggest a barrier of smallness, inside which we cannot investigate the structure of the universe using classical language and concepts. The barrier does not imply that physics cannot make sense inside that tiny duration of time, but that time itself (and space) ceases to have the meaning usually associated with it. This strange and baffling region beyond our present understanding is called the quantum era. The onset of quantum phenomena could prove to be the most crucial feature of all in determining the fate of the universe. Indeed many physicists believe that quantum effects remove the existence of a creation altogether, thereby rendering the universe infinitely old. These issues will be further discussed in chapter 11. The quantum era is usually regarded, purely on general grounds, as occurring inside regions which are twenty powers of ten smaller than the atomic nucleus, and over time intervals forty-three powers of ten smaller than one second. These numbers are small by any account. To get some idea of sizes, at the end of the quantum era, the entire observable universe was squeezed into a volume no larger than that now occupied by a single atomic nucleus. Each cubic centimetre of space contained a mass in kilograms of one followed by about ninety noughts.

To deal properly with quantum theory would take us way beyond the scope of this book. The subject is particularly abstract and hard to understand, and can only be properly expounded in terms of very sophisticated mathematics. It is only possible to present here just a brief outline of some of the easier underlying concepts, and only then by straining some of the analogies.

Quantum theory is not just an esoteric piece of abstact speculation concerning the early universe, it is a revolution in physical science, which has had more impact than any other theory of physics. What began as an *ad hoc* explanation of the thermal properties of heat and light radiation, made by the German physicist Max Planck, has since been developed into a major re-adjustment of the scientific picture of the world. On a practical level the theory explains at a stroke the detailed features of atomic structure, molecular bonds and chemistry, nuclear processes, subatomic particle interactions, the behaviour of liquid helium, the laser, the transistor, the conduction of electricity and many, many more phenomena of both 'everyday' and laboratory varieties. On an intellectual level the theory leads to a model of matter which has some startling, almost unbelievable features.

One of the more bizarre, and also significant, new possibilities of quantum matter is that energy can appear and disappear for fleeting moments. The way in which this happens is embodied in the famous uncertainty principle of Werner Heisenberg. Among other things this principle tells us that the world is inherently unpredictable. No matter how much information is available about a system, its future behaviour cannot be deduced except as a *probability*. The world is therefore subject to statistical fluctuations, much like throwing dice, where occasionally one will cast two or three sixes in a row. These quantum fluctuations are not usually noticed in the ordinary world, because they operate on a microscopic scale, but the detailed behaviour of atoms and molecules strongly depends upon their existence, and they are well-verified experimentally.

Heisenberg's principle asserts that, for a short enough time, the energy which a system possesses is unpredictable, to the extent of a precise numerical value known as Planck's constant (after Max Planck). To involve anything exciting, this duration must be very small indeed. One consequence is that, over very short time intervals, an entire subatomic particle can literally disappear from the universe, only to reappear again a short while later. Conversely particles of all types can briefly appear in empty space, and then simply fade away again. These phantom particles can actually be turned into real particles if enough energy can be given to them by some means. This is, in fact, the mechanism of particle genesis already mentioned in the previous section, where the tidal effects of space waves supply the energy to create matter out of empty space.

One familiar phenomenon involving this curious evanescence occurs, of all places, on the faces of luminous wrist watches. Luminous watches emit light as a consequence of being slightly radioactive. That is, they produce small quantities of alpha-rays, which as already mentioned, are electric particles ejected from the nuclei of very heavy atoms, such as radium and uranium. And therein lies the puzzle. How do the alpha particles escape from the uranium and radium nuclei? The paradox is an immediate one, for if the principle 'what can get out must be able to get in' is applied, it would be expected that bombarding, say, uranium with a strong beam of alpha-rays would lead to the steady disappearance of those particles as they are absorbed back into nuclei identical to those from which they had so recently emerged. This does not happen. Detailed calculations show why. The alpha particle does not have enough energy to directly break through the electric and nuclear force barrier which surrounds all uranium nuclei. This barrier operates both ways: it keeps internal alpha particles inside, and stops stray alpha particles entering the nucleus from outside. So we return to the puzzle: how does the particle get out?

Quantum theory supplies the answer. The alpha particle, according to Heisenberg's principle, can disappear for a very brief duration: in fact, for a mere million billion billionth of a second. But this is still long enough for its 'phantom image' to travel a short distance, so that when the alpha particle reappears a split second later, it finds itself outside the barrier. The statistical nature of the process is evident in the fact that radioactive substances have a fixed 'half-life', which means that each individual atom has the same probability that a 'disappearance' fluctuation of the type just described will occur.

Of course the description given above is really only a rough picture but it is good enough for understanding what might have happened to the universe at the earliest moment about which one can sensibly conjecture. This is the quantum era. The interval is now so small that the quantum energy which appeared and disappeared was actually comparable in intensity to the energy of the whole universe. When this happened, space and time would have broken apart. Space and time as we know them are not meaningful entities before this moment.

There can be few results in science more startling than the scenario of the universe coming apart at a very early moment, under the relentless impact of quantum energy. Beyond this point lies the world of quantum gravity, a subject too abstract to be properly included in the scope of this book. Many scientists have addressed themselves to the problem of what effect quantum processes might have on the early universe before this moment, but at present the results are muddled and inconclusive. These scientists are motivated by an insatiable desire to understand always what lies beyond the limit of present theory — perhaps in a few years we shall have the answer. Probably whatever lies beyond the threshold of the quantum era, it will not involve the concepts of space and time at all, but will use some more elementary structure out of which space and time will be built, just as matter is built up out of atoms. Whatever new ideas emerge, they are bound to place a whole new perspective on our view of the creation.

3.   Order out of chaos

The belief in Armageddon is common to many cultural traditions. In recent years science has also come to predict a kind of cosmic Armageddon in which the present world order will be destroyed by the remorseless processes of nature, controlled by the forces of gravity, electromagnetism and nuclear interactions. It predicts that far in the future, the complex organization and activity of the universe will cease, in a more or less violent fashion according to circumstance, and a collapse or disintegration into chaos will inevitably occur. To understand why and how order will give way to chaos, it is first necessary to examine the mechanisms whereby this order was first established in the cosmos.

As we saw in chapter 1, cosmic order spans many levels of complexity and scale, from minute biological organisms to galaxies. The remarkable quantity of structures and the degree of organization around us have led many people to believe that the world was created as a very special place, an idea which is clearly in accordance with traditional religious explanations of nature. On the other hand, as described in the previous chapter, the scientific account of the creation offers the contrary picture of a universe created in fiery chaos, subsequently generating the presently observed arrangement of matter and energy out of this structureless, primeval fire. The way in which the present world order arose out of primeval chaos is now understood in outline, and involves some recent discoveries in cosmology, astrophysics, geology and biology. A careful study of these disciplines and the interaction between them has enabled us to build up a consistent picture of a universe gradually establishing organization and ordered activity over the several billion years which followed the plasma era.

The largest arrangements of matter into organized units are the galaxies. The existence of these entities, all of comparable shape and size, is as remarkable as it is conspicuous. The origin of their regular distribution and motion in space was discussed briefly in the previous chapter, but this is only part of the story, for we also have to explain how they formed in the first place. This is a serious problem for astronomers, and at the moment there is only a partial answer. One basic principle is well understood: under the action of gravity, any sufficiently large irregularities present in the cosmological material would tend to grow in size and become more pronounced. The reason for this is that gravity is always attractive and gains more power as the mass increases. Consequently as a region of the universe accumulates matter, its gravitating effect grows, so that it attracts more matter even faster; the process therefore tends to escalate naturally.

It was once thought that the existence of galaxies could be explained on the basis of this mechanism alone. If we suppose that in the primeval epoch material was spread out more or less uniformly through all of space, then as the temperature dropped, blobs of matter would have begun to accumulate by purely random gravitational clustering, although it is now realized that a random process like this would probably take much longer than the age of the universe to be effective. One way of resolving this difficulty is to assume that the universe began with irregularities of various sizes at the outset, and that complicated selective processes have favoured the growth of those which have typical galactic dimensions. This idea suggests a picture of primeval chaos being incompletely smoothed away in the big bang itself.

Once the growth of irregularities had begun, the blobs of gas would have shrunk quite rapidly as they fell inwards on themselves under the action of gravity. There would, of course, have been competition between this restraining force and the tendency for the material to take part in the general cosmological expansion. The contraction, however, would not continue indefinitely: random spinning motions arising from turbulence and irregularities of movement would tend to become accentuated as the size of the gas clouds shrank, in much the same way that an ice skater increases the speed of rotation by contracting the arms. Eventually an equilibrium between the centrifugal force and gravitational attraction would be reached, and the final configuration would then be a flattened, rotating disc, which is precisely the structure observed for many galaxies.

One mystery which has not been properly explained concerns the spiral arms which are exhibited by many galaxies, including our own Milky Way. The problem is that the material near the galactic centre is rotating faster than the edges, so that the arms should wind up after a few revolutions. Recently it has been suggested that the spiral arms should not be treated as co-ordinated entities moving in unison, but as a local aggregation region where stars have become somewhat impeded in their slow migration round the centre. The regions in which this crowding occurs move around the galaxy in a wave, so that the whole assembly is rather like a crowded thoroughfare, in which a celebrity strolls around at less than average walking speed, causing a slight local jam as curious people slow down to join the crowd for a while and then move on.

In our own galaxy, the Earth is at present located in a region on the edge of one of the spiral arms about two-thirds from the centre, which is situated 30,000 light years away towards, and well beyond, the constellation of Sagittarius. The sun makes one revolution around the centre of the Milky Way about every 250 million years, and so far has made about twenty circuits. The centre of the galaxy spins rather faster, perhaps one revolution every twenty million years, while other galaxies with less pronounced spiral structure seem to rotate more than twice as fast as this.

Galaxies vary rather widely in morphology. Some, which are elliptical-shaped, can be 100 times larger than the Milky Way, while at the other extreme, small irregular galaxies may have less than one thousandth of the material of our own. Two mini-galaxies of this sort were noticed by the explorer Ferdinand Magellan during his voyage round the world. These patches of light, known as the Magellanic Clouds, are only readily visible from the southern hemisphere, and are really satellites of the Milky Way. Galaxies rarely seem to have formed in isolation. Most of them belong to clusters of one sort or another, which may vary in number from three or four up to several dozen. Our own belongs to a group of nineteen, scattered over a region of space about three million light years across. About fifty similar clusters seem to have formed into an elliptically-shaped local supercluster, which measures over 100 million light years across and 30 million light years in thickness.

The galaxies probably assumed their present overall arrangement within a few hundred million years after the big bang. The same principle which produced the growth of galactic-sized irregularities also operated over much smaller dimensions, resulting in fragmentations of approximately spherical gas clouds during the early stages when they were still contracting. So it was that before the characteristically flattened, rotating galactic discs appeared, dozens of smaller spherical clouds of gas separated out inside the much larger galactic region. Successive fragmentation on still smaller scales eventually produced the glowing balls of gas that we now call stars.

Stars are the most conspicuous sign of cosmic organization, and their study has dominated astronomy for centuries. In recent years astronomers have gained a fairly detailed understanding of their structure and evolution. To the ancients, the stars appeared immutable, the expression 'the fixed stars' being commonly, if somewhat anachronistically, used by astronomers until quite recently. It is now known that the stars do change with time, though usually very slowly. Later we shall see that they occasionally suffer catastrophic changes, but for the most part they burn with a steady light for millions of years.

In spite of superficial appearances, the stars are not fixed in space for, as already remarked, the entire galaxy is in a state of perpetual rotation. Those in our neighbourhood of the galaxy — the only ones visible individually to the naked eye — are moving more or less together around the centre of the Milky Way. Nearer to the galactic centre, the stars are moving a little faster than the sun, while those more remote from the centre move slower, so by carrying out careful observations of nearby stars over many decades slight changes in their positions in relation to the more distant stars have been revealed. This 'proper' motion, as it is called, went quite unnoticed by ancient astronomers, who did not possess the precision instruments to detect it. The stars are so immensely distant that even proper motions of the nearby ones measuring several thousand miles per hour relative to the Earth can be quite unobservable over a human lifetime.

With the growth of modern astrophysics, scientists have come to realize that the stars were not simply made once and for all, but are continually forming, evolving and changing, over enormous time scales. Starmaking is apparently a continuing process, which means that astronomers can observe at first hand the birth of new stars. By direct observation, we can get some idea of what the universe was like in the early stages just after the galaxy formed, when the first stars began to appear.

On a clear night it is possible to see with the naked eye a place in our galaxy where star genesis is at present in progress — in the constellation of Orion, the legendary hunter, which dominates the southern sky of the northern hemisphere in winter time. Orion possesses a line of three stars inclined somewhat to the horizontal, forming the 'belt' of the hunter. A little below the belt is Orion's 'sword', a near vertical row of three fainter star-like objects. A closer look reveals that the middle member of the three is not a star at all, but a fuzzy patch, and through binoculars it can be seen as a glowing, fan-shaped cloud known as the Great Nebula in Orion. This nebula, however, is not another galaxy, for although early astronomers could not tell the difference, we now know that Orion's nebula is a gigantic stellar nursery inside our own galaxy — a huge cloud of luminous gas one hundred million million miles (17 light years) across, and 1,500 light years away. The nebula is much farther away than the stars in Orion, which are all located in our immediate galactic suburb.

Nearly all the young, bright stars which are at present forming in the Milky Way and other galaxies seem to be situated in the spiral arms. Photographs show bright beads of luminous gas strung out along the spiral appendages, probably caused by the turbulence and compression stirred up by the additional stars in the relatively more crowded arms. When the stars form from these gas clouds, they tend to occur in clusters, often numbering many thousands. The clusters are frequently fairly loose, and break apart after a few million years, although many double or triple groupings remain. The Pleiades is a well-known cluster of several hundred young stars, and an interesting indication of their youthful activity is the fact that Shakespeare describes them in *Henry IV*, Part I, as 'the seven stars', whereas only six are now visible to the naked eye. Indeed, even as early as the beginning of the nineteenth century Lord Byron, in his poem *Beppo,* refers to 'the lost Pleiad seen no more', so evidently it had faded out during the preceding century, an irregular behaviour typical of young, unstable stars.

In contrast to the loose clusters of recently formed stars are the so-called globular clusters — impressive, highly compact balls consisting of several hundred thousand very old stars. These were among the first

Order out of chaos

stars to appear in the universe, formed from the primeval gases when
the galaxy was still nearly spherical, and separating out from the
cosmological material over ten billion years ago. Globular clusters are
therefore found in a spherical halo surrounding the flattened discs of
the main galactic masses. About one hundred are known in the halo
surrounding our Milky Way, varying in diameter from about 50 to 300
light years.

It is fascinating to imagine how the night sky would appear in the
centre of a globular cluster. Instead of the sprinkling of stars which are
visible from the Earth, the sky there would be studded with thousands
of brilliant multicoloured lights spread out in all directions in space.
The density of stars at the centre of a globular cluster is high — perhaps
thirty stars in each cubic light year — which is several thousand times
the density near the sun. Nevertheless the individual stars are still
separated by immense distances, so that two globular clusters could
pass right through each other without any stars colliding. One particular cluster in the constellation of Hercules can actually be seen with the
unaided eye on a clear night, appearing faint, fuzzy and starlike. It is an
arresting thought when gazing at it to know that one is looking at some
of the oldest stars in the universe, formed from the primordial star-stuff
erupting from the big bang, billions of years before the sun existed.

It is now clear to astronomers that our galaxy, and other similar
spiral types, are really two structures superimposed. One component
represents the very first stars, which formed when the great galactic gas
cloud was still roughly spherical in shape and imploding rather fast.
These old stars, which include those in the globular clusters, are
therefore distributed in a more or less spherical pattern, with a high
concentration near the galactic centre, and a sparser halo round about,
stretching right out into the intergalactic spaces. The halo stars tend to
be moving very fast as they fall rapidly towards the middle of the
galaxy, are swung round there by the gravity of the high mass concentration and then shoot out towards intergalactic space once more. This
cyclical high speed behaviour reflects the original rapid imploding
motion of the protogalaxy ten billion years ago.

The second component of the galaxy consists of the disc-shaped
region containing the spiral arms and gas clouds. This feature consists
of mainly second generation stars, together with the raw material for
future generations. It formed somewhat later, when the implosion had
resulted in an enhanced rotation and a tendency to spread into a

flattened shape. Some astronomers believe there may have been giant 'superstars' which formed even before the galaxy separated out as a well-defined entity. According to this view the superstars would have burnt up their nuclear fuel at a prodigious rate and disappeared from sight before even the globular clusters appeared.

Some galaxies show a dark band across the centre. This is not a 'hole' in the galaxy where the stars are missing, but indicates huge regions of gas and dust which strongly absorb the starlight from beyond. One such region in our galaxy, giving a strong impression of a 'hole in the sky', is known as the Coal Sack and is situated in the constellation called Crux. Another, in Cygnus, is conspicuously visible, almost overhead in the northern hemisphere, about mid-evening in autumn, and appears as a great inky gap in the otherwise bright band of the Milky Way.

For many years astronomers were greatly puzzled about the source of the enormous quantities of energy which stars are continually pouring out into space in the form of heat and light radiation. To take the sun as an example of a typical star, the total power output from its surface is unimaginable: about a million billion billion kilowatts. Only the tiniest fraction (about two billionths) of all this energy falls on Earth, but even this quantity is in itself large enough. More sunlight energy arrives every hour than all the Earth's power stations produce in a year.

The source of all this beneficent energy is not immediately apparent. Early theoretical models of the sun were extremely naive, and at one time astronomers believed that it consisted of a lump of burning coal, or perhaps burning hydrogen. This was clearly inadequate: at present power output the whole mass would be burned out in a few thousand years. About a hundred years ago Lord Kelvin and H. L. von Helmholtz put forward the idea that the power of the sun could come from its own contraction. When a gas is compressed, it heats up, so that if the sun began, like all stars, as a huge distended ball of gas, several thousand times its present size, it would slowly shrink under its own weight. The effect of this shrinkage would be to increase the temperature and the pressure near the centre by converting gravitational energy into heat. The central regions of the ball would then start to emit heat and light radiation, which would slowly filter through the outer layers, heating them up as it went, eventually reaching the surface and pouring out into empty space beyond. The energy would thus be supplied by the sun's own gravity. It was calculated that a shrinkage of only a few hundred miles per year was necessary to sustain the known power output of the sun at a steady rate. As the sun is nearly a million miles across, this amount of contraction would be barely noticeable. In this way, it was concluded, the sun could have kept burning for several million years.

Shortcomings of the contraction theory became apparent when geologists obtained fossil evidence that the Earth must have existed, not for a few million, but for several billion years. Some new source of energy, hitherto unsuspected, had to be operating in the sun to keep it shining at its present rate for such an extended period. No energy source of this capacity was known on Earth until the middle of this century, when it was suggested by Einstein, on the basis of his theory of relativity, that matter and energy could be interconverted. In the previous chapter an example was given where heat energy in the primeval fireball created many types of subatomic particles. At still earlier moments, the conjectured 'space tides' dissipated their energy by creating matter. We have also seen how the opposite process can occur when matter and antimatter annihilate each other to produce a burst of energy.

The central feature of this interconversion is that tiny amounts of matter will produce enormous quantities of energy. One kilogram, for example, will convert into twenty-five billion kilowatt hours of energy, which is enough to run all the cities in Britain for several weeks. The principle that energy has mass is now well-established, although under everyday circumstances it is far too small to notice. A person walking at average speed gains in weight the equivalent of many billions of atoms because of their energy of motion. Inside particle accelerators, where subatomic particles are whirled round at almost the speed of light, the weight of their energy can be many times the weight of the particles at rest, a phenomenon that has to be allowed for by engineers in the design of these machines.

Whenever energy is liberated, its source becomes lighter as a result. For example, if one were to burn a kilogram lump of coal inside a sealed transparent container, the whole system would end up lighter by about three ten-millionths of a gram. This mass is accounted for by the energy which has flowed away through the walls of the container in the form of heat and light. Using this new principle, it is easy to calculate that the sun is losing about four million tons every second, although this is barely noticeable in such a gigantic object, which contains a total mass of about a billion billion billion tons.

To explain this prodigious disappearance of mass, a much more powerful process than ordinary chemical burning is necessary. Chemical effects depend on electrical forces between atoms, but by the early part of this century physicists realized that a much more powerful force lay locked up in the nuclei of atoms — the nuclear 'glue'. If this force were operating in the burning process, then the energy output from each atom might be many millions of times greater than chemical energies. A clue to the existence of nuclear energy comes from a very simple observation. It is known that the nucleus of the helium atom contains only four particles: two protons and two neutrons. The weights of these particles are known fairly accurately, and so is the weight of the helium atom. It turns out that when the four individual particles are assembled together as a helium nucleus, their combined weight is about one per cent less than the sum of their separate weights. This loss of one per cent in mass must appear somewhere as a considerable quantity of energy, emitted from the system at the moment that the four particles first combine together.

It has long been known that the sun is composed mainly of hydrogen and helium, the latter being originally discovered in the sun before it was found on Earth. If there is a mechanism that somehow converts the free protons from the hydrogen atoms into helium nuclei, then a mass loss to the sun of four million tons a second could be accounted for by the conversion of about 600 million tons of hydrogen into helium every second. This amount of hydrogen loss could easily be supported for several billion years without exhausting the sun's stock.

The precise details of the nuclear energy mechanism were not fully understood until after the second world war. It is not possible for protons (hydrogen nuclei) to be combined unaccompanied because they have a strong electric repulsion for each other. Helium nuclei contain two neutrons as well as the two protons and neutrons do not exist in the sun in free abundance. One proposal, put forward by the Nobel Laureate Hans Bethe in the late 1930s, depends on small amounts of carbon being present and acting as a sort of catalyst. The details of this so-called carbon cycle are complicated, but at the end of the cycle the carbon is left unchanged and the hydrogen converted into helium. This process is now known not to apply to the sun, but it does operate in stars which are somewhat hotter. The chain of nuclear reactions occurring inside the sun depends only on the existence of hydrogen, and is a direct conversion to helium, called the proton-proton chain. During this process some of the protons turn into neutrons, a surprising transmutation possible only when other particles are present. The mechanism involves the emission of a small particle called a positron, which is the antimatter companion of the electron, taking away the electric charge of the proton to leave it as a neutron. During some of these transmutations, neutrinos — those elusive, sub-atomic will-o'-the-wisps — are also ejected, a significant point to be discussed later.

This 'hydrogen burning' is, therefore, not at all like ordinary chemical burning, in which whole atoms stick together and release energy. In the more powerful nuclear process it is a direct fusion of the atomic nuclei into new species of atoms which is occurring. In both cases it is necessary to add some heat to initiate the burning reactions. Nuclear fusion is much more powerful than chemical fusion, and the temperature needed is correspondingly greater. Calculations show that temperatures of over several million degrees are necessary for the proton-proton chain to operate, and still higher (at least fifteen million degrees) for the carbon cycle. For this reason it is known that the centre of the sun must be extremely hot. The temperature of the surface of the sun, and of other stars, can be measured directly from the quality of the light radiation emitted. In the case of the sun the surface temperature is about 6000 degrees. There is obviously a strong temperature gradient inside, causing heat energy to flow from the centre where it is liberated in the fusion process, to the edges, and out into space. The actual hydrogen burning takes place only in a small core in the centre.

Studies of nuclear physics have therefore revealed what makes the stars shine. The sun is a gigantic nuclear furnace, sustained by hydrogen fusion power, the same process that supplies the energy of the hydrogen bomb. In this sense the sun is equivalent to the controlled explosion of ten billion large hydrogen bombs every second, running continuously for billions of years — a mammoth powerhouse by any account.

It is now possible to explain how the stars form. Initially a slow contraction of a large ball of hydrogen gas gradually heats up the interior until it reaches several million degrees, a process typically taking 100 million years, which eventually triggers the nuclear reactions. The contraction then stops and the star settles down at a more or less constant size and energy output. Astronomers believe that some erratically behaved stars, called T Tauri stars, are still in the process of gravitational contraction in the pre-nuclear stage, whereas all normal stars are burning with fusion power.

There is still only a rudimentary understanding of the final stages of star formation. It seems likely that the sun started as a slowly rotating ball of gas about the size of the solar system, several thousand times its present dimensions. As it contracted, it began to spin progressively more rapidly — once again by analogy with the ice skater. In due course this rotation would be so powerful that the equatorial surface regions of the protosun would become disrupted and eject a disc of material, rather like sparks flying off a catherine wheel. The lighter elements, such as hydrogen, would have passed to the edges of the disc, while the very small amounts of heavier elements, such as iron, carbon, silicon, nickel, even gold and uranium, which must all have been present, remained fairly near the centre. Magnetic coupling effects would have resulted in a gradual reduction of the rotation rate of the sun itself, while the disc would have compensated by spinning up and moving outwards.

It is from this spinning disc that the planets apparently formed. The big, light planets such as Jupiter and Saturn emerged out of the large bulk of light elements near the edge of the disc, while the smaller quantities of heavy elements nearer the sun formed into the little planets like Earth and Mars. We have a good idea how long ago this happened by measuring the extent to which various radioactive substances, such as uranium, have decayed since the Earth formed. It turns out to be about four-and-a-half billion years ago. Meteorites and moon rocks also seem to be about this old, and the sun itself may be dated at a comparable age by various computational methods involving the theory of stellar structure. This shows that the solar system, particularly the Earth, is only about one-third of the age of the universe and perhaps half the age of the galaxy. The stars in the globular cluster in Hercules were ancient before the Earth even came into existence.

The disc around the sun contained all sorts of materials slowly condensing into planetoids. The gas, dust, rock and debris were caught up in turbulent eddies and formed into agglomerations under impact and gravitational attraction. Gradually these small pieces fused into larger bodies, which in their turn united to form planets. For millions of years the newly-formed Earth must have suffered horrendous cataclysms as huge chunks of material, perhaps many miles across, hammered down on the virgin surface, raising great mountains of molten rock. The energy of these impacts would have kept the Earth molten, enabling the dense substances like iron and nickel to sink to the centre, and the more tenuous silicates to migrate to the surface to form a solid crust. Noxious gases bubbled up from the rocks to clothe the planet in a dense, choking atmosphere, which was periodically stripped away into space by eruptions and flares from the nascent sun. Eventually these solar birthpangs ceased as the sun settled down into its stable, hydrogen-burning phase.

It is fortunate for us that the cosmic bombardment has long since ceased, for the effect of impact by a small planetoid would be devastating. Even the fall of a few kilograms of rock can cause a fireball visible for many miles. In 1968 the asteroid Icarus, a modest object only half a mile or so across, passed a few million miles from the Earth, which is a very close encounter by astronomical standards, because only a slight deviation from its actual orbit would have brought Icarus into collision with the Earth. It would probably have fallen into the ocean, which is a disturbing prospect, for the impact would have resulted in tremendous waves, many miles high.

Some indication of the power of impact from falling rocks during the formation of the solar system may be obtained from inspecting the surfaces of other planets. Even a casual glance at the moon gives the impression of a rugged, disfigured terrain. Low power binoculars reveal a tangled jumble of pockmarks, scars and craters, some of them hundreds of miles in diameter. This record on the face of the moon bears silent witness to the violent cataclysms under bombardment from space which occurred at the dawn of the solar system. When we look at the face of the moon we see a frozen picture of the events which took place over four billion years ago when the Earth was still in the process of condensing from the solar disc. The reason for the remarkable preservation of this prehistoric record lies in the total absence of any atmosphere on the moon. The Earth too must have once presented a similar appearance, but aeons of weathering have eroded away the last vestiges of these birth scars, and only the occasional more recent fall of a meteorite leaves a puny reminder of the former ferocity of the bombardment. Recent spaceflights to Mars and Mercury reveal a similar situation. Both of these planets have only tenuous atmospheres, and there too the disfigurement has survived.

With the formation of the solar system, our tiny corner of the universe achieved the most recent level of astronomical organization: nine planets rotating in an orderly fashion in nearly circular orbits around a stable ball of glowing gas. This is as far as gravitational processes have gone in structuring and organizing matter. After this, further development could only take place with the help of the weak and strong nuclear forces and electromagnetic forces, particularly those involving chemical processes. Nuclear processes power the sun. The essential ingredient for the further growth of organization is a thermodynamic disequilibrium, which in the case of the solar system (and any other star systems with planets) is maintained by the heat output from the solar interior. This constant flow of heat controls nearly all the processes and changes which occur on Earth, with the exception of tidal and volcanic events. The proximity of a hot sun in an otherwise cold universe keeps a thermal imbalance on the Earth, a disequilibrium which is the key to the formation and maintenance of all terrestrial life.

It is not known precisely how or when life first appeared on Earth. Sometime in the first one-and-a-half billion years after the formation of the planet, one or more of a variety of chemical processes could have triggered the beginning of a long and complicated series of molecular rearrangements ending in the first living, self-replicating organism. In the year 1952, a remarkable experiment took place inside a sealed glass flask in the G. H. Jones Chemical Laboratory at the University of Chicago. The content of the flask was a deep red, soupy looking liquid, which began as pure water and had boiled steadily for a whole week in an apparatus filled with a mixture of poisonous gases: methane, ammonia and hydrogen. During that week the contents of the apparatus were taking the first step on the long road to the creation of life. Two chemists, Stanley Miller and Harold Urey, were attempting an ambitious and exciting experiment — to simulate the conditions on the primeval Earth of four billion years ago.

Traces of living organisms appear in rocks three-and-a-half billion years old, so sometime in the preceding billion years something took place in the deadly environment of the freshly-cooled Earth akin to the processes which were occurring in the flask at the University of Chicago. The Earth's atmosphere probably consisted of methane, ammonia, hydrogen, water vapour and perhaps other gases as well, but almost certainly no oxygen. No life as we know it could have survived in those hostile conditions.

Miller and Urey did not expect such a simple experiment to create life, a process which probably took millions of years. What they found was that, even in one week, many of the basic molecular building blocks of complex organic molecules appeared in their primeval soup. The technique which they employed was to steadily boil the liquid in the flask, allow the water vapour to mix with the other gases, and pass through a small chamber in which an electrical discharge took place, simulating the effect of electric storms in the atmosphere of the primitive Earth. These discharges supplied the energy necessary to convert the atmospheric materials into prebiological molecular units.

Since 1953, many biologists have come to believe that, given long enough, the formation of life under the conditions prevailing on the primeval Earth was inevitable. Several sources of energy were available to initiate the necessary chemical rearrangements: lightning, volcanic heat, ultra-violet light from the sun, and cosmic rays, for example. Many mysteries still surround the formation of truly living things, for it is a long way from the simple molecules formed in the Chicago apparatus to the first self-replicating molecule. One puzzle concerns a curious property apparently possessed by all living organisms. When polarized light is passed through a solution of organic substances obtained from living systems, it is twisted in a characteristic fashion, which is best expressed by saying that these organic molecules are always left-handed, whereas artificially-made replica molecules can be either left- or right-handed.

In recent years astronomers have been excited by the discovery of organic molecules in interstellar space. Radio telescopes have detected emissions from more than two dozen rather complicated molecules of the type that occur in living systems, and even alcohol has been found. As yet, there is no complete understanding of how these molecules have formed, or what their general significance may be, but it now seems that the chemical basis for living matter may well have already existed prior to the Earth's formation.

When the first tiny living thing eventually formed out of successive syntheses of simple molecular building blocks, it probably reproduced and spread rapidly over the planet, eating up the less advanced contents of the primeval soup. The Earth was still a dangerous place, especially with the deadly ultra-violet radiation pouring in from the sun, but as new varieties of living matter emerged, a curious pollution of the planet began. The chemical composition of the atmosphere became drastically altered by the activities of certain organisms — the precursors of green plants — which produce oxygen by using sunlight to power a chemical reaction called photosynthesis. One important effect of the arrival of oxygen in the atmosphere was the appearance of a layer of ozone — the triatomic molecular form of oxygen — high up above the air which effectively blocks out the ultra-violet rays of the sun. Thereafter, the way was open for organisms to develop towards the general pattern which we observe today, with plants using the energy of sunlight to generate organic tissue and release oxygen, and animals feeding on other organic matter, using the oxygen to burn it to release the energy originally captured from the sunlight.

The road from the first replicating, complex organic molecule to man is a long one lasting perhaps four billion years, maybe eighty or ninety per cent of the age of the planet, and a sizeable fraction of the age of the universe. For almost all of this time-span life on Earth never got beyond simple marine organisms. Only in the last four or five hundred million years have creatures crawled and plants grown over the land masses of our planet, and a large fraction of this time was dominated by reptile life, such as dinosaurs, which survived for over a hundred million years. Mammals appeared only about a hundred and fifty million years ago, and man about five million years ago. Civilization is a mere few thousand years old.

During this immense period, the Earth did not remain inert: restless activity produced mountain chains, oceans, rivers and valleys. The Earth's crust is only a wafer-thin surface on a molten interior, with a central temperature greater than at the surface of the sun, which powers a variety of activity on the surface ranging from sudden violent cataclysms such as earthquakes and vulcanicity to slow forceful movements which eventually grind away whole continents. The idea of the surface of the Earth moving about, driven by convective forces from deep under the ground, is both awesome and alarming, but geological time-scales are so great that in practice these movements do not amount to more than a few centimetres per year. The continents as such do not move about on their own, but should be envisaged as attached to plates which may include portions of the ocean floor as well. These plates are believed to float around on the fluid support of the mantle beneath the crust. The interface regions between them are areas of continual geological activity as the gradual motions cause different plates to grind

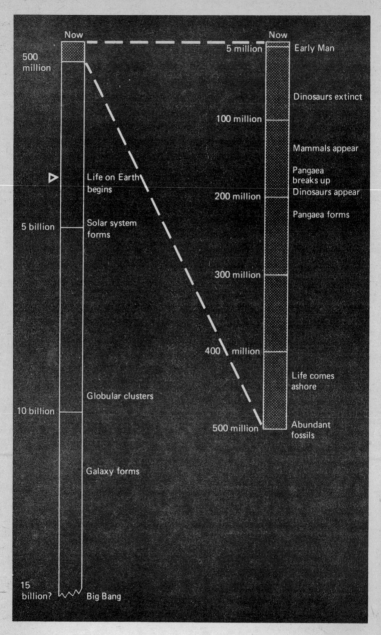

Now

500 million

Now
5 million — Early Man

Dinosaurs extinct

100 million

Mammals appear

Pangaea breaks up
Life on Earth begins
200 million — Dinosaurs appear
Pangaea forms

5 billion

Solar system forms

300 million

400 million

Life comes ashore

Globular clusters

10 billion

500 million — Abundant fossils

Galaxy forms

15 billion?   Big Bang

68

against, or ride over, each other. This is precisely what is happening along the San Andreas fault in California.

In the remote past, the features of the Earth looked very different from now. About two hundred and twenty-five million years ago this movement resulted in all the continents being temporarily joined together in one huge landmass which geologists call Pangaea, a super-continent enclosed by just one ocean, Panthalassa. The formation of Pangaea came about piecemeal over millions of years, with continental-sized masses crashing unceremoniously into one another as they were propelled slowly but forcefully across the Earth's surface. Four hundred and eighty million years ago, what is now North America ploughed into Europe, buckling up the crust along the region of impact into great mountain ranges which still survive in the old granite hills and mountains of Scotland and Norway. Two hundred million years after this, the African plate smashed into the fused American-European land mass, and drove up other mountain ranges which include the Appalachians of North America. About one hundred and eighty million years ago Pangaea began to break up. At first it split into two large pieces, Laurasia and Gondwanaland, and then great rifts appeared in Gondwana: with Africa and South America moving northwards, India crashed so violently into Laurasia that the Himalayas – the world's greatest and most spectacular mountain range – was produced. Further bifurcation and redistribution finally drove the continents into their present arrangement.

By piecing together information from several disciplines, modern science can provide in broad outline a description of the way in which the universe has progressed, in slow stages over billions of years, from the featureless fire of the primeval big bang to the complexity of the present world order. An analysis of how all these ordering processes will continue in the future provides a fairly detailed account of the fate of the universe. Much of this account is necessarily parochial, because we view the cosmos from our perspective on Earth, but astronomers now believe that the experiences of the solar system are typical of most star systems in our galaxy and others. It has long been known that the

Figure 4   Time chart
This shows how long ago in years some important events occurred. The arrow marks the approximate epoch at which the light which we now see left the most distant galaxies currently observable in optical telescopes, on the assumption that their red shift correctly indicates their distance according to Hubble's law. If the same principle is applied to the mysterious quasars, one obtains times earlier than ten billion years.

sun is the source of nearly all the important organization and activity on the surface of the Earth, so that the fate of much of the universe is typified by the behaviour of the sun. When stars like the sun cease to function, then the universe as we now know it will have ended for good.

4.   A star called Sol

If we could travel to the Andromeda nebula and look back at our galaxy, its appearance would resemble that of Andromeda itself (rather like the photograph shown in plate 12). The sun would not be conspicuous as a special object in this great assembly, and only an enormous telescope would reveal its feeble glow among the myriad of other similar stars. Nevertheless however insignificant and unremarkable solar-type stars are, the sun has a special significance for us. Although the galaxy is the largest arrangement of matter, it is at the level of stars that the most important organization occurs. Life on Earth is directly and intimately connected with the sun. It is the thermodynamic disequilibrium which arises as a result of the sun's intense heat production which drives biological systems on the surface of our planet.

As far as the Earth is concerned, cosmic catastrophe will arrive with the sun's demise. Whatever may happen to the universe at large, nothing can prevent the sun from burning itself to extinction in the fullness of time. To predict the nature and timing of this local calamity, it is necessary to understand fully the structure and evolution of the sun, and stars similar to it. This is a very difficult undertaking, for many complex processes are occurring inside the sun, whereas we can only see what is happening at its surface. Fortunately some amazing new theoretical and experimental techniques have enabled astronomers in the last few years to build up a very detailed model of the sun, so that the future of the solar system, and perhaps of the human species, can now be outlined with some confidence.

For centuries, probably millennia, people worshipped the sun as a god, recognizing how dependent the existence of life was on the beneficent heat and light which the sun supplies. They gained reassurance from its dependability, they gazed in awe at its splendour and brilliance as it rose each day to banish the lesser moon and star gods from the sky. Centuries of sun worship lie buried in the roots of our culture. Many important religious festivals, some of them Christian, are thinly disguised acquisitions from solar worship, and even the rise of science took a long time to demolish the notion of a privileged solar status. Copernicus demoted the Earth to the status of a satellite of the sun, but then enthroned the sun itself at the centre of the universe. Even as late as 1900 the Dutch astronomer J. C. Kapteyn, from a systematic study of the distribution of stars in the Milky Way, pronounced that the sun lay at the centre of the galactic system.

Modern astronomers regard the sun as a member of a class of stars, and knowledge about the behaviour of the sun has been gleaned from a systematic study of stellar structure. We obviously have a vested interest in the sun's condition, because even minor changes could result in catastrophe for the human race. Only recently have scientists come to suspect that past alterations in the solar heat may have been responsible for periods of glaciation and biological impoverishment. Ice ages can be as little as ten thousand years or so apart and civilization appeared on the Earth towards the end of the last ice age. We may be due for another soon and it is to be hoped that such an event would not mark the end of civilization. Whether or not expectations of a future ice age are misconceived, as some scientists believe they are, a proper understanding of the sun and its behaviour is clearly of major concern to us all. The sun is the key element in our survival.

One of the sun's more remarkable features is its stability. It has existed for five billion years, during most of which time some form of life has inhabited the Earth. Presumably no very drastic change in the solar condition has occurred in this time, or life would have been obliterated. The sun is not, of course, totally unchanging: it continually showers radiation into space but it seems to do this steadily. A steady state is always preserved by some sort of balance: for example, a river can flow in a steady state if it is fed with water from the tributaries at the same rate that it discharges into the sea. However, just as rivers occasionally overflow or run dry because the balance between feeding and discharge is upset by variations in rainfall, so in the case of the sun an imbalance in the outflow of energy would have drastic consequences for the Earth.

Fortunately there is a very simple stabilizing mechanism to prevent such sudden solar changes from occurring. Since the energy source of the sun is the nuclear furnace in its core, the rate at which the furnace produces energy depends on the temperature of the core. If too much energy were produced, the surface of the sun would not present a sufficiently large area to radiate away the additional heat into space. Consequently the internal pressure would rise, like a boiler over-heating. But unlike a boiler, the sun is free to expand under this pressure, and so it would start to inflate like a balloon. This inflation would in turn reduce the internal temperature, because all gases cool when they are expanded. The energy production in the interior would then fall to accommodate to the new, lower temperature, and thereby bring the energy flowing out of the sun back into balance.

The dependability of the sun is vital to us, and taken completely for granted by most people. Superficially it never seems to change, but a closer examination reveals that it is really in a state of restless torment. Galileo was the first recorded person to turn a telescope on the sun, and was eventually blinded as a consequence (the reader should never attempt to look at the sun through binoculars or a telescope). He noted what resembled rice grains on the surface, though we now know that this curious texturing is a sign that the surface is not smooth, as it appears to the naked eye, but furiously boiling. Every few minutes globules of white hot gases rise to the surface and cool, then descend again. This region of turbulence extends for many thousands of miles beneath the surface.

From time to time, more permanent features erupt among this boiling morass. These are sunspots, which can be seen with the naked eye in favourable conditions. Early observers thought that they were seeing opaque bodies crossing the face of the sun as viewed from Earth. Some astronomers believed, and still do, that there is an undiscovered planet inside the orbit of Mercury. Such an object would be exceedingly difficult to see, even with a telescope, because of its proximity to the solar glare, but if it passed between the Earth and the sun it would show up as a small black dot moving gradually against the solar disc, a phenomenon which occurs from time to time in the case of Mercury and Venus. It was in order to observe a solar transit of Venus that James Cook sailed to the Pacific, in 1769, to conduct careful observations (the transit was not visible from Europe). So convinced was the nineteenth-century astronomer Heinrich Schwabe that an intra-mercurian planet existed that he spent twenty years keeping meticulous records of all the spots which appeared on the face of the sun. The long-sought-after planet was even given the name Vulcan, in expectation of its impending discovery, but Vulcan's existence has never been verified. The sunspots were found to be located on the solar surface itself and are now known to be great patches of relatively cool gas, perhaps thousands of miles across, spasmodically bubbling to the surface. The spots are closely associated with magnetic vortices, as may be deduced from the quality of their light, which reveals intense magnetic fields surrounding them. Although the spots appear black, this is only by contrast with the white heat of the surrounding solar surface; they are still at a temperature of several thousand degrees, emitting light strongly.

The origin of sunspots is a mystery. Through a telescope it seems as though they represent a calm patch among the seething turbulence of the surface. An even greater mystery is why they tend to recur in a strange eleven-year cycle, first noted by Schwabe and later confirmed by careful observations over the years. Sunspot maximum occurred about 1970 and minimum around 1975. The cycles are associated both with numbers of spots and their magnetic structure. The spots themselves often appear in little groups and last for durations which range from a few hours to several weeks. Galileo was the first person to notice that the spots move across the face of the sun's disc, and from this deduced correctly that the sun is rotating, in a rather unusual way: the equatorial (middle) region completes one revolution every twenty-five days, but the polar regions spin slower than this. Thus it does not rotate as a solid body.

Above the boiling surface the sun possesses an atmosphere. This can only be seen properly during a total eclipse, when the glare from the main surface is hidden by the moon. Observations then show a reddish, glowing layer of gas a few thousand miles thick, surrounded by an intensely hot, wispy, tenuous, shifting halo which extends out millions of miles into space; indeed, it has no real edge. This is the famous solar corona, which is the magnificent spectacle sought by eclipse-watchers and much beloved of photographers. It makes the eclipsed sun one of the most breathtakingly beautiful sights in the universe. During an eclipse the true ferocity of the sun's restlessness is exposed, when titanic eruptions of gas are often seen shooting explosively away from the solar surface and then falling back again. These 'prominences' or jets of gas may spurt millions of miles out into space and they indicate that violent storms are taking place in the atmosphere over the boiling solar surface.

Occasionally an eruption on the solar surface itself breaks out and results in a flare which looks like a bright white blotch and lasts for about half an hour, spreading over an area of millions of square miles. Its appearance signals that a burst of energetic radiation has been shot out into space and the resulting rays, which consist mainly of protons, sweep through the solar system. When they strike the upper atmosphere of the Earth, they cause intense magnetic storms and displays of aurora borealis (northern lights) as well as disrupt radio communications. Disturbances in the sun's atmosphere tend to be associated with sunspot activity; when there are many spots, the sun becomes a rather turbulent place. Other stars are known to undergo a similar activity, in many cases more violent than on the sun. When flares occur on small, dim stars they cause a proportionately greater disturbance, sometimes appearing as a sudden, dramatic increase in brilliance which is even detectable on Earth, in contrast to solar flares which are relatively insignificant.

In spite of the violence of all this activity in the immediate vicinity of the sun, the relative remoteness of the Earth, with its cocoon of air, usually keeps the terrestrial surface reasonably safe from solar vicissitudes. Nevertheless, there can be exceptions: for example, some protection against the jets of protons ejected by flares is given by the Earth's magnetic field, which tends to deflect the energetic rays towards the poles. The evidence of paleontology, however, shows that reversals of the Earth's magnetic field take place sporadically, and for a period of many centuries the magnetic shield may be considerably weakened, leaving the proton stream free to pepper the high atmosphere. It has been suggested that the production of nitric oxide which results from this bombardment may be sufficiently prolific to deplete the vital ozone layer through chemical reactions, thereby causing the Earth's surface to be drenched temporarily by the ever-present ultraviolet radiation from the sun. This could have very serious consequences for living things. Indeed there is some evidence that whole species of animals have become extinct during magnetic reversals. In recent years much concern has been voiced about the possible harmful effects of canister sprays on the ozone layer. It is ironical that domestic deodorants might well prove to be as deadly as solar flares to life on Earth.

For more than a century speculation has abounded on the relationship between solar activity and terrestrial disturbances, even catastrophes such as earthquakes or ice ages. There is some evidence that the weather is affected by solar flares, through an as yet unknown mechanism involving the geomagnetic field. One possibility of a close physical link between the sun and the Earth has recently been discussed. Although the surface of the sun proper has a temperature of only about 6000 degrees, the atmosphere above the solar surface is so hot — up to a million degrees — that a constant stream of subatomic particles, mainly protons, is emanating from this energetic region. This incessant solar wind sweeps past the Earth, and couples the magnetic field of the sun to the terrestrial magnetic field in a complicated way. So it is that the sun discharges a steady breeze punctuated by occasional blasts from solar flares.

It is probable that the wind from the sun blows both good and bad fortune for the human race, but the precise way in which it affects our weather is still a mystery. One idea which has been suggested invokes the intrusion of interstellar gas clouds into the solar system. These clouds have already been discussed in connection with star formation. They hang around the spiral arms of the galaxy, having masses about the same as a thousand suns, but spread out in a tenuous patch with only between ten and a thousand atoms per cubic centimetre. This low density would be regarded as an excellent vacuum on Earth, but it is perhaps still dense enough to cause dramatic effects. As the sun orbits around the galaxy, it encounters a spiral arm every few hundred million years, and during its sojourn in this region may become engulfed by these gas clouds several times. The effect on the solar system during this temporary immersion would be to trap the solar wind inside a 'bubble' and prevent it from reaching the Earth, at least for some of the year. The same mechanism would operate to trap the more energetic gales from solar flares. The upshot of this 'windbreak' is to upset the ionization balance and perhaps the ozone layer above the Earth, thereby possibly triggering an ice age. At present we just do not know, but in view of the dire consequences of renewed large-scale glaciation for our civilization it seems well worth trying to understand these processes in more detail.

When the sun 'ruffles its fur' the Earth seems diminutive and exposed by comparison with the enormous forces of the solar surface, but these forces are minute in comparison with what is happening in the interior of the sun, down inside the nuclear furnace. The power-house at the centre controls the sun's condition and behaviour, so what happens there determines the fate of the sun and human civilization as well. A proper understanding of the sun requires a knowledge of its interior and the processes which occur there. This presents a great challenge to astronomers because the boiling surface layers preclude any direct visual observation of the interior. Until recently it was only by using mathematics that anything about the nature of the nuclear core could be deduced. Calculations using complicated models have gradually provided a comprehensive picture of the interior of many stars, including the sun. This entails examining the laws of nuclear physics to determine the intricate details of all the nuclear reactions which might occur at temperatures of several million degrees and to estimate the way in which the energy released from the reactions flows away from the core towards the surface. Certain assumptions are made about the chemical composition of the sun, the proportion of hydrogen, helium and the minute traces of heavier elements, which turn out to have a profound effect, and the emanation of all this energy in the form of radiation from the surface is calculated on the basis of knowledge about the solar atmosphere. Then other known quantities, such as the total mass of the sun, are fed into the equations and the result of all this information is a solar mathematical model — a whole family of them, to be precise. If, for example, somebody decides that an important nuclear reaction has been omitted from consideration, it can be inserted into the model (punched into the computer) and the consequences of the belated inclusion computed. All of these results can then be used to calculate the expected properties of the sun, particularly those to which we have direct access at the solar surface, and a comparison can be made with observations.

On this basis theoretical astronomers have concluded that the boiling layer of the sun extends to about a third of the way to the centre. Inside this layer energy flows more smoothly in the form of electromagnetic radiation. This radiation is very energetic (being mainly X-rays) on account of the high interior temperatures of many millions of degrees. The pressure is high too — a million million kilograms to the square centimetre.

The nuclear processes apparently occur in a spherical core several thousands of miles across. This core contains most of the helium, being the repository of spent hydrogen fuel — opinions differ as to what extent mixing of the core helium with the other constituents occurs. It is here, many thousands of miles beneath the boiling surface, that all the energy is being generated. How can we study such an inaccessible place?

The light from the sun is no help, because the sun is a plasma with a high opacity, like the cosmological material during the primeval fireball. The free electric particles from the ionized gases interact strongly with light and trap it for millions of years in the densely packed material of the solar interior, so it is not possible for the light to travel directly out from the core. There is something, however, which can travel straight out, something which passes right through the thousands of miles of overlying material as if there were no obstacle — neutrinos. The sun is powered by the proton-proton reaction, which results in the conversion of hydrogen into helium, and this process involves two transmutations of protons into neutrons for every helium nucleus synthesized. Each transmutation emits a neutrino along with energy in the form of gamma-rays, positrons and so on. While most of the energy remains locked inside the high-pressure matter for millions of years, the neutrinos are scarcely affected by this great bulk of material, even though it is far denser than anything we can produce on Earth. It follows that the centre of the sun rains a continuous shower of neutrinos straight out into space, carrying direct information about the situation in the solar core.

If it were possible to stop the neutrinos and examine them, we could in some sense look right into the middle of the sun. Nor is there any shortage of them: every second the sun ejects ten billion billion billion billion. Each square centimetre of our bodies is penetrated every second by seventy billion neutrinos, each of which, eight minutes previously, emerged from a proton in the centre of the sun. Every time one glances at the sun, more solar neutrinos pass through the eye every second than there are people in the world. Fortunately they are extremely insubstantial: out of the seventy billion striking each square centimetre of the Earth every second, only about seven are actually stopped by the Earth, the rest just pass straight through. This is where the problem lies. The very property which makes the neutrinos interesting — their ability to travel relatively unobstructed from the centre of the sun — also imposes a formidable obstacle to their detection. If the whole Earth only stops a few, how can we absorb enough of them in a laboratory to study them?

In an attempt to solve this problem, Raymond Davis, Jr., of the Brookhaven National Laboratory, has been experimenting with a 100,000-gallon tank of cleaning fluid in a South Dakota gold mine, five thousand feet below ground. Using this somewhat unlikely equipment and location, Davis is able to study the interior of the sun by counting *individually* the few neutrinos which actually are stopped by the cleaning fluid. The fluid itself is perchloro-ethylene, but it is the 'chloro' part which is the crucial ingredient. A solitary neutrino among countless billions may be stopped by this great tank of fluid by colliding with one of the neutrons in the chlorine nuclei of the cleaning fluid atoms. The neutron is then converted to a proton in a transmutation which is essentially the reverse of what is happening in the sun. The vital step occurs when the newly-created proton balances up its positive electric charge by ejecting an electron.

The conversion of a neutron to a proton in the chlorine nucleus changes the chlorine into a completely different chemical element altogether — argon. There is therefore one atom of argon floating around somewhere in 100,000 gallons of cleaning fluid. The next step is to try to spot this single argon atom among the one thousand billion billion billion perchloro-ethylene molecules. To accomplish this daunting task, use is made of the fact that argon and chlorine are quite different chemically; in fact, the argon atom does not unite with the chlorine or other substances. This means that when the tank is emptied the argon atom can be separated from the cleaning fluid by passing it through a cold charcoal trap.

The next problem is to know when the argon atom is there in the trap, another daunting task, but not an insuperable one, for the argon is radioactive with a half-life of about one month. It decays by capturing an electron from any surrounding material and converting itself back again to chlorine, but this time with a difference. The reconstituted chlorine nucleus is in an excited state, 'bubbling' with excess energy supplied by the neutrino in the original impact, and therefore ultimately by the sun's interior. Before long the nucleus divests itself of the energy by projecting out one of the atomic electrons orbiting nearby. The aim is to detect this fast-moving electron, which is a relatively straightforward task because it can produce a 'click' in a Geiger counter.

Although this whole method of detecting neutrinos might appear extremely complicated it is certainly satisfactory as long as the tank is kept well away from other sources of nuclear reactions, such as cosmic rays. For this reason, the experiment is conducted one mile underground in the Homestake Gold Mine, beneath a sufficient depth of rock to absorb all extraneous ionizing radiations. When Davis first set up his equipment, he was expecting to see at least six events a day in his Geiger counter. Instead he only got about one: this discrepency has been a source of profound puzzlement to astronomers for some time and explanations have ranged over several branches of physics. It has been suggested that possibly we do not understand neutrinos, or that there are nuclear processes which are being overlooked. It may also be that the core of the sun is being sporadically churned up by convection currents, or — most radically of all — perhaps our understanding of the internal structure of the sun is totally misconceived, and the central temperature is well below what has been predicted. It is still too soon to pronounce on this disturbing mystery.

Very recently there has emerged the possibility of an entirely independent way of studying the interior of the sun. Several groups of astronomers have discovered that the sun appears to be engaging in a remarkable wobble motion, or slow 'ringing'. The effect is very slight but still detectable with special instruments, which show that the ringing may involve several notes simultaneously, one wobble lasting about 48 minutes, another about 2 hours 40 minutes, which are very low vibration frequencies by any standards. As yet there is no explanation for these vibrations, although they may be caused by the boiling motions of the outer layers. The significance of the ringing motions is that astronomers can perhaps do for the sun what geologists have long done for the Earth — conduct seismology analyses. Just as terrestrial seismology (the study of wave propagation through the Earth's interior) has enabled a detailed picture of its core to be established, so solar seismology should provide a valuable cross-check on the condition of the furnace in the solar core. With luck, this new technique will help solve the riddle of the missing neutrinos.

To most people the sun is unique, but to astronomers it is just another star. Stars come in many colours and sizes and carry picturesque names like red giant, blue giant, subdwarf, white dwarf. Our sun is classed as a dwarf star, though it is not exceptionally small, being among the bigger dwarfs in the solar neighbourhood. Small, dwarf stars

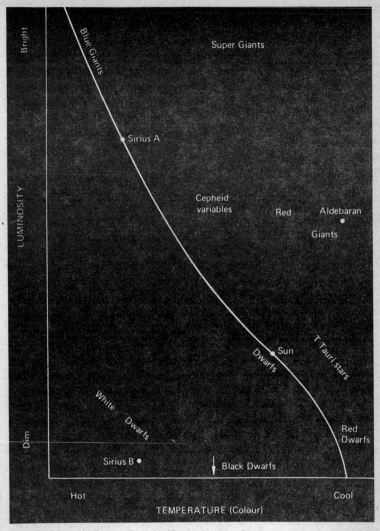

Figure 5 Schematic diagram of star classification (not to scale)
Star types may be characterized by the temperature (roughly their colour) and how much light
they radiate: for example, cool bright stars such as red giants are located in the upper
right-hand corner, whereas hot dim stars such as white dwarfs are at bottom left. Most stars
spend their early and middle life in a condition which places them along the slanting line (the
sun is at present like this): this is the stable, hydrogen-burning phase. The position along the
line is determined by the mass: high mass stars are found in the blue giant region, low mass stars
among the dwarfs. The other regions of the diagram are only populated when the 'ordinary'
stars burn up a lot of their hydrogen, and start to evolve away from the slanting line (see Fig. 7).

are generally more common than big, giant stars, but big stars tend to be the bright ones and so appear more conspicuous. Out of the 100 brightest stars that we see in the sky, the sun is the third dimmest intrinsically. By studying stars as a whole, we can gain great insight into the nature, behaviour and history of our own sun. Many other stars are quite different from the sun, and life on a planet around some of these stars would be bizarre in the extreme.

One interesting star is Aldebaran, the bright red star in the constellation of Taurus (the Bull), not far from the Pleiades. It is a red giant more than 200 times as large as the sun. Aldebaran is by no means the largest star known: Betelgeuse, in the constellation of Orion, is another familiar red star, dwarfing even Aldebaran in comparison, for it is a supergiant, almost as large as our entire solar system and more than 500 times bigger than the sun. At 650 light years distance it is ten times farther away than Aldebaran but appears to us somewhat brighter because it is so much more luminous. Although Betelgeuse is more than fifty times more massive than the sun, it is so distended that its outer layers are little more than a red hot vacuum, so there is really no well-defined surface. Furthermore, Betelgeuse changes in size from time to time; and, unlike the sun, which has a core of helium, it has a heart of iron.

The brightest star in the sky is Sirius, the great dog star. It is not a particularly large star, but it is very close, only 8.7 light years away. In 1834 the astronomer Friedrich Bessel noticed a very curious thing about Sirius: being so close, it can be seen to move as part of the general pattern of rotation of all the stars in our neighbourhood around the galaxy. The fact of motion was not unexpected, but what was surprising was an unusual wiggle in the movement. Bessel guessed the significance of this uneven motion: Sirius must be accompanied on its long galactic orbit by another star which was too dim for him to see, but the presence of which is suggested by the disturbance of Sirius' motion. In the year 1862 the mathematical predictions were verified and the new and faintly luminous companion star was observed for the first time by Alvan G. Clark while testing a new telescope lens. Sirius is therefore really a double star: the bright one is now called Sirius A and the faint one Sirius B.

What makes Sirius B so fascinating is its extreme faintness. It is evidently about the same temperature as Sirius A, so the only explanation is that the dim companion is exceedingly small — about one-fiftieth of the size of the sun, or about twice the size of the Earth. Nevertheless the mass of Sirius B is approximately the same as the sun, thus presenting the extraordinary prospect of a star with an equivalent quantity of material as the sun, but compressed to an enormous density. There are now many of these highly compact stars, called white dwarfs, known to astronomers. Nor is Sirius B by any means the smallest star of this type: others are known which are only one half the size of the Earth, on which a thimbleful of matter would weigh over a million tons.

The range of sizes from Sirius B to Betelgeuse is enormous – clearly stars are extremely variegated objects. The sun is very much in the middle league as stars go. If we were to travel to the next nearest star (four light years away in the constellation of Centaurus), the sun would appear in the constellation of Cassiopeiae as bright as most other bright stars (it would be very much closer than these). Surface temperatures of stars also vary over a wide range: some are as low as an industrial furnace, say 3000 degrees, while others are very much hotter, perhaps 40,000 degrees. The cool ones have a red colour, the hot ones are blue. Vega, the very bright star in the constellation of Lyra, which in Britain is almost directly overhead during late summer evenings, is an example of a hot blue giant star, in marked contrast to the red stars Betelgeuse and Aldebaran. The luminosities also vary greatly from the dimmest black dwarf, to the incredible Deneb, a supergiant 30,000 times more luminous than the sun, and still appearing as a bright star in Cygnus in spite of its remoteness of 1500 light years.

To regard the sun as a member of a family of stars places the Earth and the world of human affairs in a proper cosmic perspective. Definite systematic relationships exist which enable astronomers to deduce, by careful observations of large numbers and varieties of stars, how the sun first formed and achieved its present condition, what makes it shine and remain stable, and how it will change in the future. The life cycles of stars are now fairly well understood; enough, at least, is known to provide a scenario for the future of the solar system. Stellar astrophysics has revealed that stars not only form and evolve, but that they die. This is an inevitable catastrophe that will in time implement the demise of the Earth, a minor local calamity which will go unnoticed by the rest of the universe, but will mark the end of human terrestrial history. All being well, the sun will not dispose of us for several billion years to come. If we do not dispose of ourselves much sooner, it is clear that the human race, with its brief two or three million years of pedigree, is only at the very dawn of its existence. The place of humanity in the universe has always been a preoccupation of thinking people. Modern science has revealed many intriguing new angles on this oldest of mysteries, and this will be the subject of the next chapter.

5. *Life in the universe*

Matter is organized at many levels. On a large scale the appearance of stars and galaxies first established order out of primeval chaos. On Earth, chemistry erupted into biology about four billion years ago, when the next level of organization was unleashed — living matter. Then, in the very recent past, a third great level of organization, much more complex and sophisticated than the previous two, has arrived: Man. Human intellectual and social activity is the most elaborate level of organization that we have so far observed. For centuries, human beings have conjectured on the nature of their role in the great scheme of things. Does Man have a part to play in the evolving cosmos, or are we here, as it were, just for the ride?

Ever since Copernicus, mankind has learnt and relearnt the bitter truth: the Earth is just an ordinary place. Astronomers now conclude that there are millions of Earth-like planets in our galaxy alone. Can we still cling to the belief that, even though the Earth, the sun and the galaxy are not special, *we* are so very special? The contrary opinion, that life and intelligence is a common and widespread phenomenon throughout the universe, boasts a record of adherents that span several centuries. The Roman poet Lucretius wrote 2000 years ago: 'We must have faith that in other regions of space there exist other Earths inhabited by other people and animals.' In the fourth century B.C., the philosopher Metrodorus said 'To consider Earth as the only populated world in infinite space is as absurd as to assert that in an entire field sown with millet only one grain will grow.' The idea of a plurality of inhabited worlds was hypothesized in the Middle Ages by Giordano Bruno, an indulgence which contributed to his untimely death at the hands of the Church in 1600.

Astronomers have frequently speculated about extraterrestrial civilizations. The great English Astronomer Royal, William Herschel, proposed that the other planets of the solar system, and even the sun, were inhabited worlds. Later, in 1877, the Italian astronomer Giovanni Schiaparelli was using a small telescope to map the surface of the planet Mars and among the mottled features on the planet's surface, he thought he saw numerous straight lines 'drawn with absolute geometric precision, as if they were the work of rule or compass'. He called these markings 'canali', being the Italian for 'channels', and the discovery was seized upon by the recently-graduated and rich American astronomer, Percival Lowell, who adopted the anglicization 'canals', proclaiming that Schiaparelli's canali were indeed aquatic artefacts of a beleagured Martian civilization, built to distribute water from the melting polar caps to the arid equatorial regions of the planet. Lowell later established an observatory at Flagstaff in Arizona in order to observe Mars more closely. Many other astronomers saw Lowell's canals too, and maps of complex linear networks were frequently produced until a very few years ago.

Belief in life on Mars became widespread among the general public. Several years after Schiaparelli's discovery, the brilliant science writer and novelist, H. G. Wells, wrote what is perhaps his best-known and most enduring science fiction narrative, *The War of the Worlds*, which describes how a group of Martians, casting envious eyes upon the equability of their neighbouring planet, journey millions of miles to Earth in a cylindrical space craft, to land on Horsell Common, near Woking, about thirty miles south-west of London. These creatures emerge and wreak havoc among the local population, using laser-style death rays to overwhelm the regiments of hussars and artillery which are brought somewhat ineffectively against them by the luckless authorities. As fate would have it, the aliens eventually succumb to the vagaries of terrestrial micro-organisms rather than artillery shells, but not before dispensing considerable destruction and terror.

The notion of terrestrial invasion by bellicose, alien life forms has haunted the public ever since, and is adopted as a recurring theme by modern science fiction writers. It is now a well-established phenomenon that reports of flying saucers reach a peak whenever Mars passes close to Earth. Public hysteria about extraterrestrial invasion reached the level of panic in 1939 when a radio production of *The War of the Worlds* was broadcast to an over-credulous New York audience. Many listeners mistakenly interpreted the sinister announcements as real government warnings about an actual invasion, and considerable alarm broke out in the city.

None of the early speculation about life elsewhere in the universe was based on scientific fact. Indeed the pre-war theories about the origin of the solar system led most scientists to regard the formation of a planet like the Earth as a more or less miraculous accident. It was thought that the sun had undergone a chance close encounter with another star some billions of years ago, as a result of which globules of material were drawn from the sun by tidal gravity forces and strewn around the solar vicinity, later to become the planets. As such a close encounter between stars is exceedingly rare in the universe, it was estimated that the probabliity of another planet similar to Earth was vanishingly small.

Modern theories of the solar system provide a completely different picture. It is now generally accepted that planetary bodies arise quite naturally during the early stages of the formation of a star, a process already described in chapter 3. Unfortunately it is not possible to see planets around other stars, even with the assistance of our most powerful telescopes. The only reason why Venus, Mars, Jupiter and Saturn appear so brilliant in the night sky is because of their relative proximity. If, however, we were to observe the solar system from as far away as another star, the small amount of reflected sunlight from the planets would be totally swamped by the glare of the sun itself. In the same way, we cannot see the small, faint light of planets around even the nearest star. Nevertheless it is possible to detect the presence of large planetary bodies indirectly, using the same method as Bessel employed for deducing the existence of Sirius B. Slight perturbations of the orbits of several nearby stars have in this way revealed invisible planetary attendants.

The post-war years have witnessed great advances in the understanding of the biochemical basis of life on Earth, and experiments such as that undertaken by Miller and Urey have encouraged the belief among scientists that, given the right conditions and a sufficient amount of time, life will inevitably form out of the basic chemicals we know to be present throughout the universe. The three ingredients — suitable planets, an abundance of heavy-element chemicals, and enormous durations of time — are probably available in vast numbers in our galaxy and beyond. The assumption of a universe, perhaps sparsely but nevertheless universally populated with intelligent living creatures, therefore seems very natural.

It is against this changing scientific background that one of the most extraordinary mythologies in history has taken root. The post-war public has been fascinated and mystified by a provocative and outrageous new concept — the unknown flying machine. Throughout history, aerial events have been accorded a mystical or religious significance. The belief that superior beings ruled beyond the sky has fostered a centuries-old tradition that extraterrestrial super-beings manifest themselves occasionally in the form of inexplicable aerial phenomena. This belief is so deep-rooted in our culture that even the impact of modern science has only changed the terminology used to describe unexplained events in the sky.

To the ancients, these superior beings were gods, and they controlled the affairs of the sky with their powers. The sky itself became identified with heaven — the domain of the gods and chosen departed souls. Indeed even today the planets, sun and moon continue to be dignified with the appellation 'heavenly bodies'. In the same vein, the word 'celestial' still carries the dual meaning of 'sky' and 'divine'. And although there is no longer any implied association between the science of celestial mechanics and the Bible stories of celestial choirs, the common terminology betrays a long tradition of the identification of the world beyond the sky with the domain of the gods.

The Christian-Judaic religions teach how angels are occasionally despatched to the Earth from heaven as messengers. Vivid descriptions of quasi-human individuals descending from the sky in unusual vehicles may be found in the Bible. The most famous of these concerns Ezekiel's encounter with four flying wheels full of eyes, from which emerged a creature in the likeness of a man. Throughout medieval times, unusual aerial events were given picturesque mystical descriptions. Comets, meteors, aurorae, ball lightning, all spectacular and sometimes alarming phenomena, were endowed with a significance ranging from superstitious concern to outright religious awe.

With the arrival of the scientific age, many of these aerial phenomena are now satisfactorily understood, though there are some notable exceptions, such as ball lightning. However, the general public are not conversant with many rare and unusual events which occur from time to time in the sky, and there is still plenty of raw material available to perpetuate the very deep-rooted superstitions and beliefs about super beings beyond the sky. The interesting departure which has character-ized the post-war years is the use of machine terminology to describe unusual aerial phenomena. Thus opaque objects become 'metallic', blobs in the sky acquire machine-like symmetries, being described as 'round', 'spherical', 'disc-shaped' or 'cigar-shaped'. Objects are not witnessed to pass across the sky or fall to the ground; instead they 'fly overhead' or 'land'. Complicated kinematic behaviour is termed 'manoeuvring' involving 'hovering', 'acceleration' and so forth. A favourite and universal term which was invented in 1948 by an American pilot, and is now applied in a blanket fashion to almost all unusual, unrecognized aerial happenings, is the famous 'flying saucer'. Both words imply an element of machine artificiality and intelligent control.

No matter how unpalatable the idea may seem to some scientists, the belief that unknown flying machines of mysterious origin are operating in the Earth's atmosphere is a widespread, enduring and tenacious one. It has not gone away in spite of its lack of scientific attention. Moreover the belief in flying saucers is surrounded by an elaborate mythology, equally as complex and sophisticated as that associated with the Greek or Roman gods, or the European witch craze of medieval times. Bookshops contain large numbers of semi-religious tomes, purporting to explain the origins, motivations and conse-quences of the intruding aviators. These accounts are conspicuous in their inconsistency, and the reader may choose from anywhere between the centre of the Earth and another galaxy as the place from which the itinerant flying machines hail.

It is remarkable that so little scientific investigation of this im-portant technological mythology has been undertaken. It is undoubt-edly one of the more intriguing sociological phenomena of modern industrial society. It could well be that we are here witnessing the use of technological language to describe what is in reality the same basic belief system as characterized the early, formative years of the world's great religions. Little or no proper scientific follow-up has been applied to the reports of unknown flying machines themselves. However, the University of Colorado did conduct a two-year study of a few dozen reports in the late 1960s. Although unable to explain about one quarter of the reports, two were actually attributed to unknown flying machines, one of which was photographed in detail (and does, indeed, *look* very much like a flying machine!).

Now all this demonstrates just how strongly the belief in superior space beings pervades modern technological society. What scientific basis is there for advanced extraterrestrial communities? Can there really be super-beings out there in space?

In the summer of 1970 a group of distinguished scientists gathered at the Ames Research Center of the National Aeronautics and Space Administration (NASA) in the United States. Their purpose was to discuss one of the most exciting and far-reaching topics in modern science: the existence of extraterrestrial life, especially intelligent life. If there is intelligent life elsewhere in the universe, how do we know where to look for it? How can we assess its ubiquity? Could we communicate, and how? The conclusions of this conference were startling. There could be many millions of other technological communities in our galaxy alone, some of them wondering, perhaps, how to contact us. The reasoning behind this intriguing conclusion involves a great deal of speculation and assessment covering several branches of modern science, but the essential reasoning is simple enough. Because the number of stars in the galaxy is so large, even if only a tiny fraction supported life-bearing planets, there could still be millions upon millions of these.

The central assumption in this speculation is that life will form and evolve on any planet with Earth-like conditions. While this is by no means certain, the fact that life appeared on Earth so soon after conditions became suitable encourages the belief that living matter may be regarded as a more or less automatic elevation of inanimate substances to a higher level of organization. If living matter really does arise inevitably and automatically under suitable circumstances, it is virtually certain that life is very common throughout the universe. Perhaps less certain is the expectation that intelligence will automatically evolve after a long enough lapse of time. On Earth, intelligence has good survival value, and is found in other creatures besides man; for example, the dolphins and whales. It is not unreasonable to suppose that on other planets intelligent creatures have evolved. Just what fraction of intelligent life forms actually establish technological communities like our own is anybody's guess. But the curious thing is that these imponderables are rather unimportant. Factors of ten or so in assessing probabilities do not really affect the general overall picture of many millions of technological communities arising in the galaxy. Far and away the most difficult and crucial question to answer is whether there are any other such communities out there *now*.

In chapter 3 it was described how stars are continually forming from interstellar gas and dust clouds throughout the galaxy. On average, over the life of the galaxy, the creation rate works out at about ten new stars a year, but actually the rate of star formation was very much greater in the past than now, and most stars are several billion years old. Even using the average figure the Ames team 'guesstimated' that the rate at which technical communities are forming in the galaxy is about one every ten years. Although completely guesswork, at least this figure is derived from well understood, or potentially well understood, science. The parameters which determine the rate at which new communities are likely to arise emerge from studies in astronomy, physics, biochemistry and biology. However, we now reach the difficult point, the crucial imponderable which determines above all else whether the galaxy contains other intelligent life at this moment: namely, how long does the average technical community survive? This is the hardest question to answer, because it depends on such imprecise behavioural subjects as politics and sociology. Once again, our own terrestrial experience is the only available guide. The appearance of advanced technology on Earth has been closely associated with the acquisition of weapons of mass destruction, while vigorous industrial activity has been accompanied by a high level of pollution and a rapid depletion of material resources. Social instabilities, both national and international, seem inevitable features of the sudden metamorphosis of our social system into the space-age, with its science-based life-style. In all, the social and political strains imposed upon modern industrial society are so great that many people think disaster is virtually certain to result.

There are several ways in which our technical society could collapse: global warfare, with use of nuclear, biological or chemical weapons, is an obvious one. Alternatively, over-industrialization leading to an insupportable level of pollution and geological deterioration would choke technology in its own produce. The breakdown of social order under the increasing strain of the unequal distribution of wealth and raw materials, over-population and food shortage is another way. The problem is that a high level of technology requires an increasingly sophisticated and complex social organization to sustain it. It then becomes all the more vulnerable to instabilities and disaffection by minority groups. This has been dramatically demonstrated in recent years by the tactics of a number of terrorist groups who can wreak havoc by the simple expedient of capturing an aircraft or blowing up a vital pipeline. If this experience is typical of technological societies, it could be that, although life is abundant throughout the galaxy, technology is rather rare. Whereas intelligence has good positive survival value, technology could actually be detrimental to survival.

This difficult problem is precisely the one on which the whole issue of extraterrestrial communities turns, for the following reason. If the pessimists are right, and we are on the point of destroying the human race, perhaps by one of the techniques described, then our technological era would have lasted a very few decades; in round figures, say ten years. If this is the typical figure, then the lifetime of technical communities is on average only equal to their rate of appearance in the galaxy. This means that, once again on average, there is only one such technical community in the galaxy at any given moment, and at present we are that one community. We would be alone in the galaxy, the most technically advanced civilization, reaching the end of its life. Millions more would follow, as the life forms on other planets eventually develop intelligence, then social organization and finally the deadly technology which immediately proceeds to effect their demise. Millions of other alien societies would have gone before us, some perhaps speculating in this very way about the equivalent fate of their galactic neighbours in space and time, but powerless to signal a warning, knowing that the very technology which could detect any signal would already imply that the edge of destruction had been reached.

There is, of course, the brighter side. Perhaps a fraction of the communities avoid technological suicide. Maybe some achieve social organization superior enough to escape mass destruction — perhaps even we may be numbered among the survivors. If the dangerous period of high technology coinciding with low social conduct is endured successfully, technical communities may last millions, or conceivably billions of years, their lifetimes controlled by natural cosmic catastrophes, rather than socio-political ones.

The sun is a typical star and is about five billion years old. Millions of other stars exist in the galaxy which are twice this age. We do not know how long it takes on average from the time of star formation to the appearance of a technical community on an associated planet, but there are no grounds for thinking that the Earth is in any way atypical. Four or five billion years is the best guess we can make in the absence of any information about communities other than our own. Even if only about one per cent of the communities survive the technological phase, the picture is totally transformed. The 'guesstimate' formula shows that the number of technical communities in the galaxy might be many millions at this moment.

Our own situation is curious. Rather than being the most advanced (and indeed the only) technical civilization in the galaxy, we would be by far the youngest. The reason for this is simple: the chances of many other communities reaching our level of technology just at this time are infinitesimal. Most of the others with technology would have been around for thousands, millions or an even greater number of years. In short, if there *is* anybody there, they are indeed super-beings. We have a remarkable choice of alternatives, according to this analysis: either we are alone in the galaxy or, if technical communities are common, we are the youngest. This is a profound conclusion, and one that could well affect our intellectual attitude to the place of mankind in the universe.

There could, of course, be vast numbers of planets with life, even intelligent life, but with no technology, and there may be a case for regarding the non-technical communities as the more intelligent. We could not know about these communities, except by travelling or sending spacecraft there. On the other hand, if there are other technical societies, they could communicate with us in a number of ways; for example, one direct and straightforward method would be for them to send us radio messages. This was the reason for Project Ozma, in which the Greenbank radio telescope was used in 1961 to try to detect radio signals from our neighbours elsewhere in the galaxy. The project was undertaken by Dr Frank Drake, an American astronomer, who spent a total of one week eavesdropping on two of our nearest neighbour stars, called Tau Ceti and Epsilon Eridani. No signals were detected, and in any case the probability of reception was exceedingly low.

A much more ambitious and systematic search of the galaxy could be successful. In 1971 an Ames Research Center conference discussed a successor to Ozma, called Project Cyclops, envisaged as a monumental array of about 1,000 radio telescopes spread over an area of dozens of square miles; a complex devoted exclusively to the search for signals from galactic communities. To appreciate the difficulties facing Project Cyclops it should be remembered that the galaxy is a very big place, and even if there are a million other communities transmitting signals to us right now, then this still only represents one star in a hundred thousand which it is worth listening to. The average density of stars in the solar neighbourhood is about one per several cubic light years, so we might have to try every likely looking star out to about 1000 light years away to stand any real chance of success. Some stars, such as the variables, could be omitted from the list, because it is hard to see how life could survive near such fluctuating heat and light sources, but even with these exceptions it is still a formidable task to examine so many stars.

The location problem itself would be relatively manageable if it was clear on what radio frequency the incoming signals might be. There is an enormous number of usable radio channels which can penetrate our atmosphere, but even if the transmitting community assumed the correct atmospheric structure for the Earth, we might still listen in to the right star and yet tune in to the wrong frequency and miss the message. At first sight, therefore, the task seems a hopeless one. In 1959, however, Guiseppe Coconni and Philip Morrison of the Massachusetts Institute of Technology put forward a proposal that put a new perspective on the communication problem. Basically the idea is that anyone wanting to communicate with us would presumably attempt to make it as easy as possible for us to receive their signals. The situation has been compared to two people in a large city trying to find each other without having arranged a prior meeting place. Each reckons that the other will go to one of the obvious landmarks — a town hall, a central railway terminus, etc. When it comes to radio communication from one planet to another, it seems reasonable to assume that the transmitting community would try to pick a transmission frequency which has some universal significance to both parties. But which frequency? What do they and we have in common in the galaxy?

If we are going to communicate by means of radio telescopes then we must have radio astronomy in common; they must be able to 'hear' what we can 'hear' with these instruments. The most conspicuous thing to hear turns out to be the ubiquitous 21 centimetre wavelength 'song of hydrogen'. Hydrogen atoms very occasionally flip the alignment of the spins of their two constituent particles (the proton and the electron), resulting in the emission of a burst of radio waves. As hydrogen is prevalent throughout the universe, the cumulative effect of these sporadic spin-flips is to create a background hiss in radio telescopes — indeed, detecting the hiss is the main method of mapping the distribution of interstellar gas clouds in the galaxy. It follows that 21 centimetres is a good universal frequency to use for communication, because it would be well-known to all radio astronomers, human or otherwise. Alternatively, twice or one-half this frequency might be tried. There are also other natural frequencies which have been suggested, but the total list is rather short. It has been calculated that, restricting attention to a limited number of wavebands, the Cyclops system could scan all the stars out to 1000 light years in about 30 years, spending about 15 minutes on each star. There is no doubt that this represents a major scientific and engineering undertaking, so that we have to be fairly sure there is a reasonable chance of success before committing vast resources to the project.

Pessimists point out that, even if there are many millions of alien civilizations capable of entering into radio communication with us, we cannot be sure that they are attempting to do so. There seems to be no way they could know of our existence, except by detecting signals from us. As the first artificial radio signals were transmitted on Earth only in the 1920s, our presence could only be known out to a distance of about fifty light years. Hence it seems most improbable that any messages are being directed deliberately at us. An alternative strategy is for them to transmit signals omnidirectionally, in the hope that some technical society on a remote planet might pick up the message. But with what motivation would all these aliens be blasting the entire galaxy with expensive radio signals for millions of years? Once they had contacted a few neighbours, it seems probable that they would direct all their attention and resources to them. In addition to all this, the assumption of the use of radio telescopes for interstellar communication between super-advanced technological civilizations seems excessively anthropomorphic and parochial. Just because radio telescopes represent the pinnacle of terrestrial technology does not mean that communities millions of years more advanced than we would also be using such methods. They may have techniques which our science knows nothing about. We cannot suppose that the latest scientific discovery happens to be the most advanced concept in existence. Radio communication has only been used on Earth for fifty years, and in a few decades we may discover something else.

In spite of all these objections, there still seems to be a case for attempting to detect evidence of other intelligent life by radio searches. While some of the above criticisms have been answered in a fairly convincing way, it is the motivational questions which are the hardest to answer. We cannot guess at the behavioural predilections of alien species many thousands, or perhaps millions of years more advanced than ourselves. Even on Earth the habits and activities of the white European colonizers were quite incomprehensible to the American Indians, for example. An extraterrestrial community might be motivated by stimuli which are utterly beyond our understanding. The only assumptions which may be made about alien behaviour are those which seem to be required on basic biological or physical grounds: for example, any life form which achieves technological capability must at least display a level of curiosity in order to achieve the necessary scientific progress. Moreover one imagines that if such a society survives the technological crisis, it will display selflessness and consideration for others. It seems reasonable to suppose, therefore, that any alien community capable of initiating interstellar communication on a grand scale would have both the desire and the consideration to do so.

If the galaxy really is populated widely, though thinly, with highly advanced technical communities, the Earth might be expected to receive visits from time to time. After all, if humans can achieve spaceflight in the solar system within 200 years of industrial revolution, imagine what might be achieved by a society with millions of years of spaceflight experience. The prospect of alien visitation is a popular one, which has received wide attention from the public in recent years. The fact that we can send space probes to other planets makes the idea all the more plausible.

Enthusiasts of extraterrestrial life have searched for evidence that spacecraft either have landed on Earth in historical times, or are operating in the Earth's atmosphere at present. One popular theory is that the celestial super-beings worshipped as gods in ancient cultures were not purely mythical, but had a basis in real events, such as contact with extraterrestrial visitors. This is an intriguing idea supported by a number of superficially persuasive pieces of evidence. Many cultures have a tradition of the gods descending from the sky in vehicles associated with luminous discharges or haloes and drawings and de-

Plate 1 Neutron stars are small. The enormous compaction of material in a neutron star is illustrated by comparison of its size with that of London. The mass of the star might be a million times that of the Earth and its gravity would therefore rapidly suck up our relatively tenuous planet into a wafer-thin layer of crushed atoms. Courtesy of Aerofilms Limited.

Plate 2 The Arecibo Radio Telescope. This giant instrument in Puerto Rico is used to detect radio waves from galaxies billions of light years away. If used as a signalling device it could communicate with a similar instrument anywhere in the galaxy. Courtesy of the Arecibo Observatory, Puerto Rico

Plate 3 Scars of cosmic bombardment. The formation of the solar system witnessed intense bombardment of the planets by rocky debris. This photograph of the surface of·Mars shows a record of the results. Similar effects can be seen on the moon and on Mercury but on the Earth such birth scars have long been obliterated by weather erosion. Courtesy of NASA

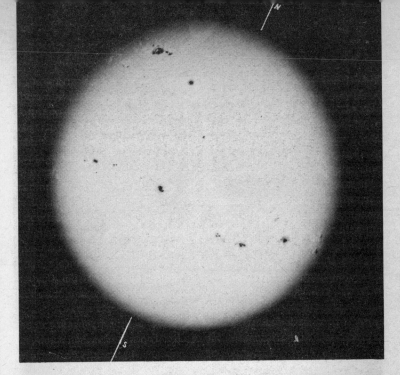

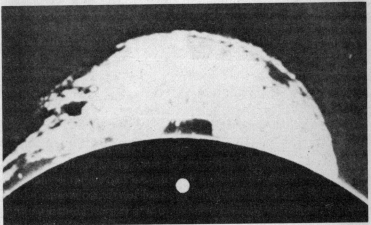

Plate 4 Sunspots. Ever since Galileo, astronomers have observed spots on the surface of the sun. The photograph clearly shows dark central regions surrounded by brighter halos. Courtesy of the Royal Greenwich Observatory

Plate 5 Solar prominence. Some idea of the fierce activity occurring near the sun's surface can be gauged from this photograph of a gigantic prominence (eruption of gas) which took place on 4 June 1946. The bright spot has been inserted for comparison with the size of the Earth. Courtesy of the High Altitude Observatory, Colorado.

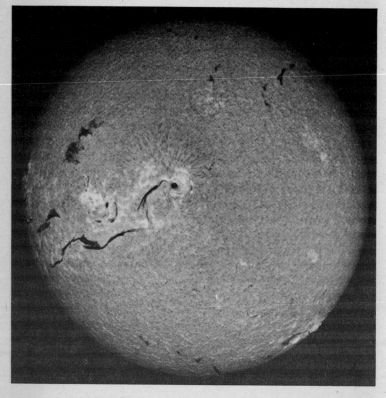

Plate 6 Activity on the sun. Photographed in hydrogen light, the mottled surface of the sun displays the turbulence of the boiling outer layers. The wispy filaments are due to erupting prominences shown in relief against the solar disc. Courtesy of the Sacramento Peak Observatory

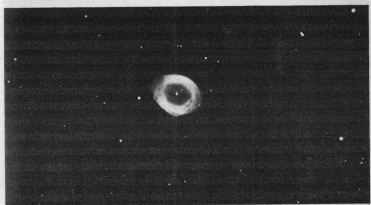

Plate 7   The Pleiades. This famous cluster of young stars is readily visible to the naked eye. The telescopic photograph shows nebulous gas surrounding some of the brighter stars. Courtesy of the Lick Observatory

Plate 8   The Ring Nebula. Occasionally dying stars explode away a roughly spherical envelope of gas to form a so-called planetary nebula. The gas is illuminated by radiation from the star which is visible at the centre. Courtesy of the Dominion Astrophysical Observatory, British Columbia

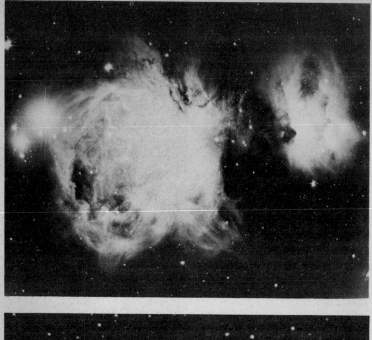

Plate 9 Great Nebula in Orion. This gigantic stellar nursery can be seen with the naked eye in the 'sword' of Orion. It contains many so-called T Tauri stars, thought to be contracting balls of gas in a pre-nuclear phase. Courtesy of the Lick Observatory

Plate 10 Crab Nebula. This cloud of gas in the constellation of Taurus represents the shattered remains of the supernova of AD 1054. The core of the exploded star still resides near the centre in the form of a rapidly rotating neutron star which produces regular radio and optical pulsations. Courtesy of the Yerkes Observatory

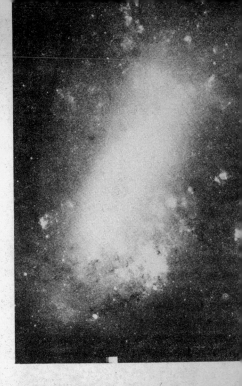

Plate 11 The Larger Magellanic Cloud. This mini-galaxy is really a satellite of the Milky Way. It is named after Magellan who noted it during his voyage round the world. Courtesy of the Boyden Observatory

Plate 12 Andromeda galaxy. This beautiful spiral galaxy is almost a twin of the Milky Way and is the only galaxy visible to the naked eye. It is nearby — only one-and-a-half million light years. Notice the two 'satellites' appearing as bright blobs in the surrounding halo of stars. Courtesy of the California Institute of Technology and the Carnegie Institution of Washington

Plate 13 Spiral galaxy. This galaxy is in the constellation of Pavo and in the photograph the faint stars and gas which make up several spiral arms can be seen to extend well out from the nucleus of the galaxy. Courtesy of the UK Schmidt Telescope Unit of the Royal Observatory, Edinburgh

Plate 14 Field of galaxies. This cluster of distant galaxies in the constellation of Pavo is about three thousand million light years away. All the individual stars also visible in the photograph are nearby members of our own galaxy. The spikes projecting from the brighter stars are photographic defects. Courtesy of the UK Schmidt Telescope Unit of the Royal Observatory, Edinburgh

scriptions of these events can readily be interpreted in terms of aerial machines of some sort. Ezekiel's description of four flying luminous wheels, the colour of beryl and full of eyes, turning as they went, sounds like a perfect description of the archetypal flying saucer. The prophet Elijah is described as ascending into the sky in a fiery chariot or carriage of some sort and the mysterious star of Bethlehem is yet another biblical account of an unidentified luminous aerial object. To most people these ancient records seem purely symbolic, but some writers have interpreted them as manifestations of alien technology. It is curious to wonder just what type of evidence one would expect to survive from an encounter with advanced extraterrestrial beings. Our present technology appears to be magic to unsophisticated tribes who live in places like New Guinea, so clearly, space-age technology would have seemed miraculous to people two or three thousand years ago, and it would not be surprising if encounters with extraterrestrials were recorded as visitations by angels or gods.

Unfortunately there is no way of knowing whether these encounters were purely symbolic or real. No physical evidence, such as abandoned artifacts, which would confirm the extraterrestrial theory have ever been found. There is also the danger that any myth or legend, from the yeti to the story of Atlantis, gains undeserved credence when recast in the language of extraterrestrial visitation. It must always be remembered that almost anything which appeared in the sky was once regarded as a manifestation of supernatural forces, and even fairly mundane objects, like comets or meteors, received the most embellished descriptions.

Turning to the idea that the Earth is being visited now by spacecraft from other planets, there is no lack of eyewitness evidence to support this contention. The number of people who have made official reports of unidentified aerial machines runs into hundreds of thousands. Furthermore, thousands of people have given accounts of what appear to be the actual landings of alien spacecraft, including in many cases detailed descriptions of their occupants. No systematic evidence has ever been produced to show that the eyewitnesses are liars or subject to delusions. The reports are made by a fairly typical cross-section of the population, but include astronauts in orbit, pilots and astronomers. Government and military organizations have collected and filed enormous quantities of these reports of which only a few have been investigated, mainly by military officers. A large fraction of the more detailed reports, particularly those with radar confirmation, remain unexplained. Apart from the Colorado University investigation, scientists have largely ignored these accounts because they are associated with a widespread, mild hysteria which feeds on the mythology of the unknown flying machine and super-beings from the sky. This hysteria is evidenced by the profusion of enthusiast clubs and organizations which are firmly committed to the belief in these beings, while bookshops display repetitious paperbacks, elaborating the whole astonishing mythology still further.

There is no doubt that the *social* phenomenon of people continually reporting unknown flying machines is a challenging modern mystery. There is no reason to suppose that the habit will not continue for the next thirty years as for the last, nor that these reports will provide any real evidence that spacecraft are operating in our atmosphere. A judgment on such a provocative idea is best made by placing the whole concept of interstellar travel into perspective.

Man has so far travelled about 1½ light seconds into space, which is the distance to the moon. At currently available rocket speeds it would take several years to travel from the Earth to the edge of the solar system, while a journey of thousands of years is necessary to reach even the nearest star, 4⅓ light years away. Clearly, therefore, interstellar travel is quite beyond our current technological capability. Nevertheless, past experience suggests that technological advancement can be very rapid, and accomplishments previously considered to be impossible have often been achieved sooner rather than later. An alien technology millions of years ahead of our own might have machines capable of travelling at speeds greatly in excess of our puny rockets. As we cannot guess the technological future even fifty years ahead, it is unwise to rule out the possibility of extraterrestrial visitation solely on technological grounds.

Even in the absence of technological constraints to the imagination, it is necessary to continue to work within the framework of the laws of physics. For fundamental reasons the speed of light is thought to be the fastest speed in the universe. Much laboratory experience confirms this and unless the whole basis of the theory of relativity — which explains, among other things, the origin of the sun's energy — is badly misconceived, then it must be accepted that the velocity of light provides a speed limit for interstellar travel. The time factor is, however, not much of a problem. A journey between the Earth and our nearest technological community is likely to take only a few hundred Earth years. This is still longer than a human lifetime but there are a number of reasons why this is not important. First, alien life forms might have, naturally or artificially, attained much longer life spans than we have. Secondly, suspended animation techniques such as freezing could probably be used for most of the voyage. Thirdly, and most curiously, there is the famous time dilation effect. The theory of relativity contains many surprises, but perhaps the most weird prediction is that time intervals are relative to one's state of motion. Crudely speaking, a clock carried in a spacecraft which travels close to the speed of light runs more slowly than a similar clock left on Earth, which leads to a bizarre effect called the twins paradox: a twin who travels to a distant star will return to find himself younger than the sibling left behind. Obviously, this 'elasticity' of time enables the astronaut to accomplish a voyage in a shorter lapse of spacecraft time than the equivalent lapse of Earth time for the same trip. This time dilation effect is readily measured, either directly by flying clocks around the Earth in fast aircraft, or indirectly by measuring the extension in the lifetimes of rapidly moving muons created in cosmic ray showers or in subatomic particle accelerators. It is a real effect.

Theory predicts that the dilation, or stretching, of elastic time increases without limit as light speed is approached. For the crew of a spacecraft, who naturally regard themselves as at rest and weightless, the effect manifests itself as a contraction of distances. For example, at 99 per cent of light speed, the distance from Earth to the nearest star appears reduced to just over half a light year instead of more than four light years. Either way of viewing it, the journey only takes a few months rocket time, but more than four years Earth time. In principle, the time dilation effect could enable a person to travel round the entire galaxy in a lifetime, but the problem is that they would return hundreds of thousands of years after departure, perhaps to find that civilization on Earth had gone, and their existence forgotten.

In spite of the promising possibilities of time dilation, a great deal of caution is necessary in assuming that travel close to the speed of light can be a successful reality. In order to attain 99 per cent of light speed, a colossal quantity of energy must be expended. As it is, the underlying laws of propulsion are strongly loaded against achieving the sort of velocities where time dilation becomes important. This is because the same factor which produces the time dilation also increases the mass of the payload, resulting in escalating energy expenditure on fuel as light speed is approached. As an example, it may be calculated that a round trip of a modest 1000 kilogram payload to the nearest star at 99 per cent of light speed would use up so much energy that all life on Earth would be annihilated in the blast of take-off. In addition to all this, something has to be done about the terrifying effects of impact with interstellar material such as meteoroids: a grain of sand colliding with a spacecraft moving at near-luminal speed would have the force of an atomic explosion.

It is still possible to envisage scenarios where the technological problems are overcome. A rocket could perhaps be launched from a zero-gravity space colony while meteoroids could be vaporized with lasers before impact. It need not, therefore, be out of the question for a spacecraft occasionally to be sent across interstellar space at nearly 186,000 miles per second. There is no doubt, however, that such an undertaking would consume major resources of the domestic community, and there would be no hope of the spacecraft returning for perhaps hundreds of their years.

From all this it should be clear that a visit to the Earth by an extraterrestrial spacecraft would be a rare and truly monumental experience. After the commitment of so much time, money and effort, it is likely that the arrival of the aliens would be treated as a really cosmic event — the physical contact between two independent cultures. The whole world would be profoundly changed. This expectation does not seems to have been fulfilled in the many hundreds of stories of alleged spacecraft landings. It is scarcely conceivable that another community should engage in a massive expedition across the galaxy, only to land in a potato field in Wiltshire for a few minutes, and then return across several hundred light years of space.

It is often pointed out that our existence on Earth could not be known far out in space. An alien civilization systematically exploring the galaxy in search of other communities might have to visit thousands or even millions of Earth-like planets before coming across one with intelligent life. Why should the Earth be graced with a call, when interstellar travel is such a rare, or even non-existent, practice? In answer to this objection, it must be realized that life has existed on Earth for over three billion years, so the chances that even a single visit has been made during that vast time span is perhaps not particularly small. Once the presence of life on Earth had been established, the entire galaxy could have been informed of the fact by radio, and the appearance of humans on this planet anticipated by many other communities long before we actually evolved.

There is also the possibility of 'unmanned' probes. The feats of micro-miniaturization in the last few years have opened up the possibility of packing enormously powerful computers into a very small volume. There seems to be no law of physics which would prevent a very sophisticated technology from producing computerized machines comparable with the human head in size and capabilities. This would necessitate the use of information storage at molecular level, but there is no objection to that in principle. The availability of such facilities would transform the situation dramatically: a very simple data gathering machine, equipped to search out and report back vital statistics about other planetary systems might be no more massive than a pea, with local on-site energy sources being used for signalling purposes. A still more fruitful procedure would be to send biological machine seeds. The idea here is that if the information for building a man can be stored in a microscopic molecule of DNA, so the information for building even quite a complicated biological machine might be compressed into something of molecular dimensions too. On arrival at a biologically suitable planet, this seed would start to grow, producing all the instruments — eyes, ears, radio transmitter and so on — needed for a complete analysis and transmission of the local conditions. The essence of efficient space travel is to confine the main use of energy and material to the other end and so avoid prohibitive transportation costs. Ideally, only the information necessary to build the machinery should be sent.

The idea of biological machines might seem over-fanciful, but it should be remembered that the Earth is full of them, beautifully adapted to their individual tasks. Cross-breeding and artificially induced mutations have already produced many man-made organisms, corn being an obvious example. Genetic manipulation promises to provide a vast field of possibilities for using organic material to perform special functions. There is no reason why a plant could not be produced which possessed powerful electrical circuits, similar to those in our bodies but capable of producing more power, which could then be used as radio transmitters, especially if they grew into a large dish shape.

The possibilities for probing the galaxy available to a civilization which had acquired these skills would be enormous. Microscopic probes or seeds could flood the galaxy, moving at near-to-light speed with acceptable energy expenditure and negligible risk of meteoric impact. Being so tiny, inertial effects would be easily overcome during violent accelerations or braking so they could simply be 'shot' out into interstellar space from an orbiting satellite. A major technological problem would be to slow the projectiles down on arrival, but there are several possibilities available. The probes might be electrically charged to enable them to spiral around in the magnetic fields of the recipient star system. Small in-flight trajectory corrections near the destination could bring them into grazing contact with tenuous planetary atmospheres. If the speed were, for instance 50 per cent of light, the total energy of motion could be considerably reduced initially by converting part of the mass into laser or some other form of energy to help produce a braking effect. These technological problems could probably be overcome. Moreover, by producing biological machines based on different chemical processes, planets as diverse in conditions as Jupiter and Venus could successfully be explored in this way. Within a few decades, a torrent of information about the nearby star systems would be obtained.

Probes of this sort may well have arrived on the Earth. Being biological they would probably have been eaten after a while, and in any case we would not expect to notice such things. It is likely that once the existence of life on Earth had been properly established, a more sophisticated package would be sent to stooge around out in orbit and conduct an investigation from the comparative safety of outer space. This much larger machine would probably be sent 'surface mail' at low rocket speeds and low cost, taking many decades or centuries to arrive. This would be quite acceptable once the certainty of an interesting subject for scrutiny had been established.

Whether or not there exist extraterrestrial communities who have attempted to communicate with each other, it seems virtually certain that in the billions of years ahead of us, such communities will arise and spread slowly throughout the universe. The ability for intelligent life to survive future cosmic catastrophes will depend on the level of technology and the control over their surroundings which these communities can achieve. We can, of course, only guess at the future of technological society by extrapolating what we know to be possible according to our present understanding of physics and biology. According to present ideas there seems to be every possibility that intelligent manipulation through technology can become a powerful force in restructuring the universe at a local level. The fate of technological society is the least well understood but, for us, most relevant aspect of the fate of the universe. Some speculations about this will be given in chapter 9. As it happens, however advanced supertechnological communities may become, and whatever their capabilities for rearranging the cosmos, a fundamental principle of physics ensures that eventual calamity can never be averted.

6.   The catastrophe principle

This book is about the rise and fall of cosmic order. A description of order at many levels has been given; cosmological, galactic, stellar, biological, intellectual, technological. With so many disparate systems, controlled by different forces on widely different length and time-scales, it might seem a hopeless task to describe any common features or systematic properties of all these dissimilar levels of structure. If there were no connecting principle or underlying conceptual link between these levels, then an account of the overall fate of the universe could not be written; it would reduce to a collection of topics in cosmology, astrophysics, geology, sociology, engineering and so forth. However, one of the greatest achievements of physical science has been the discovery of some very fundamental properties and laws which are of such general character that they can be applied to systems as diverse as a star and a man. Using these laws very broad conclusions about the fate of the cosmos may be drawn on purely general grounds.

The unifying concept is order, but the nature of this order is quite different at the various levels. At the cosmological level, order means simplicity and uniformity — a smooth pattern of expansion of the universe on a large scale. At the smaller levels, order means complex organization and the specialized arrangement of matter and energy, whether it be a star releasing energy in its core and transporting it to the cooler surface layers, a living cell engaging in metabolisms, or a techno-logical community operating an interstellar telecommunications network. What is needed, therefore, is a precise, mathematical definition of order which may be applied to all of these disparate systems.

The first step in achieving this definition was taken in the interests, of all things, of engineering. Cost-conscious industrialists of the nineteenth century were concerned about acquiring a proper mathematical treatment of the idea of useful energy. It had long been appreciated that energy can assume a variety of forms — chemical, electrical, mechanical, gravitational and so on — and that energy can be converted from one form to another: for example, a steam locomotive converts the chemical energy of coal into mechanical energy of motion. It was also known that total energy is always conserved when it changes in form. In the real world, machines always operate at less than 100 per cent efficiency, which means that some energy is always wasted with each successive conversion. The energy does not disappear, it merely dissipates; that is, we lose control of it. In short, it ceases to be useful energy. Heat is a form of energy, and many devices have been invented to convert heat into other forms — steam turbines for generating electricity is one example. The efficiency of heat engines came under close scrutiny from physicists and mathematicians during the nineteenth century, and one of their most important conclusions was that the efficiency of even the most perfect heat engines must always be less than 100 per cent, often considerably less, for very fundamental reasons of physics.

To understand this, it is helpful to consider a specific example, such as the heat content of a bucket of water. If the bucket is placed in a refrigerator, the water will freeze because some heat energy has been removed from it. If the energy is put back, the ice will melt again. The fact that a bucket of water contains heat energy when it is at room temperature is no help to us if we want to use that energy for some purpose, such as driving a motor, for the heat content of the water is not in useful form. On the other hand, when the bucket is placed in a cold environment, some heat energy can be extracted and put to use. For example, the cold air in the vicinity of the warm water will heat up and expand, and could be used to exert a pressure on a membrane, or move a piston. The crucial feature which makes the heat energy of the water useful when it is in the refrigerator but not at room temperature, is the presence of a temperature difference between the water and its surroundings. It is the non-uniformity in the distribution of the heat energy which enables the heat to do work. In the room, the contents of the bucket and the room are at a uniform temperature, so there is no net heat flow between bucket and room. This is an expression of a simple but far-reaching physical principle: the spontaneous heat flow between bodies is always from hot to cold. When two bodies reach the same temperature the heat flow stops, and we can then say that thermodynamic equilibrium has been achieved. When equilibrium prevails, no further useful changes can occur without outside interference. For instance, a temperature difference cannot open up spontaneously between a bucket of water and the surrounding air, because it would involve heat flowing from cold to hot at some stage, in order to cool down the bucket and heat up the air, or vice versa.

The general principle of heat flow is known as the second law of thermodynamics (the first law of thermodynamics merely says that heat is a form of energy which can be converted to other forms without change in the total energy quantity). Another way of describing the content of the second law is to say that useful things can be done by heat energy when it is ordered or arranged in a non-uniform way. When the heat is spread uniformly through the system, equilibrium prevails, but if it is concentrated in one place, then heat flow occurs and the system evolves or changes in some way. This change will continue so long as there is a thermodynamic disequilibrium such as a temperature difference. This means that, as far as heat flow is concerned, the essence of activity is disequilibrium; when equilibrium is achieved, activity ceases.

At this stage an important distinction must be made between microscopic and macroscopic activity. Even in equilibrium there is still plenty of microscopic activity present — atoms are still jiggling around, colliding, and emitting and absorbing radiation — but this happens in a purely random fashion. There is no cooperative behaviour involving very large numbers of atoms. What is of interest to us is organized activity, which really means macroscopic activity. For example, convection currents taking place inside a bucket of cooling water involve the cooperative motions of billions upon billions of atoms in an orderly pattern of flow. Organized activity, therefore, only occurs when there is thermodynamic disequilibrium.

In order to make these ideas more precise, physicists have invented a quantitative measure of order and disorder to describe the degree of macroscopic organization or structured arrangement in a system. This quantity is given the name entropy, which is actually a measure of the degree of disarrangement. Sometimes it is helpful to think of entropy as disorder, but it is worth clarifying this point right at the outset. The everyday use of the word disorder can be ambiguous, because what is regarded as an orderly arrangement by one person may be regarded as quite chaotic by another. A coded message, for instance, is a jumble of letters to the uninitiated, but an intelligent communication for someone who knows the code. It is, therefore, better to think of entropy as the opposite of information. Generally speaking, an ordered system (low entropy) has a high information content in the simple sense that it requires a great deal of information to describe its arrangement. In contrast a disordered system requires little information. The thermal properties of a bucket of water in a room at a uniform temperature are described by just one bit of information — the common temperature. This is a high entropy, or disordered system, disorder meaning here 'no order'. Although the individual atoms are flying around chaotically when equilibrium prevails macroscopically, complete disorder really means the cessation of activity.

To take a final example, a liquid which is spattered with coloured dye may present what is regarded in everyday language as a disordered appearance, but in fact it has a high information content because its surface features require a great deal of description to specify their precise arrangement. In contrast, when the dye has spread uniformly through the system it has become highly disordered, the entropy has risen, and the information content is very low. In fact, just one bit of information — the overall uniform concentration of dye — is needed to describe the system. The informational properties in this example are vividly demonstrated by the possibility that a non-uniform distribution of dye on the water surface could be used to spell out a lengthy message, whereas a uniform spread cannot convey any information at all except that the dye is there, with a certain concentration.

Using the concept of entropy, a systematic understanding of the organizational properties of an enormous variety of physical systems can be obtained. A single, powerful principle — the second law of thermodynamics — originally limited to the narrow context of heat engines, is now believed to apply to everything in the universe. For this universal application the second law can be stated in a very general way: in any change which occurs in the universe, the total entropy always increases. What is curious about this second law is that it is unique among the fundamental laws of nature. All the others are concerned with the conservation of properties — the perpetuation of various qualities during physical processes. Only the second law of thermodynamics deals directly with the way in which things alter irreversibly, and it therefore forms the very foundation for the explanation of all change — whether progress, growth and evolution or catastrophic collapse and decay. It provides the descriptive framework for the understanding of how all things begin and end, and through this the basic property of time which distinguishes past from future. By applying these principles on a cosmic scale, we shall discover how the fate of the universe is written into the second law of thermodynamics.

Some idea of the power of the second law can be obtained by applying it to a few simple, well-known phenomena. We have already seen that the tendency for heat to dissipate away and temperature differences to diminish provides an example of the growth of entropy or disorder, because the smoothed-out distribution of heat is less ordered then when it is concentrated into certain regions. In other words, whenever heat flows from hot to cold, the entropy rises. This was the original context of the second law, but it is easy to see that it applies equally well even when there are no temperature differences. To take an example already discussed, if some spots of dye are placed in water they start out in an orderly arrangement, but as time goes on the dye begins to diffuse through the water, eventually spreading itself in a uniform concentration. The information about the orignal arrangement of dye is then completely lost.

One way of describing the increase of entropy is to say that the change is irreversible. This is not to say that the system cannot be put back to its original condition, but it does mean that it will not return to its former condition of its own accord. In the case of a bucket of water which cools down and freezes inside a refrigerator, it is clearly possible to melt the water again by taking the bucket out of the refrigerator. We would not, however, expect the water to melt again so long as it remained in a sub-zero environment. Again the dye diffused through the water may be restored to its original local concentration by distilling the water off, collecting the dye and dropping it back into the water in blobs, but the spontaneous migration of all the dye particles back to one place would be considered miraculous.

Irreversible changes occur all around us in daily life; the list is endless, and so just a few random examples will be given. An egg which drops on the floor and breaks, a sandcastle washed away by the tide, a snowman melted by the sun — in all cases the original ordered system becomes disordered. To restore the original order is possible, but may be exceedingly difficult and depends upon technological competence. According to the second law, any restoration of the original orderly arrangement has to be paid for with at least as great an increase in entropy elsewhere; thus, for example, to rebuild a sandcastle requires the consumption of energy by the builder, which is obtained by the burning of food molecules in his body cells through metabolism. The order achieved by the sand is more than compensated by the disorder suffered by the food molecules which are disintegrated in the process. This reflects the general experience that to get anything done in the world, one needs to use up energy to do it. The resulting degradation of useful energy into dissipated energy is just another aspect of the second law.

Failure to draw up a proper balance sheet for entropy often leads to apparent violations of the second law. For example, at first sight the growth of a crystal seems to offer a clear exception to the increasing-disorder principle. A crystal is a very highly ordered array of atoms which can be made to grow spontaneously out of a disordered liquid concentrate. Careful study shows that the formation of the crystal produces a certain amount of heat energy, and that this heat is lost when it dissipates away into the surroundings. The rise in entropy from the heat loss more than compensates for the increase in order represented by the crystal.

Perhaps the most obvious apparent contradiction of the second law of thermodynamics, and one which has puzzled many scientists, concerns living systems. The gradual evolution of the species from simple-celled organisms to the variety of complex life-forms which we observe on Earth today appears to run directly counter to the principle of the breakdown of organization. A proper understanding of the thermodynamic basis of life is essential for explaining both how sophisticated organisms such as human beings have appeared in the universe, and for determining the fate of all living things in the future. We shall see that biological, and even social and technological systems, are all subject to the same entropy principle as inanimate matter.

The chemical ingredients of a human being would only fetch a few pounds on the open market. There is nothing rare or unusual about the substances from which we are made — carbon, hydrogen, oxygen, some trace elements — all exist around us in relative abundance. The crucial feature about a living organism is not its constituents, but the way in which they are assembled into an elaborate, organized and cooperative system. The simplest bacterium is so complex that it is quite beyond the ability of laboratory scientists to construct one piecemeal from the raw materials. If all the manipulative abilities available to our technology can only produce a few simple organic molecules, how can nature, without access to any technology at all, spontaneously produce a system as complicated as a human being? Every year three hundred million new humans appear on the Earth, each representing an enormous increase in the information content of the universe, for the information required to produce the human body — the most complex arrangement of matter and energy that we know — is unimaginably large. Where has all this information come from?

Although scientists have frequently speculated that living matter violates the second law of thermodynamics, it can be shown that the growth of information in biology is more than compensated by the entropy produced in the evolutionary process. The origin of biological information in living organisms can be traced to a combination of selection mechanisms, replication and random mutations. For every bit of new information necessary to improve the complexity and sophistication of a particular species, a large amount of entropy is generated by the mechanism of natural wastage.

The essence of the transformation from the first living thing to man is evolution. The large variety of life we now observe on this planet, with each species so well adapted to its particular ecological niche, seems to have all arisen from the same basic precursor organisms. The fossil record shows how there were once common ancestors between, for example, crocodiles and alligators, sheep and goats and, most poignant of all, monkeys and men. Tracing the record back into the still more distant past reveals how, billions of years ago, the ancestors of all the present rich life forms were the same simple little creatures. Evidence for this slow evolutionary transformation is easy enough to establish, the difficulty is to explain how it happened; to understand how nature is supposed to know that, for example, the polar bear should be the same colour as snow, and how she acquires the information to make a white bear in the first place.

The Miller and Urey experiment described in chapter 3 shows how the prebiotic molecules can be assembled by accident in about a week: when all the ingredients are mixed together, random combinations of molecules eventually produce amino acids and nucleotides. Even though the end product is a result of chance configurations of atoms, the accident is almost inevitable. One way of expressing this is to say that the information content of the Miller and Urey 'soup' was very low, and since the molecules are so simple, it is not hard to envisage their spontaneous assembly. Nature, therefore, does not need to 'know' a great deal to achieve this. On the other hand, a man or a polar bear has an information content countless billions of times greater, and it is too much to expect these complex systems to have arisen purely by accident.

The explanation was discovered in the nineteenth century simultaneously by Charles Darwin and Alfred Wallace, who argued that evolution has occurred by a long series of controlled accidents, so that man has not arisen from a single, sudden transformation, but by a slow succession of gradual adaptations. The underlying principle is easily described with the help of an analogy. Suppose an inexperienced artist wishes to make an alabaster mould of a man, and he finds from experience that after a few dozen attempts he can satisfactorily fashion a head, not by virtue of any manipulative or artistic skill, but purely by trial and error. After a few more dozen attempts he can produce a successful leg. Many, many moulds later he at last has a mould with both a good head and one good leg. At this point, however, discouragement sets in: he may toil for years before being lucky enough to produce all the appropriate members, properly formed, in the same mould. Then he hits upon an entirely different strategy: he works through a few dozen moulds in the same trial and error fashion, until he happens to produce one with a good right arm. Instead of discarding this as incomplete, he makes a hundred identical moulds, all of which are at least better than the pile of moulds with no good features at all. He then sets to work on these one hundred good moulds, one by one refashioning them at random, and eventually he obtains a mould with the original good right arm, and a good left leg too. Immediately he makes one hundred copies of this, and sets to work again. In due course, before too long, the perfect mould is produced — the entire alabaster man may be cast. The basic principle of the new strategy is that, although each small part of the alabaster man is fashioned purely by accident, a selection process was used to preserve the good features and to discard the bad. In this way, by a succession of controlled accidents, the perfect end product was produced.

Darwin explained how all living creatures are subject to random remodelling, called mutation. The reason for this is now understood. The information for building the creature is stored in a very long molecule called DNA (short for deoxyribonucleic acid), which has the structure of a double helix formed out of millions of atoms joined together in a very complicated arrangement. The genetic differences between an elephant and an ant can be traced to the different arrangements of the atoms in their respective DNA molecules. From time to time, however, atoms in the DNA get displaced through some random accident, such as impact from a cosmic ray particle, and when this happens the offspring of the creature will be a mutant. In most cases, the change will be a disaster — the loss of a limb, or a malformed internal organ, for example — but very occasionally the accident will result in a beneficial change. This is unlikely to be the case in normal times, because most creatures are already so well adapted to their particular existence that they can hardly be improved, but when some upheaval is occurring, such as a change in climate, vegetation, water supply or the appearance of new predators, then the occasional muta- tion could be beneficial. For instance, at the approach of an ice age, lighter coloured mutants are better off because they blend more effectively with the snow and ice.

We now reach the crucial point: just as the artist discards his imperfect moulds, so nature discards her imperfect mutants. The harsh reality of survival ensures that only the fittest, the ones more adapted to the prevailing ecological conditions, live long enough to reproduce and pass on their characteristics to their offspring. A three-legged gazelle would not be able to reach adulthood and reproduce other three-legged gazelles, because it would be eaten by a lion long before. A slightly more long-legged gazelle might, however, have a definite advan- tage in this respect over others, because of its ability to run away faster. In this way, rare advantageous mutations — accidents — have a selective advantage. This natural selection ensures that either each species will slowly adapt over many generations to the particular conditions which obtain, or else become extinct.

It is now possible to answer the difficult question of where the information to build a man has come from. During the billions of years that life has existed on Earth, millions upon millions of little accidents have been selectively preserved and combined, like the gradual perfec- tion of the moulds. The information has been fed into the organism by the environment through the natural selection process. The DNA which carries the information to make a man contains the entire record of the evolution of our species from the primeval soup. This is a great deal of information, but the DNA molecule is so intricate that it has the equivalent storage capacity of a very large computer indeed.

Similar reasoning may be applied to society. Every step in the construction of more complex social and industrial organization must be paid for by an increase in entropy somewhere. To take one example of this, consider the construction of a railway system, in which the achievement of an ordered network of communications demands the price of large-scale excavation, and despoilation of some of the environment. As industry consumes, so the world's resources become irreversibly depleted. Clearly life and technology can only continue so long as the entropy of the environment is allowed to rise. Because of this crucial restriction, technological communities must always be situated in regions of thermodynamic disequilibrium, which in our case is the sun.

A careful examination of all systems which evolve order reveals that a compensatory increase of entropy takes place somewhere else in the universe. This raises the question of what happens when we apply the second law of thermodynamics to the universe as a whole. Considering any large, typical region of space containing many galaxies, we can ask what consequences for their future behaviour and activity follow from the requirement that their entropy always increases. Before this is done, however, a very profound paradox must be resolved. The second law requires that in any change all physical systems end up producing more disorder than order, yet the universe has managed to do just the opposite by creating order out of primeval chaos. Nor can we look to some other place for a compensatory increase in entropy, because the universe includes everything there is. Does this mean that the second law fails on a cosmic scale? This is the single most important question in determining the eventual fate of the universe.

One way of approaching the paradox is to use the concept of information. The universe is a very special place, with an enormous information content — information about galaxies, stars, planets, living things, intelligence — where did all this information come from? It evidently was not present when the universe began because, if the cosmic background heat radiation is any indication, the primeval fireball was in thermal equilibrium, which is described by just one bit of information (the temperature). According to the second law, information is lost as entropy increases, yet in the cosmic situation it seems to have appeared out of nowhere. There is no doubt that this is one of the most basic enigmas in cosmology.

In explaining the resolution of the paradox, it is helpful to draw an analogy between the universe and a clock. Clocks only work if they are wound up, when they perform normally for a while but eventually, in accordance with the fundamental law of entropy increase, will run down and stop. One way of expressing this change is to say that a working clock is engaging in organized activity, with the cog-wheels turning, the hands rotating, etc. but in due course this organized activity becomes converted into disorganized activity, as friction between the moving components dissipates the energy stored up during the winding process.

The energy reappears as heat energy in the working parts, but in this form it powers only the disorganized activity of random atomic motions. A similar phenomenon occurs on a cosmic scale. Stars, rather like clocks, are organized systems, whose stored energy is slowly dissipated away into space through the radiation of heat and light. So long as the sun shines, its energy is useful, because it is ordered. The radiated energy does not disappear, but becomes disordered by spreading itself about in space and cooling to the temperature of its surroundings. In this form it is no longer useful.

Expressed in clock language, the paradox of the origin of the world order, or cosmic information, reduces to the question of how the universe got 'wound up' in the first place. A condition of equilibrium, in which all organized activity ceases, corresponds to a clock being unwound, and this was the situation for the universe during the primeval phase. The winding must have occurred in the subsequent epochs, but the mechanism can only be understood by a detailed study of the processes which took place in the fireball. This is the reason why the early stages of the universe are so important for determining its ultimate fate, because that was the time when the universe became 'wound up'. What we now observe is the universe slowly unwinding itself and running down.

Although a full explanation of the winding process requires a knowledge of physics beyond the scope of this book, the main principles can be understood. The basic mechanism involves the expansion motion of the primeval fireball, which was explosively rapid in the very early stages. At that time the universe was so hot that processes in the fireball

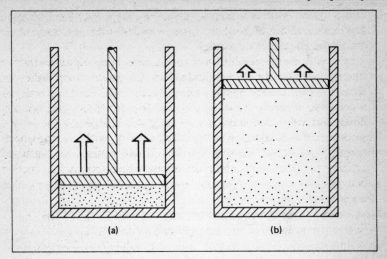

(a)   (b)

Figure 6 Winding up the universe
The mechanism which enabled order to arise out of primeval chaos has a close analogue in the
piston and cylinder arrangement shown above. The motion of the piston represents the
expanding universe: it starts off very rapidly and then slows down. The gas confined beneath
the piston represents the cosmological material in the primeval fireball.

In (a), the gas is very compressed and very hot, so that although the piston is withdrawn
rapidly, the fast-moving molecules quickly respond to maintain uniformity and equilibrium:
no structure or organized activity appears; the information content remains low. In (b), by
contrast, the expanded gas has been cooled and is also very tenuous, with its molecules moving
slowly. Even though the piston (representing the expansion of the universe) is also withdrawn
more slowly, it is now much faster than the response time needed by the gas to reach
equilibrium. Consequently the sluggish gas molecules are for ever vainly trying to catch up with
the retreating piston. As the expansion proceeds, the lag gets greater and greater. The gas is no
longer uniform, but has broken up into a more structured arrangement, with turbulent activity
and a high information content.

In the real universe there is no piston — the expansion occurs uniformly everywhere
throughout the cosmological material; nevertheless, the basic idea of the microscopic processes lagging more and more behind the changing conditions, is the same.

happened very fast; all the complicated particle motions and interactions became telescoped without limit at progressively earlier
moments. Therefore although the expansion was explosive, it was still
very much slower than the processes going on in the hot fluid, and it
was possible for the contents of the universe to adjust themselves
almost instantaneously to the expansion, so maintaining equilibrium.
In due course, however, as the temperature began to fall, the various
processes which were going on became somewhat sluggish in the cooler

conditions and could not keep pace with the expansion. At this stage the contents of the universe began to get out of step, and they have been out of step ever since, lagging farther and farther behind. It is precisely this disequilibrium between the expanding universe and its contents which constitutes the winding mechanism.

It is now possible to see how information and order have appeared in the universe apparently against the prediction of the second law of thermodynamics. The second law only applies to undisturbed systems, and in the cosmological case the expansion of the universe disturbed the equilibrium which prevailed initially and enabled new information to appear by allowing the entropy to rise in compensation. Every time that some new organization arises in the universe, whether it be the formation of a star or the evolution of some new species, a compensatory amount of entropy occurs somewhere else. If the expansion of the universe stopped, this increasing entropy would rise to a maximum and equilibrium would prevail once more, but so long as the expansion continues, no equilibrium can be reached and new organization can continue to appear.

Unfortunately the winding mechanism from the cosmological expansion is no longer as effective as it was, and on balance the universe is now running down much faster than it is being 'wound up'. New activity and order caused by the expansion is too small to make much difference to the general pattern of disintegration and collapse of organization which lies ahead. Beginning with the stars, and spreading throughout the cosmos, the decline and fall of the universe will be remorseless and inevitable.

7.   *Stardoom*

All stars face ultimate catastrophe and eventual death. For billions of years they may act as sources of free energy, but gradually and inexorably they must run down and cease their activity. This fate is required on quite general grounds by the second law of thermodynamics, which predicts that the thermodynamic disequilibrium which keeps the stars hot when the surrounding space is cold cannot last for ever; sooner or later a uniform temperature must be approached. Although the second law requires this inescapable end, it does not make any prediction about the nature of the star's demise. It is fairly obvious to everyone that if stars shine by nuclear burning, eventually their fuel will be exhausted. What is not generally realized is the variety of spectacular ways in which this exhaustion is achieved, or the bizarre nature of the celestial corpses which remain once the stars have died.

Astronomers have recourse to two methods for studying the death of stars: the construction of mathematical models, and straightforward observation. The fact that we can watch stars dying as well as being born may come as a surprise, but many stars are much older than the sun. In addition, there is a definite relation between the lifetime of a star and its mass. The reason for this is that more massive stars are heavier, so they require a greater internal pressure to support the extra weight of the outer layers. This in turn requires a greater compression and a higher temperature (because all gases heat up when compressed), which causes the nuclear fuel to burn faster. Furthermore, massive stars are usually large in size, too, so they can radiate a great deal of energy from their extensive surfaces. Some stars are about one hundred times more massive than the sun and their lifetime might be as little as one hundred thousand years.

The first critical stage which marks the beginning of the end for a star is when it suffers, literally, its first heart attack. The normal state of a star such as the sun is the phase of hydrogen burning. During this period the star is in a very stable condition, steadily converting hydrogen to helium near its centre. The sun will remain in this condition for about another four or five billion years, until the hydrogen fuel in the central regions becomes depleted. The freshly produced helium forms itself into a core, which being unable to supply energy by nuclear processes, starts to contract under its own weight. The actual details of what follows are complicated, and depend to some extent on the mass and composition of the star, but the general pattern is the same. As the core shrinks, its temperature gradually rises. Nuclear burning still takes place, but it now operates in a thin shell surrounding the core. The effect of these internal readjustments is to cause the outer layers of the star to expand steadily, cooling in the process. There is then the curious situation in which the core of the star shrinks and becomes hotter, while the surface swells and becomes cooler. The cooling of the surface changes the colour of the star to red: the star has now become a red giant, like Aldebaran.

In relatively low mass stars such as the sun, this turn of events is accompanied by a considerable increase in luminosity, and so although the sun will become intrinsically cooler, it will radiate much more energy. Eventually it will grow perhaps 1500 times as bright as it is now. The enhanced luminosity will lead to a greater flux of heat striking the surface of the Earth, and life on our planet will then become imperilled. The elevated temperatures will soon melt the polar caps, flooding large coastal areas of the continents, and the equatorial temperatures will gradually become insufferable for living things. For many millions of years, evolution will no doubt continue to select organisms capable of withstanding progressively higher temperatures, but eventually, with the continents reduced to parched desert, the oceans will boil and the atmosphere will be filled with steam clouds. It is hard to see how life as we know it could continue under these hostile conditions. Perhaps near the polar regions life will hang on for a few more million years, but there will be no escape from the incineration.

Studies of other stars, together with mathematical reconstructions, indicate that the sun could become so distended that it will actually engulf the Earth in its outer layers. In any case, long before this happened, the Earth would be slowly but irresistibly vaporized. The planet which played host to several billion years of life will have disappeared for ever.

If the descendants of humanity are still inhabiting the Earth in those days, they will have plenty of warning of the impending disaster. The early stages of the solar expansion take place very slowly, lasting many hundreds of millions of years. After this the pace quickens, until the star reaches the red giant stage and enters on a career of rapid and spectacular evolution. It is doubtful if life could survive anywhere in the solar system during this next phase. The benign stability which characterized the early history of the sun will have given way to catastrophic changes quite unsuitable for biological life, although machine intelligence could no doubt continue on the outer planets such as Pluto.

The origin of these changes must be sought in the sun's contracting core. As more and more helium is added to the core from the hydrogen-burning shell, the weight of the core grows and in order to support this additional weight, the central pressure must rise. For a while this comes about by the contraction process, which elevates the central temperature: as the temperature rises, so does the pressure. However, when the density of the core reaches about 1000 times that of water, a curious new phenomenon occurs: the highly compressed material of the core becomes excessively stiff. The reason for this sudden stiffening is a subtle one connected with the microscopic quantum mechanical properties of the electrons in the core.

Physicists have discovered that there are two distinct types of matter, with rather dissimilar properties. The differences can be sought in the internal behaviour of the individual particles of matter. Sub-atomic particles of the same variety have long been known to be indistinguishable − all electrons, for example, are identical − except in one respect. It was discovered in the 1920s from the study of atomic spectra that electrons could exist in two different states, even when engaging in identical motion. The distinction between the two states cannot therefore be a property of the way they move, but must reside in some internal property of the particle. A closer analysis has revealed that in many respects this internal property bears some resemblance to a rotation; electrons are in some sense spinning. This spin, however, is a peculiar phenomenon differing in two crucial respects from, say, the spin of the Earth. The first enigmatic feature is that the electron has to spin completely round twice — not merely once — in order to return to the same condition as before. This paradoxical notion was mentioned on p. 43 in connection with neutrinos, and it is very hard to visualize accurately. Nevertheless, it may be given a clear mathematical description and fits in well with theoretical ideas about the nature of rotation; it can also be measured directly by experiment. The second peculiarity about electron spin arises from the laws of quantum mechanics. Whereas the axis of rotation of an ordinary spinning body can apparently lie in any direction whatsoever, the electron can only spin in one of two directions, which we can picturesquely describe as 'up' and 'down'.

The restriction of electron spin to two directions provides the explanation of the double-state property observed in atomic spectra; this is a property also shared by protons, neutrons and neutrinos. The quantum theory not only restricts the possible directions of spin, it also fixes its magnitude: spin can only come in integral multiples of a basic unit. Electrons and protons, for example, have one unit of spin, while the photon of light and some heavy mesons have two units. Whereas the graviton has four units, some particles, such as the pion, have no spin at all. This is where the division into two classes of matter becomes important. It turns out that the properties of matter consisting of particles with an even number of spin units, or no spin at all, is quite different from matter made of odd spin particles. In particular, odd spin particles cannot be packed together very easily, a feature embodied in a famous principle discovered by the physicist Wolfgang Pauli and now known as the exclusion principle.

The Pauli exclusion principle not only controls the fate of stars, it is the basis of all atomic structure and chemistry. It states that no two odd-spin particles of the same type can occupy the same state, which means that, roughly speaking, no two electrons can be squashed together in the same region of space. For this reason the electrons in atoms stack up around one another in shells, rather like the skins of an onion. If the principle failed to operate, the stacks would collapse and chemistry would be impossible. This means that the same stiffness which supports the electron shells in the atom also supports the weight of the helium core in an ageing star.

Physicists call the quantum stiffness due to the exclusion principle 'degeneracy pressure', to distinguish it from ordinary thermal pressure. Degeneracy pressure does not occur for even-spin particles — for example, any number of photons may be compressed together — and is the reason why light may build up to form a wave. In the core of a star the electron degeneracy pressure has the effect of halting the slow contraction, as well as influencing the star's stability. Unlike ordinary matter, which rapidly dissipates energy as it is produced, the extra-stiff degenerate matter will contain the energy until such an enormous temperature has been achieved that the degeneracy pressure disappears. In this way the conditions are set for the red giant to become a monstrous bomb.

So long as the temperature of the core of a red giant remains below eighty million degrees, the fuse does not ignite. If, however, the slowly rising temperature at the centre reaches this critical level, a new nuclear reaction is initiated — helium fusion. In the same way that hydrogen acts as a nuclear fuel by fusing to form helium, so helium in its turn can fuse to form still heavier nuclei, especially carbon, which can arise as a direct result of a simultaneous encounter between three helium nuclei. The energy needed to overcome their electric repulsion is several times greater than for hydrogen nuclei (protons) because there are more electric particles involved (six instead of two) — which is why such a high temperature is necessary.

Helium burning is less efficient than hydrogen burning, but its effect is much more dramatic because of the instability of the degenerate helium core. As soon as helium burning begins, the temperature of the core rises sharply as the stiff material is unable to expand rapidly enough to take up the sudden extra energy being produced. The elevated temperature then ignites the whole core within the space of a few minutes in a sort of stellar flash fire. The helium flash enhances the energy production of the star by perhaps a hundred billion times, an output which would be utterly catastrophic if it did not take place buried beneath thousands of miles of material. As it happens, the weight of the star's overlying layers traps the explosion and within seconds brings it under control. All the energy becomes dissipated by working on the core, inflating it back to a normal condition in which there is no longer any degeneracy pressure. The effect of this spasm in the heart of the star completely changes its internal structure and subsequent development, bringing about a new phase of both helium and hydrogen burning. In the case of the sun, the luminosity will settle

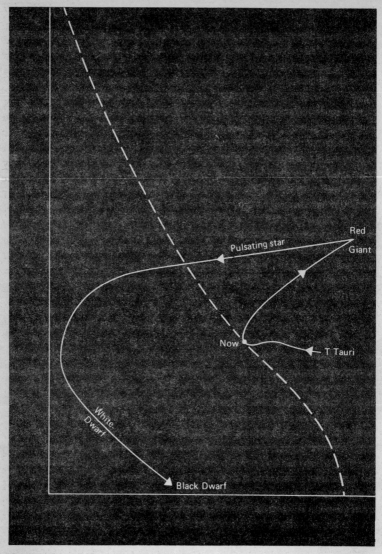

Figure 7 Life and death of an ordinary star

Although individual details may vary widely, the general pattern of stellar evolution for ordinary dwarf stars such as the sun is outlined above. Starting as a shrinking cloud of gas (T Tauri star) the star settles down for several billion years of stable activity. Then it swells up and moves off to the right of the diagram, becoming a red giant. After the helium flash it moves rapidly to the left, becoming a hot blue star, perhaps pulsating or blowing off shells down in this new phase to about one hundred times its present value, and the colour will change from red to blue, indicating a surface temperature many thousands of degrees hotter than at present. The sun will then be a blue giant. During this time the surface of Pluto will have a temperature comparable to that of the Earth at present.

The same general pattern of evolution is followed by all stars, although individual details may vary widely. In particular, the duration of the hydrogen burning phase depends sensitively on the mass of the star: very low mass stars may take as much as a thousand times longer than the sun to reach the red giant stage. Furthermore, some stars may never attain a sufficiently great internal temperature to ignite the helium flash, and will simply cool down instead. Whatever the details or duration of their evolution, all stars are subject to the second law of thermodynamics, according to which they cannot go on burning for ever; the time must eventually come when the star will die. The death throes may be more or less violent according to circumstances. Most stars of moderate mass will pass on from the helium burning phase through a succession of complicated nuclear reactions, building up heavier and heavier elements in a sequence of shells. There is, therefore, a general tendency for stars to continue to become hotter. Each heavier element synthesized requires heavier nuclear fuel, with a progressively lower energy release and higher electric nuclear barrier to be overcome. As a result, ever higher temperatures are necessary to initiate the less and less efficient nuclear burning. It is rather like a bonfire starting by burning paraffin, going on to wood, and then having to contend with damp leaves; all are combustible, but a more vigorous fire is needed to ignite the less inflammable fuels.

With the completion of each stage of burning, the core of the star shrinks still more to keep up the all important balances of pressure and energy flow. Whenever the star runs out of energy, it must start to shrink under its own gravity until the temperature is sufficiently high to burn what fuel is available. By the time that elements like oxygen begin to burn, the temperature is approaching a billion degrees — about one hundred times hotter than the centre of the sun in its present state.

---

of gas. Eventually, with all the nuclear fuel exhausted, it cools down to become a white dwarf then, after an enormous duration, gradually fades into a black dwarf. The rate at which the star evolves depends critically on its mass (and hence its position on the sloping line). High mass stars from the blue giant region swell up and become red supergiants many thousands of times faster than the sun will.

When the temperature rises above a billion degrees, an important new source of instability sets in. The conditions are now comparable to the primeval fireball at about one second — the end of the lepton era. At this stage the temperature is so high that the radiation energy is in the form of X-rays. The energy is sufficient to produce electron-positron pairs through the matter creation process, and some of the pairs then annihilate again and produce a neutrino-antineutrino pair. Other processes also produce neutrinos: in one of these, the core of the star literally becomes radioactive and starts to decay through neutrino emission.

The combined effect of all these processes is to transport vast quantities of energy away from the centre of the star. The reason for this is the incredible penetration property of neutrinos, most of which pass straight through the outer layers of the star and away into space. This energy loss from the centre accelerates the nuclear processes and forces up the internal temperature still more, while the core of the star shrinks faster and faster to compensate through gravity for the increasing drain on the star's energy. But the higher the temperature rises the more prolifically the neutrinos shower away into space. The star has now reached a great crisis. As the temperature climbs, the rate of shrinkage accelerates. Whereas the evolutionary changes following the helium flash take millions of years, the star now changes its internal structure appreciably in a few months. The stage is set for the next catastrophe, but on a much more violent level than the first.

The fate of the star now hangs in the balance, the determining factor being nuclear physics. The supply of energy from nuclear processes cannot continue indefinitely; eventually the equilibrium form of matter is reached, when the nuclei assume the most stable and tightly bound state and the maximum amount of energy has been extracted from the nuclear synthesis process. At this point elements like iron are formed. Although nuclei heavier than iron can be produced, they require a net energy input for their synthesis, so they do not add to the heat of the stellar furnace. When the temperature reaches about three billion degrees, nuclear reactions occur in complex profusion. A type of thermodynamic equilibrium then sets in, where all types of nuclei are produced in balanced ratios. Much of the centre of the star converts rapidly into iron, with some very heavy elements built up in small quantities by the capture of stray neutrons.

These nuclear processes have all been studied in great detail with the help of computer calculations and mathematical models, and in particular, estimates have been made of the relative abundances of the different nuclei produced. In this way conditions in the centre of a star at this time are reckoned to be far beyond anything available in the laboratory, with the temperature a thousand times higher than at the centre of a hydrogen bomb and the pressure a million billion times greater than at the bottom of the deepest ocean on Earth.

When the core starts to shrink more and more rapidly, the temperature soon soars to eight billion degrees, when a remarkable effect occurs. The iron, so painstakingly synthesized in stages over millions of years, cannot stand the high temperature, and the nuclei start to break up under the impact of ever more energetic gamma rays. Within a matter of minutes, nearly all the iron disintegrates back into helium, with the result that all the vast quantity of energy released in building up the heavy elements has suddenly to be paid back.

The moment of reckoning has arrived — there is a devastating disappearance of energy from the core of the star. The result is catastrophe: the centre of the star collapses, not gradually over many years, but suddenly in a few seconds. The already compact core simply falls in on itself under its own weight and the shock waves generated by this awesome implosion are enough to create large quantities of neutrinos out of the shock energy. Whereas a star in normal condition would be transparent to these particles, the compaction at the centre is now so great that a thimbleful of matter contains a million tons. Under these densities the neutrinos can only travel about a hundred metres before being absorbed. Consequently a powerful tide of neutrinos, spreading out from the core, transports the energy released by the implosion forcefully through the outer layers of the star, causing them to explode violently. In the ensuing cataclysm the star commits suicide in a most spectacular way. The energy released in the explosion causes the star to increase its luminosity by a million million times, making it outshine a whole galaxy for a few days. The outer material is blown violently into space to form a glowing nebula of hot gas, known to astronomers as a supernova. So bright are these explosions that they can easily be detected in other distant galaxies, and when they occur in our own galaxy they are readily visible in the sky. If the nearest star became a supernova, it would rival the sun in brightness in our sky.

The most famous supernova is that recorded by Chinese astronomers in AD 1054. It was visible in the daytime for several months, outshining even the brilliant planet Venus. It was called 'Guest Star' or 'New Star' (nova being the Latin equivalent), although of course it was not the birth, but rather the death, of a star. The Chinese noted the position of the supernova in the sky: it lay in the constellation that we call the Crab. Through a telescope it is now possible to see the remains of the Crab Nebula consisting of a ragged cloud which represents the shattered debris of the explosion, still hurtling outwards at several miles per second many centuries later. Nothing else conspicuous remains of the original star. The last supernova seen in our galaxy was recorded in 1604 by Kepler, and another is expected any time.

Having traced the fate of the outer layers of the star after the supernova explosion, we should now look at what happens to the centre of the star whose catastrophic implosion began the supernova event. We might expect to find a remnant of the core at the centre of the nebula, but exposed, stripped of the star's outer layers. Such an object would have to be extremely dense and compact, because the core was left imploding from a density of around one million tons per cubic centimetre. The first supernova remnant was accidentally discovered in 1967, when a group of astronomers working under the direction of Anthony Hewish of Cambridge University were building some radio equipment to detect the 'twinkling' of distant radio sources. While operating one of the antenna arrays, one of Hewish's students, Miss Jocelyn Bell, spotted a slightly peculiar fuzzy trace on the print-out record. When she found other examples of fuzzy trace, she checked and determined that the signal producing it always occurred at the same time in the astronomical day, which is not the same time as the terrestrial day, being about four minutes shorter. The reason for this is that during one day the Earth has travelled a short way — about one degree — in its orbit round the sun, so the sun's orientation relative to the distant stars, as seen from the Earth, shifts by the same amount, causing the sun to gradually pass, over the months, through the constellations of the zodiac. It takes about four minutes for the daily reorientation to be corrected by the spin of the Earth on its own axis, so the solar day is about four minutes longer than the astronomical day. The association of the strange radio pulses with the latter suggested that the source of the signals was either a distant astronomical object, or other radio astronomers, working by the astronomical clock.

The most remarkable feature about these radio signals was not just their astronomical connection, but the fact that each consisted of a highly regular sequence of pulses. The immediate conclusion reached by Hewish and Bell was that the pulses were artificial radio signals of some sort. Hewish wrote discreetly to other radio astronomy groups to see if they were transmitting something similar, and they were not. A dramatic new possibility presented itself: perhaps Miss Bell had detected the first artificial radio message from another civilization in the galaxy. If this were so, it would have the most profound implications.

Hewish was suddenly faced with an unenviable responsibility. He decided to proceed carefully and made no announcement. If the signals did originate from an extraterrestrial community, then they would presumably alter slightly as the transmitting planet orbited its star. The source was provisionally named LGM for 'little green men', and kept under quiet surveillance for several months. When the character of the signals remained unaltered, the astronomers began to realize that they must be natural in origin and therefore associated with a star of some sort. Finally, a second pulsing source was found in another part of the sky. The coincidence was too great for there to be two separate civilizations transmitting to Earth simultaneously, and the star explanation was no longer in doubt. In February 1968 Hewish and his group announced their discovery to the world.

The identification of an astronomical source with the radio pulses now presented a great enigma since some of the pulses occur many times a second with very great precision. The problem was to identify the type of star which could generate such powerful regular radio pulses so rapidly. Regular pulsations of stars are well known — the Cepheid variables, for example, oscillate and change their optical brightness in a very systematic way, but cases like this involve a time scale of hours or days. In order to oscillate more than once a second a star would need to be very highly compact — more dense than even a white dwarf.

Within a short time the astronomer Thomas Gold put forward the model of a highly shrunken star with a magnetic field locked into it. The star rotates rapidly, and as it does so the magnetic field is swept around at great speed. Close to the star and linked to it by the magnetic field is a cloud of plasma. The magnetic field coupling to the plasma rotates with the star and causes the charged particles in the plasma to spin around with it. The electrons in the plasma emit radio energy concentrated in a very narrow beam and so cause radio pulses. As the star rotates, the beam sweeps around like a lighthouse, and every time it passes in the direction of the Earth we detect a pulse. The pulses therefore do not come from the star itself, but from the surrounding plasma. These cosmic dynamos are now known as pulsars.

In order to understand the nature of the star which drives the pulsar, we should remember that the star itself must be very small and dense, with a high surface gravity sufficient to prevent the material near the periphery from being flung off by centrifugal force.

Calculations soon show that such a star would have to be only a few miles across, which raises the incredible spectacle of an object with perhaps the mass of the sun, squashed up into less than the size of London. The gravity of such an object is so strong that if one were dropped on to London, it would suck up the whole Earth in a matter of seconds. Indeed the vast bulk of the Earth would be squashed flat into a skin around the surface of the tiny star measuring about a centimetre in thickness. The material is so dense that a thimbleful would weigh more than a fleet of ocean liners on Earth.

The densities involved in this phenomenon are equalled only by nuclear material. Special interest therefore attaches to the nature of the pressure which holds the star up under such immense gravitational attraction. In these conditions the electron degeneracy pressure fails to support the weight of the overlying layers. The gravity is so strong that it crushes even the individual atoms into neutrons. The star is therefore just like a gigantic atomic nucleus made entirely of neutrons — a neutron star.

The idea of neutron stars was first proposed in the 1930s on the basis of theoretical models, but it was only when pulsars were discovered that the idea was taken more seriously. By now it is widely accepted that neutron stars lie at the centre of the pulsar mechanism, and for some years a great deal of theoretical study has been devoted to modelling their properties. While many aspects of the theory are tentative, the general internal structure of these objects is reasonably clear. The surface, which consists of a layer several metres thick and has the properties of a metal, has frozen into it the magnetic field which drives the pulsar. Below lies a solid crust about a mile deep consisting of neutron crystals nearly a billion billion times tougher than steel.

Most of the neutron star, however, is not solid, but consists of a remarkable substance called a superfluid. In the laboratory, superfluids of ordinary atoms may be produced at excessively low temperatures. In the star we have a superfluid of ultradense neutrons whose properties can only be inferred from mathematical analysis. The feature which distinguishes a superfluid from an ordinary fluid is its total absence of friction, an effect which arises, roughly speaking, from a macroscopic organization of quantum behaviour. Finally, the core of the neutron star may contain other subatomic particles in a condition as yet only dimly understood.

As the neutron star rotates and emits radiation, it loses energy, giving rise to a braking effect, causing a steady reduction in the rotation rate. The deceleration is rather small — the first pulsar discovered is slowing down by only forty-four billionths of a second per year, but such is the regularity of the pulses that even this can be detected. It is an indication that pulsars fade out after tens of millions of years, although there can be occasional sudden irregularities in the rotation rate. One of these occurred in the early spring of 1969 when a pulsar in the constellation of Vela suddenly actually increased its rotation rate, quite unexpectedly. While this phenomenon is not properly understood, some astronomers think it is associated with a neutron starquake, a minor readjustment in the crust material of the star. If neutron stars really are supernova remnants then we might expect to find pulsars at the centre of the debris from a supernova explosion. In 1968 great excitement was created by the discovery of a pulsar in the middle of the Crab Nebula, thus dramatically confirming this theory. The Crab pulsar is the fastest known — it pulses thirty times a second — a feature explained by its very recent formation less than one thousand years ago. It has, therefore, had very little time to decelerate by the braking process. Because of its high rotation rate it is also very bright and can actually be seen through a moderate telescope as a rapidly flashing source.

It is now believed, on the basis of these discoveries, that neutron stars are dead stars — the natural end-state of stars which are massive enough to reach a central temperature of several billion degrees before exploding. In several tens of billions of years from now, many of the stars we see in the sky will have burnt out and exploded apart, leaving a neutron remnant, as the sole reminder of their existence. After dissipating its rotational energy through the pulsar mechanism, each dead star will fall silent; the end of a long career of organized activity will have arrived, and the second law of thermodynamics will have claimed another victim. Though the neutron star may sit in space for all of eternity, the second law forbids it to do anything more.

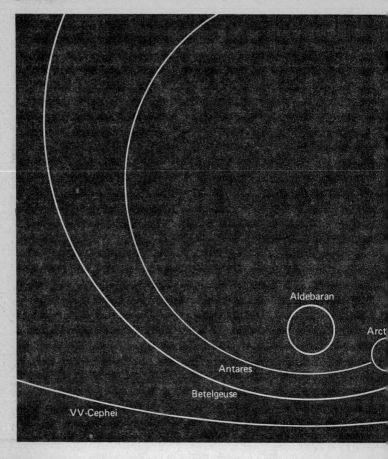

Figure 8 Stars vary widely in size
This chart shows the enormous range of sizes for stars. Some, like Betelgeuse, would engulf the entire solar system, while at the other extreme, the tiny neutron star is dwarfed by the Earth.

Not all stars end their days as neutrons. Some are not massive enough to reach even the helium flash, while others — those which contain up to about six solar masses — may not follow the course described earlier in this chapter right through to the supernova stage. In some cases the surface layers of the star may explode in a less violent fashion without any collapse of the core. This results in the formation of a roughly

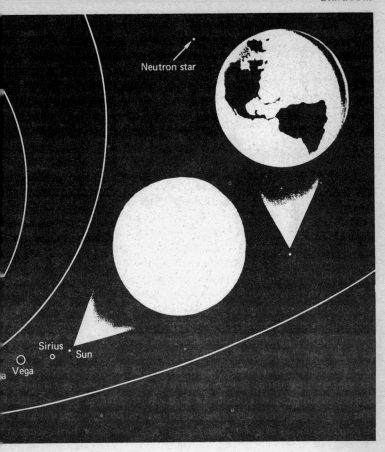

Neutron star

Sirius
Sun
Vega
a

spherical shell of gas which is blown off to form what astronomers call a planetary nebula, the most famous of these being the so-called 'Ring' nebula in the constellation of Lyra, which is just visible in a four-inch telescope. The expulsion of gaseous shells may occur several times and greatly diminish the total mass content of the star. The force of gravity is still inexorable of course, and once the nuclear energy supply of these more moderate mass stars has been depleted, they will start to contract in the usual way. However, as long as their final masses do not exceed about 1.4 times the mass of the sun, they can settle down to a stable equilibrium, held up by electron degeneracy pressure. Such stars are still very compact — perhaps the size of the Earth — but nowhere near as dense as a neutron star. Known as white dwarfs (see chapter 4) they can be very hot, possibly 40,000 degrees at their surface, and they therefore continue to radiate. Slowly, however, they cool as their energy supply is gradually depleted, a process which may take as long as a hundred billion years. As they approach the temperature of surrounding space and fade out, all that remains is a black dwarf. The second law has claimed another victim.

For the stars that die as neutron stars or black dwarfs, the catastrophic end can be both violent and spasmodic, involving extremes of temperature, pressure and density, as well as slow and uneventful cooling and decay. In all cases gravity is the agent which ultimately controls events. In fact a star in the popular sense must be regarded as nothing more than a brief interlude between a dispersed cloud of gas and a ball of crushed matter. The fundamental activity which is occurring throughout the universe is the collapse of matter into tightly concentrated blobs. The fact that nuclear processes intervene to provide a stay of execution in the form of a luminous star for a few billion years may be vital for the existence of life, but it is only a temporary victory against the inexorable power of gravity trying to drag the object in on itself.

The second law of thermodynamics ensures that this interesting luminous activity must eventually run down. The fight against gravity cannot be sustained for ever. Eventually compaction will prevail and the star will die, the manner of its death depending on circumstances. The all-powerful nature of gravity is curious, for it is by far the weakest of known forces. Indeed if it were not for the fact that gravity only attracts, we should never have discovered it at all. But the cumulative effect of an always-attractive force is without limit, and gravity is capable of overwhelming all the other known forces of nature once it has taken control. In white dwarfs and neutron stars, the cumulative power of the stars' gravity is not enough to overwhelm the quantum degeneracy pressure, and the weight of the star, dense though it is, can be withstood by the core. It is possible to definitely predict, however, that if at the end of its life a star contains a greater quantity of matter than about three suns, then nothing can prevent a catastrophic gravitational collapse of a nature still more bizarre than the phenomena described in this chapter.

8.   Black holes and superholes

Of all the catastrophes that can overtake a star, total gravitational collapse is the most awesome. It represents not just the end of the star, but the end of matter. The second law predicts the inevitable spread of disorder, or rise of entropy, and it follows from this that the organized activity of the universe must be steadily lost. In gravitational collapse, vast quantities of information and ordered structure disappear almost instantaneously from the universe, to be lost irretrievably. In order to understand the physical basis of this phenomenon, we must look into the nature of gravity as revealed by Einstein's general theory of relativity.

Most people regard gravity as a force which can be felt, for example, pulling us down towards the surface of the Earth. Newton explained that objects fall towards the ground because they are forced downwards by the Earth's gravity, which causes them to accelerate vertically ever faster. The same gravitational force which pulls on an apple also pulls on the moon, which is why it remains in the vicinity of the Earth instead of flying off through space. Newton offered no explanation of how the Earth's gravity could reach out across empty space and attract the moon, but modern physicists think in terms of a gravitational field, envisaged by some as a sort of invisible halo of force fading out gradually from the gravitating centre, whether it be the Earth, the sun, a neutron star or a galaxy.

As we saw in chapter 2, Newton developed his physical ideas about gravity into precise mathematical relationships so that detailed calculations, such as the motion of planets in the solar system, could be made. The theory was very successful and remained unchallenged for two centuries, but when Einstein discovered the theory of relativity in 1906 it was realized that Newton's picture of gravity must be wrong, one crucial shortcoming being that it must act instantaneously at a distance. Experiments conducted about the turn of the century, combined with Einstein's brilliant theoretical work, established beyond doubt that no physical influence can exceed the speed of light without reversing the order of cause and effect. As this is quite unthinkable, it rules out the possibility of instantaneous action at a distance on which Newton's concept of gravity is founded. In attempting to construct a replacement theory, Einstein was greatly impressed by a feature of gravity which Newton had regarded as merely a coincidence. This is not a subtle feature but a familiar one first articulated by Galileo: the well-known fact that objects of different weights and densities when dropped simultaneously from the same height strike the ground simultaneously. It is only approximately true near the surface of the Earth, because air resistance interferes, but this is just a complicating effect quite unrelated to the nature of gravity and may be avoided by dropping objects in a vacuum.

Some people have an intuitive misconception that heavy objects ought to fall faster than light ones. What really happens, however, is that heavy objects have a greater inertia and so are harder to accelerate. The net effect is exactly compensatory, so that although heavy objects are pulled downwards more strongly, they respond to this force more sluggishly. Careful observation shows that they really do fall in the same way as light bodies; in other words, when objects are freely falling under the action of gravity, their motion does not depend on the mass or composition of the body. This characteristic of gravity sharply distinguishes it from any other force, and it suggested to Einstein that perhaps the explanation for gravity should not be sought in the properties of the falling bodies themselves, but in the nature of the space through which they fall.

As gravity varies from place to place, so there are variations in the paths along which objects move, a phenomenon called the tidal effect, because the variation of the moon's gravity across the surface of the Earth raises the ocean tides. Einstein searched for some property of space and time which could explain how the paths of freely falling bodies could vary from place to place. This variation might be a twisting and turning effect or an expansion, a contraction or shearing. As remarked in chapter 1, Einstein proposed that space and time are in a rough sense elastic and can suffer distortions in the presence of a gravitating mass. The space-time curvature in the vicinity of the mass twists and bends the paths of freely falling bodies. According to this view we should no longer regard the Earth as being forced into a curved path around the sun by the force of gravity, but as falling freely through bent space-time, in which the distortion carries the Earth away from straight-line motion into a curved path. Gravity is, therefore, reduced to geometry and is not a force at all.

The distortion of space and time in the presence of gravitating bodies can be checked in the solar system from three different experiments. The first was conducted by the British astronomer Sir Arthur Eddington during a total eclipse of the sun in 1919. This observation concerns the deflection of a light ray passing close to the surface of the sun and appears as a displacement in the position of a distant star, caused by viewing it through the bent space around the sun. The deflection is very small, but confirms Einstein's theory. The second test, which can even be carried out on Earth, is a check on the effect of gravity on time. The stronger gravity near the surface of the Earth causes time to run more slowly than at a greater altitude, and this can be verified by careful comparison of nuclear clocks. A gamma ray with very sharply defined frequency from an atomic nucleus is sent up a tower, at the top of which its frequency is compared with that from a similar nucleus. Clocks really do run slower near the surface of the Earth where the gravity is higher. The third test checks for curved space round the sun by examining the orbits of the planets. Mercury is nearest to the sun, and a discrepancy in its orbital motion had long been known to astronomers. Einstein's theory predicted the exact amount of twisting effect of space curvature on the planet's motion. In the solar system all three effects are very small and of little importance, because even the gravity of the sun is not great enough to cause large space-time distortions, but close to superdense objects like neutron stars distortion of space and time becomes appreciable.

In the previous chapter it was mentioned that degeneracy pressure, of either electrons or neutrons, could not support a star the mass of which is more than three times that of the sun. The vital question is, what happens to such a star? If there is no way of withstanding its own gravity, a star must collapse catastrophically. This is what happens at the centre of a supernova during the formation of a neutron star, but there the mass of the core is low enough for the neutron degeneracy pressure eventually to halt the collapse. For a slightly more massive star this support is insufficient and the collapse continues uncontrollably, causing the surface gravity to rise progressively faster and the star to become increasingly more compact. The time-scale involved is very short: in a matter of only thousandths of a second a point is reached where the distortion of space-time near the surface of the collapsing star becomes so great that strange new phenomena occur.

The first effect concerns the dilation of time already mentioned in connection with the Earth's gravity. On the surface of a spherical collapsing star the rate at which time runs relative to a distant place decelerates exponentially; that is, by halving the 'clock' rate every ten thousandth of a second for a typical star. Within the blink of an eye, time at the surface as gauged against a distant clock virtually grinds to a halt, and events there seem to a far-off observer to be frozen in time. Consequently the collapse of the star itself will, as far as the outside world is concerned, seem to come to an abrupt stop. The radius of the star at which this happens is known as the Schwarzschild radius after the German astronomer Karl Schwarzschild, and is proportional to the total mass. For an object with the same mass as the sun it is about one mile — even smaller than a neutron star.

The apparent freezing of events on a collapsing star should not convey the impression that time and activity actually stop there. An observer on the surface of the star would not regard time as behaving unusually. What happens is that star time and the time at a distant place get out of step by an amount which grows greater at an accelerating rate. All time is now known to be relative to an observer's situation and state of motion. Normally, of course, we do not notice any discrepancies between measurements of time intervals made by different observers because the effect is small in everday life, but in circumstances as drastic as total gravitational collapse, the time-scale disparity becomes unlimited. One immediate consequence of this is a sudden reduction in the frequency of light waves coming from the star, resulting in a change in the colour quality of the light — a shift towards the red end of the spectrum. The red shift increases very rapidly indeed — the frequency halves itself every ten thousandth of a second — and within a very short while the collapsing star no longer emits visible light at all. When the wavelength passes even beyond the radio region, the star will have become totally black, its surface features being invisible. The same process which brings the star's time-scale to a halt also brings the emission of light to a halt.

Many ingenious methods have been proposed whereby a distant observer could obtain information about the invisible collapsing star. One suggestion is to shine a strong light on to it. Unfortunately, however, the same time distortion which operates at the surface of the star would also affect the incoming light. As measured by the distant observer, this light would never catch up with the collapsing star — even if the observer waited for all eternity — so the illuminating beam would never return to reveal the retreating surface.

An alternative strategy which has been investigated mathematically is to station an accomplice on the surface of the star as it collapses, and arrange for him to try to send various signals. Although in reality no observer could withstand the rigours of gravitational collapse, let alone carry out any signalling in the few thousandths of a second which are available in his frame of reference, the imaginary situation is useful for the sake of argument. If the falling observer attempted to signal what was happening in the star by placing electric charges in a coded pattern, the distant observer would be prevented from reading the pattern. The reason is that the distortion of space around the object bends the electric field of the charges to such an extent that they all appear to be concentrated in a single point at the centre. Similar effects occur if other forces are used; nuclear force fields cannot be read and gravitational messages using gravity waves or patterns of heavy objects are equally futile. The only information about the object that a distant observer can obtain is the total mass, total electric charge and the total angular momentum, if it is rotating. Nothing about the internal state can be discerned. Even the strategy of lowering a grab on a rope to claw up some of the star will fail, for it can be proved that no rope in the universe is strong enough to withstand the gravitational forces.

These strange limitations are better understood by examining (using mathematics) events as witnessed by the falling observer. For him there is no time dilation, so the star seems to shrink in size at an alarming rate. Its gravity is so intense at the enormous compression involved that a typical star halves its radius in a few thousandths of a second, dragged inwards on itself under its own weight, pulling the observer down with it. He notices nothing unusual as he passes through the Schwarzschild radius, for it has no local significance, but once he is inside, however, his fate is sealed — he can never escape again to the outside universe, nor can he even signal his fate to the distant observer. No information at all can reach the outside world from inside the Schwarzschild radius. In the short time that it has taken for him to fall this far, all of eternity has passed in the universe he so recently left.

The region inside the Schwarzschild radius has the bizarre property that even light is not swift enough to avoid being dragged inwards by the intense gravity. A light pulse emitted by the star in an outward direction, away from the centre, will actually find itself travelling backwards towards the star, not away from it, drawn irresistibly on to the collapsing body. It is rather like a runner on a moving track: as fast as he moves forwards relative to the track, he is swept backwards by the movement of the track itself. In the vicinity of the collapsing star, this distortion in the motion of light rays is another effect of curved space-time, caused by the gravity of the star.

According to the theory of relativity, all material bodies must move slower than light. As the surface of the star is made of matter, it too must continue to move towards the centre, otherwise the outward-directed light pulse, which is actually moving inwards, would cross the surface, which means that the material of the surface would have to 'travel' faster than light just to remain at a fixed radius. The star must, therefore, inevitably continue to shrink, and no force in the universe can stabilize it in a static condition. The collapse is now truly inexorable; in a sense the roles of space and time become interchanged inside the Schwarzschild radius, so the surface of the star can no more avoid shrinking than the flow of time can, in the outside world, be halted. Furthermore, the shrinkage accelerates at an ever increasing rate.

We are now faced with a profound puzzle. What happens when the surface of the star has shrunk to nothing? When this occurs, all of the star's mass is concentrated into a single mathematical point at an infinite density. The curvature of space-time also rises without limit. Space-time cannot exist under these circumstances and it is, as it were, torn apart by the unlimited tidal forces of gravity. The star has encountered what mathematicians call a singularity, which is a region where space-time comes to an end. It is not possible to say what lies beyond a singularity, for all of physics breaks down there. It is generally believed that a singularity lay at the beginning of the big bang, discussed in chapter 2, which may be thought of as the time-reverse of the singularity encountered by the star; the former marks the entrance of matter into the universe at the creation whereas the latter marks its exit.

After the singularity has formed, the region inside the Schwarzschild radius is empty; the star has apparently shrunk to a point and disappeared for ever. The gravity still remains, though, trapping everything that falls through this critical radius and preventing any light or information from escaping. This strange region of space-time is, therefore, both black and vacuous — a 'black hole' in modern jargon. Black holes have received wide attention from scientists and public alike in recent years. They have been studied in great detail by mathematicians and physicists who wish to probe their unusual features using mathematical models, and by astronomers who are searching for them in space.

Great interest attaches to the part played by the surface at the Schwarzschild radius in trapping all information inside the black hole. Because a distant observer cannot see or know about any of the events which take place inside this surface, it is called an event horizon. The event horizon separates events in space-time to which we have access from those to which we do not. Events taking place inside the black hole, being inaccessible, cannot affect the outside world in any way — they are causally disconnected from it. The reverse is not true, however, for the outside world can influence what happens inside the black hole, for example by matter and light falling into it, though they are unable to return to the outside world. The event horizon therefore acts like a one-way barrier, allowing the free passage of ingoing material only. Anything that falls into the black hole makes it bigger; that is to say, the event horizon grows. The fate of the infalling matter is violent in the extreme, for the same tidal forces which raise and lower the oceans on the Earth operate strongly over very small distances inside a black hole. A hapless observer falling headlong into one would find his head, being nearer to the gravitating centre, pulled more strongly than his feet. He would therefore be stretched with increasing vigour. He would also be crushed as his body was squeezed down into the diminishing volume near the singularity. His fate is similar to that of the original star, which has long since disappeared, and he soon crashes into the singularity and out of the universe.

From the viewpoint of an observer in the outside world, the slowing down of events near the Schwarzschild radius caused by the unlimited distortion of time there implies that the falling observer will appear to take an infinite duration to reach the event horizon. In effect, though, he disappears from the outside universe in a tiny fraction of a second, because the red shift of light grows at an escalating rate. There is no way that the distant observer can reach his colleague, though he knows that he has not yet crossed inside the horizon, because even travelling at near the speed of light he would find that by the time he reached the horizon in pursuit, his friend would have long since crossed over into the black hole. This point is particularly important, for it means that information can effectively disappear down a black hole almost instantaneously. The sudden loss of information represents a gain in entropy, so the black hole may be viewed as the ultimate consequence of the second law of thermodynamics — not only the cessation of activity by matter, but its total disappearance.

A measure of the total entropy of a black hole is the area of its event horizon, which increases whenever matter or energy falls into it. The second law of thermodynamics, which requires that entropy must always increase in any process, can be applied directly to black holes to predict that they will tend to grow bigger (increase their area) under very general circumstances, and not just when they accrete matter from their surroundings. For example, when two holes collide and coalesce, the product black hole will have a total area bigger than the combined area of the original pair. The same principle forbids a black hole to bifurcate, which implies that coalescence is irreversible.

It is still possible for a black hole to shrink, however, if the entropy of its surroundings is taken into account, for then the total entropy of the whole system can still rise, even though that of the black hole decreases. If the hole shrinks, it must divest itself of some mass, or energy, because the area of the event horizon is proportional to the square of the mass. This energy must appear somehow in the surrounding environment in the form of high entropy radiation emitted from the hole. As explained in chapter 6, the highest entropy attainable is in the form of thermal equilibrium radiation at a uniform temperature, recognizable from its characteristic spectrum. In 1974, the British mathematician Stephen Hawking, whilst investigating the quantum theory of black holes, made the astonishing discovery that quantum processes should indeed cause the hole to emit thermal equilibrium radiation at a definite temperature. Evidently black holes are not black after all.

The quantum process discovered by Hawking predicts that black holes will slowly evaporate and shrink as they emit energy, a situation which at first seems to contradict the nature of the event horizon, for if nothing can escape from a black hole, how can thermal radiation be emitted? The resolution of this paradox turns on the rather abstract notion of negative energy. According to classical physics, a black hole can only reduce its mass by ejecting energy, which is impossible because of the restriction of the event horizon. Quantum physics, however, provides for another possibility: instead of energy flowing out, negative energy can flow in. In this way the radiation can be produced outside the black hole, where it is able to escape to the world beyond, and paid for by an influx of negative energy which reduces the black hole mass at the appropriate rate.

The negative energy is created by the gravity of the object, and exists even around ordinary objects such as stars, or the Earth, although it is exceedingly small. Normally it has no noticeable effect because it is static, but if the object implodes to form a black hole, the negative energy will fall in through the event horizon like everything else, and thereby cause the appearance of positive energy in the form of Hawking's thermal radiation outside the black hole.

The evaporation effect is very small, for the temperature of a black hole about the mass of the sun is less than one millionth of a degree above absolute zero. If black holes of this size exist then they will be growing larger, not smaller, because the temperature of the surrounding universe is at least three degrees due to the primeval background radiation. Unlike most objects, black holes grow hotter when they radiate heat, so small holes have a higher temperature than big ones. It has been conjectured by Hawking that mini-holes may have formed during the big bang, when very high densities occurred. A typical mini-hole might be the size of an atomic nucleus, and contain a mass equivalent to Mount Everest. Such an object would be intensely hot, with a temperature of about ten million million degrees, unequalled by anything since the primeval universe. It would therefore radiate very strongly and lose mass at a prodigious rate, raising the fascinating question of what happens to it in the end. At the time of writing this question cannot be answered with any confidence because quantum gravity effects (the disruption of space-time mentioned at the end of chapter 2) will play an important part. According to one point of view the black hole will evaporate away completely, thereby exposing the singularity at the centre when the horizon shrinks to nothing. Just what the consequences of a naked singularity might be is anybody's guess — perhaps this just disappears too — in which case the matter which imploded to form the black hole in the first place will have completely vanished, leaving only the thermal radiation as a reminder of its erstwhile existence.

There is little doubt that black holes will play an important part in the collapse of the cosmos. Many astronomers believe that most massive stars will end their lives in this way, though this will not happen to the sun, which is destined to become a white dwarf instead. There may also be superholes lurking in the galaxy somewhere, with a mass equivalent of millions of suns. A few years ago there was a flurry of excitement when the American physicist Joseph Weber claimed to have detected gravitational waves emanating from the centre of the galaxy, similar to those produced in the big bang but with much longer wavelength. Theoretical studies indicated that they could be generated as ripples in space-time caused by the violent impact between a star and a superhole. The hole, assumed to reside at the galactic centre, eats the star and grows larger, while some of the extra mass is radiated away as gravitational waves. If Weber were right it would provide strong evidence for the existence of a superhole in our galaxy. Unfortunately the results of his experiment have not been confirmed by other workers, and the status of these particular gravitational waves is still uncertain.

Superholes have a voracious and insatiable appetite, and with enough time they could consume a major fraction of the galaxy. Although many stars will escape implosion themselves, it seems likely that they will eventually succumb to gravity and be swallowed up by a large black hole somewhere.

In spite of their cannibalistic tendencies, black holes represent an enormous source of available energy, particularly if they rotate. It is thought that neutron stars spin as fast as several times a second, so if a black hole formed from the collapse of a star it seems probable that it would spin still faster than this, possessing a rotational energy equal to the total present energy output of the sun for ten million years. The difference is that while the sun radiates its energy away at an enormous rate, a large black hole retains its rotational energy more or less indefinitely, apart from a tiny leakage due to the evaporation process. There is, therefore, no better way of storing energy than dumping it in a black hole — the problem is then, how to extract it again.

One mechanism whereby the black hole can release some of its rotational energy was discovered by the British mathematician Roger Penrose. In principle the strategy is simple enough: a particle of matter is dropped close to the event horizon surface where it is exploded into two pieces, one of which is sacrificed down the hole. If the trajectory is chosen very carefully, a great deal of energy can be delivered to the remaining piece, which finds itself projected away from the object at very high velocity. This energy is supplied partly by the mass of the sacrificed component, and partly by the rotational energy of the black hole, which ends up lighter than before. The Penrose process does not contradict the universal second law of thermodynamics, however, even though the black hole loses mass, because the size of a rotating black hole depends on its rate of spin as well as its total mass-energy content. It turns out that the faster a black hole rotates, the smaller its event horizon surface area becomes. Consequently when its spin rate is reduced by the Penrose mechanism, the area actually increases, even though the total mass-energy decreases.

It is possible to carry out the reverse process, and increase the rotation rate of the black hole by injecting matter into it in such a way as to supply extra angular momentum and mass, to see if this reduces the area of the event horizon. Investigations have been carried out to discover whether this or some other process can be used to spin up a black hole so much that the horizon disappears altogether, leaving a naked singularity. In all cases the answer seems to be no; it is as though nature abhors a naked singularity and always operates to prevent the unseemly removal of the event horizon screen. Some writers have dwelt morosely on the dire consequences for the rest of the universe if a singularity were to become naked. Because singularities are associated with a complete breakdown of the laws of nature, it is claimed that any influence at all might emerge from such a thing, and in the unpredictable world which followed, anything might happen. Others, with a more sceptical attitude, have suggested that perhaps singularities do not form anyway.

The fate of a traveller who ventures into a rotating black hole is still more fantastic. As the event horizon is approached, a region called the 'ergosphere', where the Penrose process can operate, is traversed. Here, the traveller finds that he is unable to avoid rotating around with the black hole — it is as though this spinning object sets up an invisible space vortex which irresistibly drags everything round with it. Even with rocket motors blazing he cannot avoid being spun around by the vortex, and if he crosses the horizon he cannot afterwards return to the outside universe. Because of the rotational motion, however, he is not drawn directly towards the central singularity, so that he does not leave the universe that way. What happens next is a matter of some dispute. According to one idealized picture of rotating black holes, he will pass right through the interior of the object and emerge on the other side in another universe.

Understandably this remarkable possibility has greatly endeared itself to some science fiction writers, the idea that there might be another universe connected to ours through a black hole having a definite appeal to many people. Unfortunately it also has a rather absurd aspect to it, for if the intrepid explorer were to drop back into the same black hole from which he had so recently emerged, he would find himself, not back in our universe, which is impossible (because to a distant observer in our universe he will not have passed through the first time yet) but in another universe. Moreover the process could be repeated *ad infinitum.* One other universe is perhaps plausible enough, but an infinity of them seems a dubious concept. The idea of a 'space-bridge' connecting our universe with others has been treated with scepticism by most physicists, because it is based on an idealized model of a rotating black hole. In the real universe it seems probable that material falling into the black hole over an extended period as well as quantum processes inside the hole would have an important effect, by causing the appearance of another singularity which would shut off the space-bridge and prevent any matter or information from travelling beyond the hole.

In recent years several studies have been undertaken to find out how a black hole can be observed. Being small and black, one formed from the collapse of a star could not be seen directly, so its existence would have to be inferred from the effects it produced in its vicinity. The best hope is to search for a black hole in a binary star system. A high proportion of stars in the galaxy are found in multiple combinations, so that from time to time one of the companions to a visible star should turn out to be a black hole. The presence of a dark compact object could be deduced by the gravitational disturbance which it exerts on the visible companion, in much the same way as the white dwarf Sirius B was discovered by Bessel. This in itself is not enough to prove the existence of a black hole in the system, but fortunately there are other

144

effects which offer more positive evidence. Strong tidal forces might disrupt the surface of the visible companion star, causing material to be drawn from it. This material would fall towards the black hole, but the orbital motion of the star would tend to sweep the gases around the hole in the form of a disc. The interior regions of the disc would be pulled gradually into the hole, heating up strongly as they went. Calculations show that the temperature of the accreted material should be high enough for X-rays to be emitted — a tell-tale sign that a black hole is at work.

One of the great technological advances in the last few years has been the development of X-ray astronomy. Because X-rays do not penetrate the Earth's atmosphere, this branch of astronomy is carried out with the help of X-ray telescopes placed in artificial satellites. Many X-ray sources of various types have been detected, including several associated with binary systems, an especially good example being Cygnus X-1 in the constellation of the Swan, another less convincing example being Epsilan Aurigae. Cygnus X-1 is a prime candidate for a black hole, though it is necessary to prove that its dark companion is not just a highly compact and very dim star, such as a neutron star or white dwarf. At present this can only be done from theoretical studies which suggest that neither a neutron star nor a white dwarf can have a mass greater than a few solar masses. Because of its gravitating effect, the mass of the dark companion in Cygnus X-1 can be evaluated if the mass of the visible star is known, which in turn depends on a correct understanding of the nature of that star. Granted all the assumptions that go to make up the latter, it appears rather probable that Cygnus X-1 really does contain a black hole.

There is also a possibility that microscopic-sized black holes can be observed by detecting the radiation which they emit through the quantum process discovered by Hawking. As already explained, these objects gradually evaporate away, getting hotter as they do so. The rate of evaporation increases rapidly as they shrink, so that in the final few moments, a great burst of energy is emitted suddenly, much of it in the form of gamma rays. In recent years, special telescopes in artificial satellites have detected gamma-ray bursts, although with different characteristics from those expected from exploding black holes.

The observation of microscopic black holes would provide interesting information about the conditions which existed in the primeval fireball, because these tiny objects would be relics of that early phase.

The lifetime for a black hole to evaporate completely away depends sensitively on its initial mass: the heavier ones take much longer to radiate all their mass-energy away and disappear. A simple calculation suggests that any holes formed in the big bang with a mass less than a million million kilograms — having a size comparable with an atomic nucleus — would have already evaporated away by now. By determining how many black holes are still around from the primeval fireball, and what their present masses are, some of the properties of the primeval material at very early epochs can be inferred.

In this chapter and the last we have examined in detail the fate of stars. While all stars are necessarily doomed by the second law of thermo-dynamics, some of them may fade out slowly and quietly as dwarfs, while others do not accept death with such equanimity; they explode spectacularly and shower the galaxy with debris, often leaving a neutron star behind. Others may suffer periodic but less drastic explosions and pass through stages of lively activity, perhaps swelling and shrinking spasmodically, or pulsating regularly. Many of these end their days as white dwarfs. Finally, the massive stars implode with a violence far greater than a supernova, but with their energy directed inwards to rip open space-time and shrink out of the universe. Even the black holes left behind are now believed to evaporate slowly away in the fullness of time.

This is the future of our universe as modern science predicts it; a mixture of violent paroxysms and slow decay. The collapse of the cosmos will eventually extinguish every feature of the universe as we know it. To what extent and for how long intelligent life can survive these events depends on the level of technology available to our descendants. Certainly the end is a very, very long time in the future. It is possible, however, that even the survivors may be overwhelmed by a still greater calamity, the ultimate catastrophe of all — the gravitational collapse of the entire universe.

9.   Technology and survival

Technology represents the supreme level of organized activity that we know and will, more than anything else, determine the ultimate fate of intelligent communities in general and human beings in particular. In attempting to predict the future of technological society, it is necessary to leave the world of well understood scientific principles and indulge in some speculative futurology. Curiously, it is far easier to predict the end state of a star than to foretell the fate of intelligent life, because the principles which control the evolution of stars are straightforward and relatively simple, whereas history has frequently proved that social futurology is hopelessly inaccurate. When it comes to technology, all that we can do is to extrapolate present trends on the basis of what we believe to be the correct laws of physics and to adopt the reasoning that anything that is possible in principle could be achieved in practice by a community with sufficient time, money and motivation. The question of whether the limits of technology will ever be attained is, of course, another matter. One thing, however, is certain: there is no lack of time available for technological communities of the future to achieve some of the speculations given here. With these important cautions in mind, some recent conjectures by astronomers, physicists and biologists will be examined.

The most immediate threat to the survival of humanity is not cosmic catastrophe, but social and political disintegration. Many people look to technology to provide an amelioration to privation and strife, measuring human progress by the degree of social organization and technological development. In a few thousand years, social organization has evolved from small tribal groups measured in hundreds, or even dozens, to the modern nation state of perhaps dozens or hundreds of millions. In spite of the unrest during this synthesis, the process has taken place fairly effortlessly. Grave problems seem to stand in the way of any attempt to organize greater numbers of people than the nation state. A further synthesis by a factor of one hundred or so would see an integrated global society. It may be that some very basic social instability sets in as soon as the population of a given social unit reaches, say, one billion. In that case, world social order will always elude mankind (unless the population falls dramatically), and the risk of self-destruction would always be present. Assuming, however, that the next step is eventually taken, and the planet is run as a single unit, the question naturally arises as to whether this is the end of the story. An idea much beloved of science fiction writers is the galactic empire, in which social organization extends beyond the bounds of one planet to encompass an entire star cluster, or even a galaxy. Frequently sci-fi stories are written about animosity and warfare between rival empires, extending terrestrial trivialities to the cosmic domain.

We have a strong vested interest to know whether galactic empires are a possibility, not because we may then strive to achieve one, but because if they are possible, someone will probably have already produced one in our own galaxy. Since human society is only about one hundred thousandth of the age of the galaxy, we are comparative newcomers. Any possible empire building will presumably have been undertaken long ago, unless we are indeed alone in the universe. This thought once prompted the physicist Enrico Fermi to ask: 'where are they?' He reasoned that if other technological communities were to exist, they would already have colonized the Earth. Knowledge about extraterrestrial life is so sparse that even the negative information that the Earth has not been colonized is useful for placing constraints on speculations about galactic communities.

It is worth examining in some detail what is involved in the establishment of a galactic empire. The rise of the nation state on Earth turned fundamentally on technological advance, particularly with regard to communications. The railway, the telegraph and modern road building are the catalysts which have enabled millions of square miles of territory to be administered, policed and supplied by a central authority. Proper social cohesion and political control between, say, the

East Coast of the United States and California could not be established whilst it took many arduous weeks on horseback to cross the Rocky Mountains. With the coming of the railways and the telegraph, the States rapidly became truly united into a nation state. Twentieth-century communication facilities such as air travel and instant satellite television coverage, as well as economic interdependence, already supply the technological basis for a world society.

The first step in establishing an extraterrestrial community would be the colonization of the planets in our solar system. We already have rockets capable of reaching any of these planets with payloads of a few people and journey times of several years, so small groups could be ferried to other planets, especially the moon, in the forseeable future. The overriding problem is how to survive in the hostile conditions there, for none of our sister planets possesses conditions anywhere near those needed for human habitation. Carl Sagan has suggested that an intelligent use of biological control might enable the planetary conditions of Mars and Venus to be drastically altered. For example, if an organism could be found to convert the atmosphere of Venus to oxygen, the 'greenhouse' heating effect produced by the overabundant carbon dioxide would be greatly reduced, allowing the temperature to fall and the polar regions to be colonized.

If these methods are not practicable, the only alternative is to construct artificial, self-contained ecosystems. In practical terms this means building airtight containers large enough to accommodate a whole community along with a sufficient diversity of plant and animal life so that some sort of ecological self-sufficiency could be achieved, because frequent trips to and from Earth are prohibitively expensive. There is still the major difficulty of constructing the colony in the first place. Engineering projects of this magnitude are difficult enough on Earth, and in the foreseeable future the cost of transportation of huge pieces of machinery even to the moon would probably be quite incalculable.

A more realistic proposal has been advanced by Gerard O'Neill of Princeton University, who suggests that instead of establishing planetary colonies, units should be constructed in outer space, preferably at the Earth-sun-moon gravitational equilibrium points. It is much easier to manipulate large and massive pieces of material in the weightless environment of free fall in space, and there is no problem of landing supplies and machinery on a host planet. Furthermore, there is a dramatic saving in fuel costs, because a planet to planet trip is much more than twice as expensive as a planet to space trip, for the simple reason that all the fuel needed to slow down the payload for a soft landing at the other end must be lifted off from Earth along with the payload itself. What O'Neill suggests is to mine the moon (or asteroids) for raw material instead. The surface gravity is much lower than that of the Earth, and chunks of rock could be despatched into space by the simple expedient of hurling them fast enough. The absence of an atmosphere on the moon means that a simple projection device would be enough for this purpose.

Once a small space station housing a few dozen people had been established, work could begin on assembling the larger units. O'Neill envisages huge cylinders, several kilometres across, slowly rotating along their axes so as to simulate the effect of the Earth's gravity at their periphery. Part of the fabric would be transparent, and large mirrors would reflect sunlight into the interior. A typical cylinder would be self-supporting and landscaped, with urban and rural areas, industry and recreational facilities. A large variety of life forms could be supported in such a construction and each could contain a human population of several thousand. The project would of course be hierarchical, with one cylinder providing an *in situ* labour force for the construction of still more. Nuclear fuel and sunlight energy would provide the power requirements, and hydrogen brought from the Earth combined with oxygen from the lunar rocks would provide an easy, cheap source of water to fill the artificial lakes. O'Neill has undertaken careful scientific and economic studies of the space colony proposal and finds that the cylinders are within present technological and financial capabilities. The first cylinder could be built within a century.

It is easy to envisage a chain of artificial worlds strung out across the solar system in this way. Physical travel between them would be much easier than a journey to Earth because of the zero gravity. The space colonies would, therefore, probably evolve a complex integrated social organization of their own, with only tenuous links with Earth. Nevertheless radio message times across the solar system are a few hours at most, so there is no reason in principle why the entire solar system should not be eventually inhabited to become a single, loose-knit, social unit containing perhaps a million million people.

Many regard this prospect as a welcome way of avoiding ecological disaster on Earth. It is argued that when this planet's resources are exhausted and its population bursting to capacity, expansion into space will remove the pressure to restrain economic and population growth. This is a fallacy. At present the population doubles every twenty or thirty years, and even if the whole of Venus could be colonized and the Earth were full to overflowing, Venus would also be crowded out in another ten years. Whether space colonies become a reality or not, simple statistics dictate that the days of unlicensed human fecundity are over.

Another major constraint is energy expenditure. Our greatest source of energy is the sun, which provides an upper limit to the amount of naturally available energy we can consume. The ultimate consuming technology based on the solar system would be one which used the sun's entire energy output. The American physicist Freeman Dyson has suggested that if some of the planets, such as Jupiter, were dismantled and spread out in a shell around the sun, nearly all the sunlight would be trapped. A human community could then inhabit the inner surface of the shell and exploit this prolific power supply. Although the idea of dismantling an entire planet might seem to be utterly beyond the bounds of sensible futurology, it is important to realize that no restriction is imposed by the laws of physics. There is no doubt that given sufficient time and money, as well as motivation, a Dyson shell could be constructed, though that does not mean it will. It is, however, amusing to note that if energy expenditure continues to rise at present rates, our power requirements will approach that of the Dyson shell in a mere 500 years. If the galaxy really is full of supertechnicians, we might expect to find signs of their technological activities even if they are not actually sending messages to us. Engineering feats like the Dyson shell could have been achieved by a civilization one billion years old, and it is interesting to ask whether we would notice such a construction. The answer is that we might, because it would appear as a very cool, distended star, radiating strongly in the infra-red part of the spectrum.

In spite of all these grandiose schemes, a solar-scale community is not a galactic empire, the establishment of which would depend first upon interstellar travel, then upon a network of communication. In chapter 5 it was pointed out how direct spaceflight between stars is unlikely ever to be a serious possibility on a large scale. There is, however, a totally different and far more promising concept in space travel — the space ark. In this variant the itinerant community forsakes all attempts to achieve a return journey at very high speeds, or indeed, to return at all. The essence of the idea is to make the spacecraft ecologically self-supporting, with the crew remaining inside it for many generations, floating gently and slowly through space, without the need for massive power facilities for propulsion. The occupants might prefer to deep freeze themselves for the duration of the voyage, which could last many thousands of years. Better still, only a skeleton trained crew need be sent, the rest of the party being stored in the form of fertilized ova, ready to be incubated on arrival. This could enable literally millions of future individuals to be transported in a reasonably modest-sized ark. The space ark could be a lilliput version of one of O'Neill's cylinders, fitted out with a propulsion system and an internal energy supply (no sunlight would be available on the trip). Alternatively, the energy requirements could be met by scooping up quantities of the tenuous interstellar hydogen which pervades all of the galaxy at very low density, and using it in a controlled nuclear fusion device. Even better, a lump of antimatter, produced before departure, could float along harmlessly a few metres outside the ark, to be plundered when necessary for its energy content.

Using space arks, a resourceful community could populate the entire galaxy within a few million years, although that would not in any sense be a galactic empire. There could be no integrated trade or travel between colonies, for even radio communication would take hundreds of thousands of years. The speed of light imposes a very basic limit to the cohesion of a social unit. For a society to be considered as an integrated organization, it must be capable of a collective response to changing affairs. In terrestrial nation states, daily crises such as economic instability, warfare, natural calamities and so forth are met with a collective response from the whole community within hours or days of their appearance. People identify with a country because they feel they can contribute to an evolving situation as part of a national effort. National affairs, such as politics, sport or technological enterprises are followed almost as they happen, and opinions are communicated rapidly throughout society. There is an intense network of information flow between the individuals in the community. When the time taken for information transmission becomes comparable with the time-scale of events, the society loses its cohesion. There is little point in a space colony knowing that one half of the Earth is at war with the other if the information does not get through for ten thousand years. The maximum size of a space community as a true empire is probably only about a light year, which represents two years of dialogue time, and is comparable to the situation on Earth in the Middle Ages when ships took about two years to travel to distant countries. One light year does not reach even half way to the nearest star.

If galactic empires are out, the Earth need have no fear of becoming someone else's 'fifty-first state'. In spite of this, there is still the question of why no space arks have arrived. Is Fermi correct that the absence of colonists on Earth implies our galactic solitude? A number of interesting answers can be given to this question. Firstly, it could always be argued that the Earth happens to be a special case. Perhaps the climate does not suit most other communities or perhaps our biological chemistry is unique; it is also possible that we live in a sparsely populated part of the galaxy and have been overlooked. None of these answers is very satisfactory, because it retreats to the pre-Copernican principle of a privileged Earth, whereas all experience dictates that our planet is typical rather than special. A more serious point is that would-be colonizers have fundamental biological problems about inhabiting host planets. It is not just a matter of touching down and climbing out of the spaceship. The chances are very remote that the host planet would be sufficiently similar to the planet of origin in atmospheric content, temperature range, radiation levels, seasonal changes and so on to be habitable without protected environments, such as space stations. Moreover micro-organisms of a quite unknown variety could be expected as a major health hazard — one thinks of the fate of Wells' martians. If the colony were in the form of a space station anyway, it would make more sense either to remain in the ark itself and build up O'Neill-type colonies, or else to establish the colony on planets with no life. In addition to all this, it may be that super-advanced technological communities which are capable of inter-stellar travel have requirements that we know nothing about. It may suit their purposes much more to reside on the solid surface of Uranus and mine frozen ammonia than to colonize the Earth.

Another consideration is that of social evolution and natural selection. On Earth, the proliferation of species is controlled by evolution and natural selection at the biological level, the rules of which are fairly well understood. We do not necessarily regard the most advanced species as the most aggressive colonizers. If mankind were destroyed, there is no evidence that the gorillas or the dolphins would take over the world. Very little is known about terrestrial, let alone alien social evolution. It could well be that selection effects exist which favour sedentary communities over itinerant ones. Perhaps the very civilizations which have the technological capability for interstellar colonization are the most unstable. It is extremely parochial to suppose that one may apply principles deduced from a few thousand years of non-technological human social evolution to the technological behaviour of galactic communities millions of years more advanced than ourselves. In short, colonization may be possible, but unusual.

Another argument which is sometimes used is to suppose that space arks have indeed arrived, and that the colonists are here, but we have not noticed. Certainly the other planets of the solar system could be teeming with colonists and we would not know. Nor would we readily notice O'Neill colonies in space, especially if they were located among all the rocky debris in the asteroid belt, which is actually the most likely place in view of the abundant raw materials available there. Would we even notice an extraterrestrial community if they were here on Earth? A civilization millions of years more technologically advanced might appear to us as our civilization does to the ants — indistinguishable from the general environment. If most of the colonies were located at the bottom of the seabed, we would only obtain occasional glimpses of their astounding activity, which would appear either quite incomprehensible, or else miraculous. No witnesses of such activity would be generally believed, just as miracles are not generally believed. A still more speculative proposal is that the colonists came four billion years ago to a barren planet, and seeded it with life — a sort of cosmic 'plant-a-tree' year — with the intention of making it habitable for someone in the distant future; in fact, along the lines of Carl Sagan's idea for Venus.

A major assumption which goes into discussions of space colonization and interstellar communication is that biological intelligence and societies represent the supreme example of organization and complexity of matter. We have to face the fact that we may only belong to a transient stratum in a whole hierarchy of levels of organizational development. The situation of the amino acids in the Miller and Urey flask in the life-genesis simulation experiment conducted at Chicago University is relevant here. Although amino acids represent a degree of structured organization, they only form an intermediate step along the path of biological evolution. Eventually, after a few million years, the amino acids combined together to trigger off a whole new form of matter with a much greater organizational potential — living matter. There is no way in which we can deduce the possibility of living matter merely by knowing the properties of its inanimate component parts. Life is a collective phenomenon which is only sparked off when a certain threshold of complexity is reached. We do not know whether there exist higher states of organization than living matter which we may in turn spark off when a certain level of complexity is attained; it is impossible to guess what this higher state of organization might be or from what it may be made. It would probably be incomprehensible to us. If there are these possibilities beyond biological intelligent life, then talk of social systems lasting for millions or billions of years is clearly nonsense, for the next level would establish supremacy long before then. There could be no communication between the two systems, any more than we can communicate with an amino acid, or for that matter a frog.

There is a strong belief among some scientists that we are already on the threshold of unleashing the next level of organization — what is known as 'machine intelligence'. There is no doubt that intelligence has developed in living systems because it has good survival value in the competitive world of biological evolution, but there is no reason to suppose that is the only place where it can occur. Artificially created intelligent machines abound in the modern world; small computers, for example, perform rudimentary tasks such as operating components on assembly lines, driving tanks, setting gunsights, etc. These operations are comparable to the reflex reactions of, say, spiders negotiating an uneven surface. We would not normally think of a spider as displaying much in the way of intelligence, and these smaller computers we regard more as simple calculators than as intelligent entities. Large computers are a different matter: they run factories, banks and companies, organize traffic and services, calculate spacecraft trajectories, compute the nuclear synthesis in stars, play chess and decide when a nation will go to war. Already computers are taking control of large areas of human affairs which are just too complicated for people. The machines perform calculations, weigh up alternative strategies, maximize efficiency and deliberate on complex technical problems many millions of times faster than any human being.

In spite of the powers of computers, many people are reluctant to call them intelligent. This depends, of course, on precisely what one means by intelligence. It is certainly true that they do not display human qualities and emotions — they do not appreciate music or poetry, and are governed by cold logic — but that is because they are deliberately made that way. At present we have no need for an illogical computer, but it would be straightforward to make one by including some randomizing element. There is no human response to a situation which cannot, in principle, be emulated by a correctly programmed and sufficiently sophisticated machine.

At present, computers are highly dependent on programming, but in recent years there has been some development of computers with direct sensing equipment. Machines already exist which have 'eyes' to locate objects in a field of vision, and are capable of manipulating an arm to move them. There seems no reason in principle why a computer could not analyse the tones of the human voice and thereby interpret speech directly. Although such facilities may be some years away, undoubtedly they will become available in due course if we desire them. In the science fiction book *2001: A Space Odyssey* by Arthur C. Clark, a computer named HAL runs a whole spaceship. The occupants are very much at the mercy of this machine, which in the course of events becomes belligerent and has to be disconnected. During the power struggle HAL is even able to lip-read the space crew's conspiracy.

Computers have a number of distinct advantages over humans in the intelligence game. Firstly, they are immortal: if a component malfunctions, it can be replaced. Secondly, there is less distinction between the personal and social capabilities of computers than in the case of humans. Computers can be connected up together — and frequently are — to enable a much greater degree of co-operation than is possible in human society. The merging of brains enables virtually unlimited intellectual power, for they no longer need to be taught individually. Each can read the information directly from the memory of another. In the third place, computers can physically decouple their sensory systems from their central processing unit. For humans, this would be rather like leaving your brain at home and sending your eyes, ears and hands to work. So long as they report back by radio what they see and hear, you do not actually have to think *in situ* to respond in the right way. Your secretary could be given orders by instructing your hands to type out the relevant messages. In this way, the sensory deprivation of computers is actually an advantage: they can sit safely in one place, with no fear of predators, and acquire information simultaneously from many different channels, including directly from the memories of other computers.

All these features have led some science writers to propose that machine intelligence will in time inevitably predominate over biological intelligence; some even argue that it is already doing so. This does not necessarily mean the demise of biological intelligence, any more than the appearance of living matter meant the end of amino acids. Indeed it has even been speculated that biological computers may be a possibility. We know the human brain is capable of incredible intellectual feats by computing at a microscopic level on organic molecules, and it is possible that genetic manipulation may advance far enough for us to be able to *grow* computers to order, though whether an organic computer would endear itself more to people than one made of integrated circuits is another matter. In any case a social symbiotic relationship between people and computers could well be mutually satisfactory. Living matter contains examples of symbiosis between different organisms to their common advantage. Computers already make our lives far more orderly and efficient; our present dependence on them is great, and growing all the time. Those that have a horror of being 'taken over' by machines should contemplate the chaos and misery which would ensue if all the plugs were pulled on all the world's computers tomorrow. If we want a complicated technological life-style, full of easy-living gadgetry and high industrial productivity, we must pay the price of forsaking our independence. We shall no longer be masters of our own fate, but will probably be too comfortable to worry.

A community in which powerful machine intelligences dominate, and biological intelligences provide the labour force, with social orderliness and comfort for payment, might have extremely good evolutionary survival value in the universe. Computers could probably run human affairs far better than humans, who have so far failed to organize themselves on a global scale without strife and conflict. The promise of no more war in return for computer control may be too appealing to forsake. If the galaxy is full of these two- (or perhaps multi-) component communities, it is probable that they would attempt to signal each other by radio. This means that any message received by us from another star system would be most likely to come from a machine. This is not as startling as it sounds. Any radio message would not consist of an orator broadcasting in English, but a mathematically coded signal. Efficiency of information transfer demands a highly complex pattern encoded in the radio wave and only a computer would be able to unscramble and analyse for us all the information content. Likewise if we were to transmit any very sophisticated information about our own culture, this would be beyond the organizational capabilities of individual people. Even at our own level of technology, therefore, the computer would be in the forefront of any interstellar dialogue. If interstellar communication exists, it will be a complex and tedious affair. Only computers — not programmed for boredom — would have the endurance to maintain years of radio searches and signal evaluation.

If most advanced communities are of this type, we would not expect any colonization. The sedentary habits of computers would tend to limit them to a life in one place, growing larger all the time with the addition of new units. Excitement would be provided by sending 'eyes' and 'ears' to other star systems and digesting the information sent back. There seems to be no limit to the size of these machine intelligences, and their power to manipulate their environment would grow with their intellectual capabilities. If one considers how much more accomplished the human brain is in comparison with, for instance, the brain of a cat — about one tenth the size — the possibilities for a huge artificial brain would be unimaginable.

In the far future, when the sun is becoming too dangerous for life to remain on Earth, technology will be needed to create new environments for our descendants — if there are any — to inhabit. As explained in chapter 6, the presence of a thermodynamic disequilibrium of some sort is essential if organized society is to continue, and the second law of thermodynamics ensures that such regions of the universe will become progressively harder to find. Although there are many ways in which a technological community can increase its longevity by prudent arrangements and preparations, there appears to be no hope of averting decline indefinitely. The same principles of physics which regulate the inexorable disintegration of ordered activity apply also to the universe as a whole, which is already gradually running down. In the next chapter we shall examine whether all activity will eventually cease, or whether the universe will be overtaken before this by total gravitational collapse.

10.   *The dying universe*

There can surely be few conclusions in science more profound than the prediction that the universe is doomed, but the principle upon which this prediction is founded — the second law of thermodynamics — is the most fundamental regulator of natural activity known to mankind. Its application determines the evolution and fate of systems as diverse as boxes of gas, sandcastles, human beings, stars — and the cosmos. The inexorable progress towards equilibrium and maximum entropy is built into the behaviour of everything; all around us we see the universe slowly but surely running down.

In the earlier chapters of this book it has been explained how modern astronomers believe that the universe was born between ten and twenty billion years ago. The mechanism whereby the universe first became 'wound up', evolving slowly from fiery chaos to orderly structure and complex activity, was traced to the explosive cosmological expansion in the primeval epochs after the big bang. This expansion continues even now, as can be seen from the systematic pattern of recession between distant galaxies. By now, however, the winding mechanism which couples the cosmological expansion to material systems is very loose and feeble, so that the dilation of space can no longer sustain the complex organization of matter and prevent the relentless disintegration of order. Unless, therefore, our whole understanding of matter and energy is totally misconceived, the inevitability of the end of the world is written into the laws of nature.

Speculation about Armageddon is not a preoccupational preserve of the scientist. For centuries, the great religions have taught of doom and destruction, of a day of reckoning when the present system of world order will be demolished, and for many believers it has frequently seemed as though the time of collapse was imminent. Even in our modern technological society, doomwatching has become a fashionable if somewhat morbid pastime. Modern science has now given precise articulation to these fears, and provides a detailed basis for cosmic eschatology — the end of the universe.

Although the second law tells us that the universe is running down, it has little to say about the rate at which the decline and fall of the world order proceeds. This information is provided only by a careful study of the important sources of thermodynamic disequilibrium, such as the stars. In the previous two chapters, the fate of the stars was examined closely, and the time-scale for their death found to be immensely long. The generally accepted scenario for the future of our corner of the universe is that the sun will gradually brighten and expand towards the end of a five-billion-year period. Its radiation will eventually destroy all life on Earth, and perhaps even the planet itself. For several more billion years its behaviour will be somewhat erratic, possibly including sudden changes of an explosive nature, or it may become unstable and pulsate in size and luminosity. The last phase of its life will be as a white dwarf, a shrunken lilliput of the stellar family, slowly cooling down over a time-scale which is long compared with even its present great age. In one hundred billion years it will simply consist of black, burnt-out matter.

During this time, stars all over the galaxy, and in other galaxies throughout the universe, will be engaging in the same basic pattern of birth, evolution and death. The more massive stars soon burn up their nuclear fuel, many of them blowing themselves apart as supernovae, or collapsing catastrophically into black holes. Indeed many massive stars have already long since died. In contrast, the smaller stars burn more slowly and can live hundreds of times longer than the sun. There is a lower limit, though, to the mass of a star. If there is insufficient weight of material to compress the core and elevate the central temperature to several million degrees, then the vital nuclear burning which provides the energy of the stars will not begin. These smaller balls of gas will slowly contract and fade out as their gravitational energy is dissipated as heat, and they will become failed stars — like the planet Jupiter, for example.

Not all the material observed in the universe is in the form of stars; much of it lies strewn in great clouds of gas and dust, from which new generations of stars can eventually form. In this way the active lifetime of the universe will be greatly extended, although it is clear that the supply of this raw material is finite and will in time become depleted. No new stars will then form and the whole galaxy will slowly begin to dim. By then the cosmological expansion will have swept the other galaxies many times farther away from us than now, so they will already appear only a tiny fraction as bright and nowhere near as big. All over the universe the stars will be going out.

Many of the dead stars will be in the form of black holes, and from time to time these will collide and coalesce, particularly near the centres of galaxies, where the density of stars is highest. Successive cannibalism will gradually create supermassive black holes into which large amounts of debris will fall. The falling matter will radiate energy away from the galaxy in the form of gravitational waves, thereby reducing the total gravity of the galaxy and causing the dead stars and smaller black holes near the galactic periphery to detach themselves and drift off into the intergalactic spaces. Probably the sun is too near the centre of our galaxy to be lost in this way; it will no doubt spend a very long time as a black dwarf and eventually collide with a black hole somewhere. Whatever happens, the remaining activity will be purely gravitational in nature — a slow accumulation of black holes taking place in a dark, cold space.

As the universe expands, so the temperature of the relic primeval heat radiation falls. After perhaps a billion billion centuries this radiation will have cooled below even the tiny temperature possessed by the black holes formed from burnt-out stars — about one ten millionth of a degree above absolute zero. When this happens there will be a renewed type of activity to lighten the darkness. The cause of this minor rejuvenation is Hawking's black-hole evaporation process described in chapter 8. There it was explained how quantum theory predicts that a black hole radiates energy as though it were in thermal equilibrium at a very low temperature. It is important to remember that the temperature increases as the size of the black hole decreases, so that as the hole slowly evaporates it becomes hotter. Under present conditions the cosmic primeval background radiation is much hotter than the temperature of black holes of solar mass, and there is a net flow of heat into these objects from the surrounding space, albeit at a tiny rate. In the very far future, however, the background radiation will be so cold that the black holes will start to lose more energy through the quantum evaporation process than they gain through sweeping up the background heat. In this way the holes will slowly but surely begin to shrink, getting hotter as they do so.

The rate at which these black holes grow hotter is staggeringly slow. After no less than ten thousand billion billion billion billion billion billion (one hundred followed by sixty-five noughts) years, they will have regained a pale shadow of their former splendour and be shining at temperatures comparable to that of the stars that they once were. They will, however, be much smaller — only a few millionths of a centimetre in size — but containing a mass equivalent to that of a large asteroid. Because of their tiny size their total luminosity will also be very small — less than that of the average firefly. They will glow like this for a million billion billion billion years until, as their temperatures climb more rapidly, they will disappear completely in a bright flash of radiation. All trace of the once resplendent star will have vanished from the universe.

The time taken by stellar black holes to evaporate is so immense that most of them will probably be eaten by bigger black holes first. If a major fraction of the galaxy ends up as a gigantic black hole about one tenth of a light year in diameter, then this object will take 10^{100} (one followed by one hundred noughts) years to evaporate. When they, too, are gone, there will be nothing left except the tiny, and diminishing, radiation left from the evaporation process. The universe will then be just black, empty, expanding space, for the whole of future eternity. The final feeble resources of free energy will be exhausted, the whole cosmic machine will have run down to a standstill and the second law of thermodynamics will have claimed its last victims. After this, equilibrium will prevail and the entropy of the universe will have risen to its maximum. There are few predictions of cosmic doom equal in gloom and futility to this slow heat death of the universe.

For many years astronomers have realized that there might be an alternative end for the universe, a fate no less catastrophic than the slow heat death, but one considerably more spectacular. It has long been known that the laws of motion do not distinguish past from future; that is, they do not operate preferentially in one direction of time rather than the other. This means that every motion of matter can in principle be reversed, including the large-scale motion of the universe itself. The force which controls the cosmological motion is gravity, and there are familiar examples of motions under the action of gravity which reverse themselves; for example, the swing of a pendulum.

If a body is propelled upwards with sufficient energy it can escape the Earth's gravity completely and fly off into space, never to return. The so-called escape velocity from Earth is about twenty-five thousand miles per hour, and in practice large rockets are necessary to achieve this speed. If a body is projected at less than the escape velocity it will inevitably fall back to Earth. This brings to mind the cosmic motion where the galaxies are flying apart from one another at considerable speed, but the question has to be asked whether this speed is great enough for them to 'escape' each other's gravity. If it is, then the universe will continue to expand more or less freely in due course, when the gravity has become so weak that it can no longer restrain the motion. If this does not happen, then the cosmological expansion will slowly decelerate until it eventually stops altogether. In that case no power in nature can prevent the universe from total collapse.

Such an awesome prospect raises profound issues about the nature of space, time and matter. The notion of a star collapsing and forming a black hole with a singularity inside is strange enough, but the catastrophic implosion of the entire universe makes the black hole pale into insignificance. The decisive factor which determines whether or not gravity will succeed in dragging the galaxies back on themselves is the total quantity of matter in the universe. If the matter density is high enough, the strength of its gravity will remorselessly slow the cosmological expansion until a point is reached where the galaxies are no longer receding from one another. They will then begin to fall together again and the universe will start to recontract, accelerating as it does so, towards total collapse.

If this actually turns out to happen, then the recontracting phase would, on a large scale, appear like the reverse of the present expansion. There would be no sudden implosion as with a collapsing star, but rather a gradual shrinkage of space over billions of years. The reason for this sluggishness is that the universe is so much more distended than a star, so that the gravitating effect between distant galaxies is at present very weak. For millions of years the recontraction would not be directly observable, because the distant galaxies would be seen as they were millions of years before, when the universe was still expanding, but in due course some of the nearby galaxies would be seen to slow their recession and start to approach. Over the next few billion years more and more galaxies would appear to move inwards, but instead of being red-shifted by the expansion, their light would now become blue-shifted and more energetic. At the same time the temperature of the primeval background heat would slowly start to rise.

Neither of these two effects would prove to be of very great significance for many billions of years. During all this time our galaxy will appear to be very much the same. The sun, of course, will have gone, but there will still be stars in profusion. The feeble light from the other galaxies and the near-zero heat of the fireball radiation will be totally inconspicuous in comparison with these bright stars. Gradually, however, as the contraction continues, the spaces between the galaxies would disappear and the galaxies themselves start to collide. One of the first to strike our galaxy would be the Great Nebula in Andromeda. For a time this great star system would be superimposed on the Milky Way, and eventually merge with it. Collisions between galaxies are observed to be occurring even now, and are not as serious as they sound, for distances between stars are so great that there are few cases of actual contact.

As the shrinkage continues, its rate increases ever faster. Soon, individual stars find their motions altered by the slow compression of the star clusters. With all the galaxies no longer distinguishable, the stars would fill the whole universe more or less uniformly, and the interstellar spaces would start to contract steadily. The night sky would be considerably more brilliant than it is now, because of both the high density of stars and the blue-shift increase in the light energy of the distant stars as they fall inwards on each other.

This spectacle would last for a few million years, but before the stars themselves start to collide, a new phenomenon takes place. The primeval background radiation, for so long totally inconspicuous, now becomes hotter all the time and is, moreover, augmented by the accumulated starlight of billions of years. The shrinkage of space is now so great that the temperature of this radiation soon rises to several thousand degrees, hotter than the surfaces of the stars themselves. When this happens the stars can no longer divest themselves of the energy being generated by nuclear processes, so their internal temperatures will rise to match the elevated temperatures of their environment. Probably explosive instabilities will set in, but in any case the remorseless rise in the temperature of the surrounding radiation would steadily vaporize the stars out of existence.

At this point the universe will have returned to a new plasma era, when it will consist of a more or less uniform density of opaque material spread throughout the whole of space. The only vestige of the universe we now know would be the presence of some black holes, which cannot be vaporized this way, and some heavy nuclei which were synthesized in the stars. But after another hundred thousand years the temperature would be rising appreciably over a few minutes. When it reaches a billion degrees, all nuclei will be destroyed; the collapse of the universe becomes frenetic. The density and temperature rise progressively faster: at ten billion degrees they will double in about a second. The higher the density becomes, the greater the gravity and the speed of implosion. The universe will now pass in reverse sequence through all the epochs of the big bang: the plasma era will give way to a lepton era, followed by a hadron era, each one occupying a shorter amount of real time than the previous one. Tremendous quantities of matter will be created out of the heat energy. Only the black holes survive this onslaught to distinguish the end of the universe from the beginning.

About one second after the temperature rises through ten billion degrees, quantum processes become important and space-time would start to break up under the tremendous tidal forces. At this point known physics comes to an end and we can say nothing about what happens next. If quantum effects are ignored, then our present understanding of gravity predicts that space-time will come to an end altogether at a singularity, and probably all the matter will be squeezed out of existence at an infinite density. If this is so, then the universe will cease to exist. This fate is quite distinct from the empty darkness which characterizes the ever-expanding model described earlier. There, all that was left was expanding empty space; here, not even space or time survives the encounter with the singularity. The universe has a future temporal extremity similar to that of its past — a birth, life and death in symmetric relation. It disappears in a furnace which is more or less the mirror of the one in which it appeared. Never was Armageddon envisaged as so thorough.

These two distinct scenarios — slow refrigeration through everlasting expansion or dramatic cremation and complete obliteration of the physical world — seem to be the two inescapable alternative fates for the universe. Both choices are catastrophic, for both will destroy the organization of the universe as we now know it. Which alternative scenario will turn out to apply to the real universe must be decided by

165

appealing to observation. Remarkably enough, it is possible to tell by fairly straightforward means what fate is in store for us.

Astronomers have adopted two separate approaches in their analysis of cosmic eschatology. The first is the direct method, and consists of determining the rate at which the cosmological expansion is slowing down with time. This can be done by observing the expansion rate in very remote regions of the universe which, because of the delay in the travel time of light, are seen as they appeared a long time ago — typically when the universe was about half its present age. The expansion rate at that time can therefore be compared with the present expansion rate, which in turn is deduced from the observation of nearby galactic recession. For many years this method has produced the answer that the expansion rate is decelerating rapidly enough to cause eventual recollapse and cremation. In spite of this there is considerable scepticism about the conclusion, because the observations are both difficult to carry out and depend to some extent on our understanding of the evolution in time of the luminosities of galaxies, whose true distance can only be determined by a comparison of intrinsic and observed luminosity. The situation can be compared with car headlights: if all cars were known to have equally powerful headlights then we could determine the distance of a car by seeing how bright its lights appear to us. The bright ones would belong to cars nearby, the dim ones to distant cars. If, however, the drivers changed the power of their lights by altering battery voltages in a systematic way as they approached, then this type of distance estimate would be wrong. Understanding the power output of a galaxy is of course incomparably more complicated than understanding the operation of car headlights, and there is the further problem that in the search for very distant galaxies which are also very faint, selection effects bias the astronomer to spot only the unusually bright galaxies rather than the average ones. In recent years both these and other problems have received considerable attention from astronomers, and the conclusion is that the uncertainties involved in deducing a recontracting universe are much greater than previously supposed.

The second method which astronomers have used to determine the fate of the universe involves the dynamics of cosmological motion, based on Einstein's general theory of relativity, which relates the geometry and behaviour of space and time to the condition of matter and energy in its vicinity. This is the theory which predicts gravitational collapse and black holes, and it is the currently accepted mathematical description of gravity. General relativity can provide a mathematical model for the large-scale motion of the cosmos which relates the characteristics of the expansion (and perhaps recontraction) to the condition of the gravitating material, such as the quantity of matter in the galaxies and the pressure of radiation. The connection between the geometrical arrangement of the cosmos and its material contents is given by Einstein's so-called field equations, which in practice are very difficult to solve, and only by making major simplifying assumptions about the geometry and distribution of matter in the universe can progress be made. Fortunately the real universe contains a remarkable symmetry which enables it to be modelled mathematically with great ease. As mentioned already in chapter 1, on a very large scale the distribution of galaxies seems to be amazingly uniform, both in direction around us and in depth from us. This property implies that the geometry of space can be described by just one quantity, the scale of distance between any two representative galaxies. As the universe expands, this distance is scaled in a fixed ratio to any other representative distance. Furthermore, because distant regions of the universe appear to contain the same type of matter in the same condition — galaxies spaced out by the same average distance — the material content of the universe can be assumed to be, on average, the same everywhere.

With these simplifying assumptions one can go on to solve Einstein's equations to determine how the distance scale of space changes with time. In the conventional theory, the gravity of all the matter in the universe restrains the expanding motion, causing it to decelerate. The amount of deceleration depends on the quantity of gravitating matter — that is, the density. In a high density universe, the gravity is sufficient to reverse the expansion and cause the universe to recontract, whereas in a low density universe expansion is slowed down but not halted. Astronomers use the word 'critical' density to mean the quantity of matter in a typical volume of space which is just enough to cause recontraction. The critical density is very low — an average of about one atom every million cubic centimetres.

In principle it is easy to use telescopes to measure the quantity of matter in some sufficiently large volume of space, but this can only provide a lower limit to the density, for it includes just the luminous matter. There may be large quantities of matter which we do not see, because it is dark, transparent or inconspicuous. Furthermore, matter is not the only source of gravity, according to the theory of general relativity; energy and pressure — from radiation, for example — also gravitate. In order to determine whether the cumulative gravity of all forms of matter, energy and pressure is enough to halt the expansion, a careful account of the different contributions has to be made.

The amount of luminous or otherwise visible material, which means all the stars and gas clouds in the galaxies, may be readily estimated, and works out at about only two per cent of the critical density. Galaxies, however, only occupy a small fraction of the universe, and it is clear that there must be some material in the intergalactic spaces, as a relic of the primordial hydrogen from the big bang, left after the galaxies formed out of the cosmological gases at the end of the plasma era. Considerable research has been devoted to detecting the intergalactic medium, but without success. It cannot exist in the form of ordinary hydrogen, because the light from certain very distant objects called quasars would be strongly absorbed by this material at various characteristic wavelengths, and this is not the case. On the other hand, ionized hydrogen is transparent to light, and so any intergalactic material must be in the form of a plasma. It is possible that this plasma contributes to the observed background of X-rays coming from all directions of space, but other sources of X-rays also exist. At the present time there is no reason to believe that there is enough intergalactic matter to achieve the critical density for recontraction to occur.

There is still the possiblity that large numbers of non-luminous objects could provide the missing 98 per cent of matter necessary for a recontracting universe. Black holes, planets, dim stars and clouds of dust could all proliferate undetected in space. Nevertheless some astronomers find it hard to imagine that there is fifty times more matter in dark objects than in visible ones, which would be the necessary proportion to achieve the critical density. There is some evidence from the examination of the local motions of galactic clusters that luminous matter may only account for about 20 per cent of all the matter in these clusters, but even five times the luminous matter density is not enough. On the other hand, there could be large numbers of black holes in galactic and intergalactic space which are completely undetectable by us. One suggestion is that during the very early epochs of the primeval fireball, microscopic black holes formed in profusion from the extremely dense cosmological material of that time, purely as a result of random fluctuations in the density of matter. Some models of this process predict that nearly all the mass of the universe could be in this hidden form, and certainly we cannot rule out the possibility that the critical density has been exceeded by these inconspicuous relics of the big bang.

Finally, it has been suggested that large amounts of energy (which gravitates like matter) may exist throughout the universe in the form of inconspicuous radiation. Of the radiation which we can detect, the total energy contributes a mass of less than one per cent of the cosmological matter, which is negligible. On the other hand, some forms of radiation are not so readily detected, one example being the background of primeval gravitons coming from very early epochs of the big bang and discussed in chapter 2. According to our present understanding, the graviton radiation should be comparable in energy with the heat radiation and so would be equally negligible, but if the estimates were wrong by a factor of a few thousand — and this is quite possible — the gravity of these gravitons could dominate the cosmic dynamics and cause the universe to collapse. The existence of all this graviton energy would be otherwise quite undetectable to us. Similarly, gravitational waves much longer than the primeval gravitons may have escaped detection. Many sources of such waves exist: for example, turbulence in the primeval fluid before the galaxies formed.

Another source of hidden mass is neutrinos. No laboratory apparatus yet available could detect cosmic neutrinos in enough abundance to exceed the density of all ordinary matter one hundredfold. Once again, theoretical studies of the big bang predict a background of primeval neutrinos, but with an energy comparable only with the heat radiation.

In the last year or two, a completely new piece of evidence concerning the mass of the universe has come to light. In chapter 2 it was described how nuclear synthesis in the primeval fireball produced a great deal of helium from the primordial hydrogen in a two-stage process: first ordinary hydrogen forms deuterium, then deuterium combines to form helium. Deuterium is also called heavy hydrogen because it is chemically the same as hydrogen but twice as heavy on account of the nuclear structure, which consists of a proton combined with a neutron rather than a single proton which exists in ordinary hydrogen. The hardest part of the helium synthesis is the first step; once the deuterium has formed, it soon combines into helium. For this reason the deuterium does not last very long, and so we do not expect it to occur in the universe in any abundance. It is found mixed with ordinary hydrogen in sea water and a great hope among physicists is that it could be used to operate a controlled fusion reactor for nuclear power.

Estimates of the deuterium abundance in the interstellar medium have been made by a group of scientists at Princeton University, who find one deuterium atom in every hundred thousand. If this is typical of the cosmic abundance it may be used to determine the fate of the universe in the following way. In the primeval fireball, the rate at which deuterium converts into helium depends directly on how often deuterium nuclei collide at high energy. This in turn is determined by the density of matter: in high density material collisions occur more often than in low density material. The fraction of deuterium nuclei which escape fusion into helium may therefore be calculated for any given density of primeval matter. Using the Princeton findings, we can fix the primeval matter density, and the present density is then easily inferred by calculating how much the universe has expanded since the helium synthesis took place. In this way, it has been estimated that if there were enough matter in the universe to cause it eventually to collapse, then there should be only about one-tenth of the deuterium found by the Princeton astronomers.

For several reasons, astronomers now seem inclined to the view that the universe will continue to expand for ever, but all the tests and estimates mentioned above are subject to errors and objections, and a clear-cut decision does not seem likely at the moment. Until we have a more detailed understanding of some of the complicated physical processes at work in the cosmos, the nature of the catastrophe which lies in our future must remain open.

From a study of Einstein's field equations it can be deduced that the occurrence or not of a cosmic recontraction and collapse is intimately connected with the question of whether the universe is finite or infinite. In chapter 1 we saw how a finite universe was discounted by Newton because it would fall into the middle under its own gravity. In his day, space was regarded as rigid and fixed, and so the question of the finitude of the universe rested on whether or not the assembly of stars or galaxies has an edge somewhere. No edge is visible, but that may be either because the Earth is located near the centre, or because the universe is so large that our telescopes do not penetrate to the periphery. Newton supposed that if there were an edge, a dark void without limits or boundaries would lie beyond. It was precisely this idea of a finite blob of stars located in an otherwise empty, infinite void that Newton rejected on mechanical grounds.

When Einstein discovered that space is not rigid and fixed, the debate about the size of the universe took on a totally different perspective. If space is considered as curved, then the universe can be finite in size without the distribution of stars having any edge or boundary at all. This novel idea is best visualized by analogy with a curved two-dimensional surface, such as the membrane of a balloon, speckled all over with spots to represent the stars or galaxies, an idea introduced in chapter 1. As the distribution of spots extends over the entire surface, there is no middle or edge to the distribution, yet the surface is clearly finite in size. From the standpoint of any one place, an observer fixed in the surface would perceive that his world did not continue for ever, for if he journeyed in any direction he could circumnavigate the surface and return to his starting point from the opposite direction. On the other hand, at no time during this journey would he encounter any barrier or edge, nor would he notice any change in the number or arrangement of spots (stars) around him. In fact, his universe would look more or less the same (spotted) wherever he went. In crude terms, he would account for this by saying that his world was not flat, but curved away in all directions and joined up with itself on the other side of the universe from wherever he happened to be.

Einstein proposed to extend this simple idea about the geometry of a surface to real three-dimensional space by supposing that the universe is curved in all directions from us and joins up on the 'other side'. Therefore in this model of space it would be possible to travel right around the universe and come back again from the opposite direction, just as a flat creature could circumnavigate the balloon. It would also, in principle, be possible to see the back of one's head through a large enough telescope by receiving light which had completed this cosmic circumnavigation. In the same way that the surface of a sphere is finite in size, so too is Einstein's universe finite in volume, so the number of stars is also finite.

Astronomers have attempted to verify Einstein's concept of a closed and finite space by measuring the sizes and numbers of distant galaxies. The curvature of space leads to a distortion of their sizes at great distances, and this should be visible to us. Unfortunately the numbers and sizes of galaxies are subject to all sorts of other, less exotic, effects and it has not yet been possible to verify the space curvature of the universe. There is, however, a curious connection between the finitude of space and the finitude of time. The curvature of space is directly related through Einstein's gravitational field equations to the density of matter in the universe, which in turn determines whether the universe will eventually collapse.

In order to try and visualize an expanding universe, it is helpful to return to the analogy of the speckled balloon which becomes slowly inflated. Each dot moves away from every other dot, but no dot is at the centre of the pattern of expansion. It is important to remember that there is not an explosion of galaxies into a pre-existing void, but a uniform inflation of space itself. It turns out that a recontracting cosmos, which ends in a space-time singularity at a finite time in the future, also has a finite size. Conversely, an ever-expanding universe would be infinite in extent — space without limit. The issue has far-reaching implications: simple mathematics requires that in an infinite universe with infinite numbers of stars there will be an infinite number of intelligent creatures to wonder about it, however small the probability that life will form elsewhere. More than that: there will be an infinite number of planets, star systems and galaxies that are almost identical copies of the Earth, solar system and Milky Way. Any reader of this book will possess an infinity of near-carbon copies, indistinguishable from himself except perhaps by the arrangement of a few atoms. So in an infinite universe, not only will there be other inhabitated planets, but we are assured on statistical grounds, an unlimited number of others arbitrarily closely resembling the Earth as it is now. If we were to travel to one such planet, we could not distinguish it from Earth. Of course, for every Earth-like planet, there are countless billions upon billions which are totally different.

Organization on a galactic scale was the first to appear in the universe and will be the first to disintegrate. Technology is the last level of organization to arise, and will probably be the last to succumb to the inevitable collapse. It is fascinating to speculate how the use of technology will stay the cosmic execution for as long as possible.

If the universe recontracts in a few billion years, then no amount of technology can avert impending doom. Manipulation of the environment may enable civilization to continue until up to perhaps a billion years from the end, when the temperature of the primeval radiation will have risen so much that the vital thermodynamic disequilibrium upon which life depends will become drastically upset. Perhaps this problem can be solved somehow, but not for long, because by a million years before the end the temperature of space will have risen to thousands of degrees and all solid bodies will start to vaporize. After that, the catastrophe accelerates quickly.

On the other hand, if the universe continues to expand, it may be hundreds of billions of years before life becomes impossible on any planet. This time span is so vast that on the scale of human activity it seems almost infinite. If it is meaningful at all to talk about our 'descendants' so far in the future, we can have no inkling as to their technological capabilities. As already remarked, with enough time, money and motivation, anything that is possible within the laws of physics can be achieved by a sufficiently advanced technology. There is plenty of time ahead of us and there can be no stronger motivation than survival, although supertechnology will continue to be largely dependent on economics. The economic structure of a society based on machine intelligence is of course rather beyond our understanding, but it is hard to imagine any limits to the technology of such a community. The only restraints on our speculations are the laws of physics which we believe to be correct. We may have got some of these wrong, but if speculations outside these laws are permitted then 'anything goes', and all ideas are equally valueless because they have no basis in known fact.

With this reservation in mind, we would not expect any technology, however sophisticated and developed, to be able to escape the second law of thermodynamics. The catastrophe might be postponed, but it can never be avoided. For planetary-dwellers, such as the inhabitants of Earth, the beginning of the end comes when their star grows into a red giant. This happens very slowly and should leave plenty of time for an orderly evacuation of the community over millions of years. This need not be a physical evacuation of individuals, but rather the establishment on another planet of a small community which is allowed to enlarge over the years while the parent community is gradually phased out over hundreds of generations. The whole operation might be traumatic, but no threat to cultural traditions and technological expertise would be posed by the eventual extinction of the home planet. The new colony could be on a more remote planet in the star system — possibly one of the moons of Saturn or Uranus would serve the inhabitants of Earth — but in view of the unstable condition of stars after the red giant stage, removal to another star system altogether would be better. If life exists throughout the universe, whether indigenously or through slow colonization by a small number of intelligent life forms, there will be increasing competition between different communities for a place near one of the dwindling numbers of suitable stars. These will be the low mass stars whose lifetime can extend for one hundred billion years to sustain nearby communities long after most of the other stars have burnt out.

A better way of avoiding direct conflict with rival, beleagured civilizations would be to gain control over a large cloud of gas and defer star formation until the original star becomes dangerous. A small mass could then be manipulated into a new dwarf star which would serve for another hundred billion years or so. Continuing in this way the community might increase its lifetime a hundred or more times.

Machine intelligence would enjoy far greater survival prospects than biological intelligence. In the first place, low mobility drastically reduces the supply of free energy needed to sustain a community of intelligent machines compared with, say, human beings, for careful manipulation and control of cosmic gas clouds could keep such a community going for about a billion billion years. Nor would they be vulnerable to the vagaries of stellar death throes: apart from supernovae explosions, very little that happens in the neighbourhood of a star could wipe out a machine community if this were well enough entrenched and protected. The simple expedient of putting the community on the dark side of a planet which has one face turned permanently away from the star would avoid all but the most cataclysmic disruptions. Perhaps by this time biological engineering will have reached such sophistication that it will not be meaningful to distinguish between machines and biological forms. No doubt biological adaptation can also be manipulated to create beings quite capable of living under extreme conditions of heat and cold, or wide variations in gravity, thereby opening up the greater part of the universe as potential habitats.

The general conclusion is that technology could extend the lifetime of intelligent organization billions of times longer than that of cosmic organization. It could not, however, continue for all eternity. Whatever ingenious devices are invented, however industriously a community devotes itself to controlling star clusters and gas clouds, eventually the supply of free energy will run out. New ways will often be invented to double the time before disaster, to add just a few more billion years, but the remorseless growth of entropy must continue and the technological organization will slowly run down. There will always be room in the universe for a small enough group of intelligent individuals, but the number and the level of activity available will slowly but surely diminish. All life ultimately faces catastrophe.

The extent to which disaster may be alleviated will depend on two key factors: how profligate the technology becomes in energy consumption and the scale of the environment over which it gains control. Once it is realized that all activity and organization depend on minimizing the increase in entropy, then the uncontrolled dissipation of energy resources will stop. This is already happening on the Earth, and its importance will grow with time. The best use of resources and zero industrial growth will enable the lifetime of the community to be greatly extended.

The acquisition and control of new sources of free energy will demand a more expanded and comprehensive technology. Each venture will therefore have to be costed in energy terms to see what the potential advantage is likely to be. For example, expanding the technological community to a big enough size to construct and maintain a Dyson shell might increase consumption so much that the extra energy gained would hardly be worthwhile. In the face of impending catastrophe, of course, such a community might adopt a totally different attitude from ours and might regard it as more desirable to increase in numbers at one time than to increase the life span of the community. It is more probable, though, that temporary advances in technology would be used to acquire new resources, followed by a period of negative growth to prolong the benefits.

We know of no limits to the scale over which technology can effectively operate. In the few short years since the Industrial Revolution, large areas of the surface of our planet have been restructured to our convenience. After several billion years it would be surprising if technology could not gain control over stellar dimensions. Technology, being limited by the laws of physics, is prevented by gravity from conducting any major restructuring of the galaxy, but manipulation of individual stars, or even star clusters, may well be possible. The ultimate objective is to reduce the fraction of entropy increase which occurs wastefully and redirect it through the technology. For example, of all the energy emitted uselessly into space by the sun, only about one billion billionth finds its way into our own inefficient technological system. To defer the cosmic catastrophe, this colossal natural wastage must be curtailed, and the reservoir of potential free energy conserved.

By far the greatest source of free energy is supplied by gravity. After the energy from the slow contraction of a star has been released, a black hole which forms at the end can still supply enormous quantities of energy under certain circumstances. If technology can gain control over black holes, or even produce them artificially, then hitherto undreamed-of possibilities emerge. For example, when two non-rotating black holes collide and coalesce, up to 29 per cent of their mass can be converted into energy. This should be compared with the paltry one per cent of the sun's mass which it radiates away in ten billion years. In other words, it is possible to extract all at once the same energy from two solar mass black holes as that emitted by a couple of dozen stars in their whole lifetime. This mind-boggling proposition is based on the fact that the entropy of the holes is in direct proportion to their surface area but their masses are in proportion to the square root of this quantity. So the total combined area (and hence entropy) need not decrease when they coalesce, even though the total mass does decrease. For these simple arithmetical reasons, it can be calculated that the second law of thermodynamics will not be violated so long as the energy extracted is less than 29 per cent of the total mass. For a given quantity of matter it is clearly more advantageous to create little black holes and make them coalesce in successive stages than merely to form two such objects, for once two black holes are united, nothing can separate them again; there is no way to divide up a black hole without decreasing the total surface area. At each stage of coalescence 29 per cent of the mass could be extracted; and the efficiency of the process increases with the number of stages employed. On the other hand, the difficulty of making small black holes increases as their size diminishes, so once again a balance has to be struck between the energy expended on creating the black holes and that available from their coalescence. Ideally a supertechnology should scour space for primordial black holes of tiny mass, and set about collecting, storing and coalescing them.

The advantage of black hole technology is that once there is a black hole, however small, it can be grown without limit just by dropping things into it. This then provides the perfect energy storehouse, because the mass may be increased by the addition of any convenient unwanted material. Unlike all other known energy storage systems, black holes cannot lose any of their energy by leakage because nothing can escape from the inside, and losses from quantum evaporation radiation are negligible. In this way it is possible to store energy almost intact for a billion billion years, and 29 per cent of the mass of the expended article of yesteryear can then be extracted for use. Black holes can, therefore, not only store energy perfectly, they run on fuel which can be anything at all in the universe, because any matter, whatever its constituents, can in principle be sacrificed and converted into a huge amount of energy.

If black holes become the currency of supertechnologies they can delay the run-down of the universe for an unimaginably long time. Nobody, of course, has the slightest idea how two black holes may be combined to yield energy, and it may be that no technology, however advanced, would be able to control the process. In any case, tame black holes could be regarded as so precious that their coalescence, and subsequent reduction in number, might be looked upon as foolish. If this were to happen, an alternative strategy might be used. Black holes can rotate up to speeds far in excess of ordinary objects; loosely speaking, they can spin nearly as fast as light. It follows that a great deal of energy — 29 per cent of the total mass, once again — can be stored in the form of rotational energy, and Roger Penrose has discovered a mechanism which enables the rotational energy to be extracted. The way in which this is done was described in chapter 8.

Using rotating black holes, supertechnologies could prolong their lifetimes so much that they would become the dominant activity of the universe for a longer period than the stars. Indeed, the epoch of the stars may come to be regarded by these extraordinary inhabitants of the future as merely a primeval phase — a brief, uncontrolled, but necessary, interlude at the dawn of history — much as we now regard the low level and uncontrolled activities of prebiological molecules like amino acids,-which inhabited the primeval soup on the Earth so long ago, as a brief but necessary interlude on the road to life.

We are used to thinking of gravity, nuclear physics, electromagnetic fields, chemistry and so on as the dominating forces which restructure and arrange the universe. Biology, however, also plays a part: the surface of the Earth has greatly changed as a consequence of biological activity. For example, the change of our atmosphere from methane and ammonia to oxygen is one result of this. Intelligent life and technology have brought about even more radical planetary transformations mountains have been levelled, seas and rivers dammed or diverted forests destroyed and deserts irrigated. There may be still higher levels of organizational activity above that of technology and based on intelligent biological organisms which are capable of still more sophisticated and complex arrangements, but in any case it would be unwise to make assumptions about limits to the power of supertechnologies. This raises the prospect of a universe over which the dominant force is, for the greater part of its existence, intelligent control. Intelligence as a cosmic organizational activity may eventually be regarded as natural and as fundamental as gravity, in the later stages of cosmic evolution.

It is interesting to imagine ourselves in the far future, at the evening of existence, looking back over the history of the cosmos. It will no doubt be seen as overwhelmingly the history of technology, in a dark, cold universe: a billion billion or more years of black hole manipulation following a mere one hundred billion years of uncontrolled stellar activity. For these individuals, machine or biological, the universe and the processes of the natural world will be indistinguishable from technology — the world will simply *be* technology. The time when the skies burned brightly with billions of untamed suns will appear as just another epoch of the primeval big bang. The universe we now know will be lost in the mists of the creation.

11.   *Worlds without end*

If the universe expands for ever, the second law of thermodynamics seems to predict that entropy will inevitably continue to rise until equilibrium is reached, when all organized activity ceases. In 1948, three brilliant young British astronomers, Hermann Bondi, Thomas Gold and Fred Hoyle, realized that there was a loophole in the argument that the inexorable rise in entropy, with its associated disintegration of order, necessarily implies that the whole universe will steadily run down to a prolonged heat death. Certainly the rise in entropy means that some regions of the universe are decaying, but this need not require that the total disorder continually increases. If a mechanism could be found to inject new information or order into the universe, then although the total entropy will continue to rise, this could be matched by the appearance of more and more new order.

These astronomers proposed a model of the universe radically different from the conventional picture of creation and evolution followed by death through slow disintegration or catastrophic collapse. It is based on a provocative and novel principle which demands that, on a very large scale, the universe remains more or less the same from epoch to epoch. To make the principle consistent with the observed irreversible evolution of the stars and galaxies, a continual supply of new order is necessary, for if the universe is required to appear the same in many billions of years time, then new galaxies will have to form to replace those which have burnt out and decayed. Where do these new galaxies come from?

Bondi, Gold and Hoyle sought to explain the unlimited supply of new galaxies necessary in their model by challenging the whole basis of modern physical cosmology. They argued that instead of all the matter in the universe appearing in one go at a singular creation event, a form of continuous creation is taking place which replenishes the dispersing matter in the universe at a steady rate. In order to produce the features of their new principle, the rate at which new matter enters the universe must be carefully adjusted so that, on average, the density of galaxies remains roughly the same as the universe expands. This demands that the rate of new galaxy formation in a fixed volume of space just compensates for the loss of galaxies through the cosmological recession, so that as the old galaxies move apart, new ones appear to fill the gaps left behind. If this process continues indefinitely, then the universe will always have the same aspect: sparsely populated with old galaxies which have receded far apart from one another, and thickly populated with younger ones. By permitting continuous creation of matter, the big-bang creation of the universe, and its subsequent death are both removed. Instead the universe simultaneously enjoys evolution and change at a local level, as individual galaxies pass through their life cycles, but on a global scale things remain the same for ever. There will always be the same density of new galaxies rejuvenating the cosmos with activity and order.

The concept of movement without overall change is called a steady state, and this theory of continuous creation became known as the steady-state theory of cosmology. For many years it rivalled the big-bang model in popularity, largely because of its novelty and philosophical appeal. One of the least important objections to the theory was the problem of where the matter which continually appears in the universe comes from. This is a problem in any cosmological theory; in the big bang it is simply assumed to occur all at once at an initial singularity. It is not enough to appeal to the creation of matter by a process of conversion out of some other form of energy, such as that discussed in chapter 2 in connection with the primeval fireball, because the supply of energy would eventually run out. Instead a genuine injection of new matter and energy into the universe is necessary. Hoyle elaborated the theory in an attempt to give a proper mathematical and physical foundation to this mysterious creation process, by inventing a new type of field, called a creation- or C-field, which has the unusual feature that it contains negative energy. When this field is coupled to ordinary matter it becomes unstable to the production of new particles together with the enhancement of the negative energy C-field. By adjusting the strength of the coupling between the C-field and the matter, Hoyle could arrange for his hypothetical field to create matter at just the right rate. Energy would always be conserved in this process, because the C-field would accumulate progressively more negative energy as the matter acquired positive energy.

The rate of production of new matter is actually very low; far too low to be observable in action if spread uniformly throughout space. To replenish the galactic density at the rate necessary to compensate for the cosmological expansion, only one atom per century needs to be created in a volume of one cubic kilometre — quite beyond any known means of detection. Sometimes it was conjectured that matter is being created, not uniformly throughout all space, but densely concentrated in compact bodies such as quasars. In the original version of the theory the newly created matter was presumed to arrive in the form of hydrogen atoms spread uniformly throughout space, but with the discovery of dense, exploding astronomical objects, some of the adherents preferred the idea of special centres of creation, where huge amounts of energetic matter gush violently into the universe. The crucial feature is to inject low entropy matter into the universe so that although the total entropy in any expanding volume of space increases with time, the entropy in a fixed volume of space remains always the same.

There is no doubt that a model of the universe which has no beginning or end provided a strong emotional appeal to both scientists and public alike. The trouble with the model is that it makes very definite predictions about the large-scale features of the cosmos which do not seem to agree with observation. Firstly, according to the underlying principle of the theory, the global aspect of the universe should remain the same epoch by epoch, implying that as we look far out into space, and hence far back in time, things in those remote regions should appear much the same as in our own galactic neighbourhood. In the early 1960s astronomers began a number of systematic surveys of distant objects to check whether the universe really is in a steady state, or whether it is evolving with time. The surveys consisted of counting the numbers of radio sources as a function of epoch, back through time (i.e. out through space) to the limits of the equipment. The results dealt a blow to the steady-state idea because they unequivocally showed that there were more radio sources in the distant past than there are now, and this contradicts the principle that the large-scale features of the universe should remain unchanging with time.

In addition to the radio-source counts, other evidence began to mount against the steady-state theory. The discovery of quasars, the acronym for quasi-stellar radio sources — highly compact and energetic objects whose precise origin and properties are still unknown — provided another observational check. Because quasars are among the most distant objects known, they carry information about very early epochs of the universe, and observation reveals that they were much more numerous in the past than now. Nevertheless the really decisive blow to the steady-state theory came with the discovery by Penzias and Wilson of the universal background heat radiation, now widely assumed to be a relic from the big bang. There seems to be no place in the steady-state theory for the presence of this background radiation.

Apart from these objections based on observation, the steady-state theory would lead to some peculiar possibilities. If there was no beginning to the universe, there can be intelligent civilizations which are arbitrarily old. If these communities remain in one galaxy, they must be extremely rare, for the old galaxies will have receded so far apart that they can only populate the universe very sparsely. In this case the community is doomed when the domestic galaxy runs out of free energy in the usual way. It is hard to imagine that these ancient civilizations would not leave the dying galaxy and spread across the universe, moving into the new galaxies as soon as they formed and produced stable star systems. Although according to the big-bang model of the universe this technological feat would presumably be quite beyond the capabilities of any civilization at this time, the infinite time available in the steady-state theory forces one to take seriously the existence of civilizations somewhere in the universe which have unlimited technological expertise. Is there evidence of these incredibly advanced communities in our galaxy? Should we suppose that they are so advanced that we cannot distinguish their activity from nature itself? With the existence of technical communities of unlimited age, it is hard to see how the universe can avoid becoming a product of its own technology.

The cumulative effect of these objections has resulted in the abandonment of the steady-state idea by most astronomers and cosmologists. In spite of this, the underlying concepts of continuous creation and the spontaneous appearance of new order as a means of avoiding the death and perhaps the birth of the universe, remain important contributions to the debate about the nature of the world we inhabit.

A completely different theory, according to which the universe has neither beginning nor end, has been proposed on the basis of a disarmingly simple extension of the conventional big-bang model. The weakness of the conventional theory is the presence of a space-time singularity at the creation event. In chapter 2 we saw how the initial singularity has been taken by some to imply that the universe did not exist at all 'before' this moment. Similarly if the universe eventually recontracts, it will collapse to a final singularity in the future, the ultimate cosmic catastrophe where space, time and matter all pass out of existence to leave behind nothing at all, not even empty space. Whether or not this approach to space-time singularities is misconceived, it is clear that the known laws of physics must break down there, and no prediction can be continued through these temporal extremities.

Some astronomers and cosmologists have conjectured that a recontracting universe may survive its encounter with the future singularity and emerge, phoenix-like, from another primeval fireball to re-expand in a new cycle of activity. Furthermore, this process of expansion and recontraction could then be repeated *ad infinitum,* thereby endowing the universe with immortality. According to this picture, the big bang in our past is relegated to just the most recent restart of an endless chain of universes, in which the cosmos oscillates in a cyclic fashion between some distended maximum size, and highly dense, hot fireballs.

The major problem with such a cyclic model is how the singularities can be avoided. Several possibilities have been suggested, all of them conjectural. The first is that quantum effects operate at sufficiently high densities, an idea which was briefly discussed in chapter 2 in connection with the big bang. The quantization of gravity would, if we had a theory of it, provide a description of quantum space-time itself, in which fluctuations of geometry occur. When the density of matter is so high that the whole observable universe is compressed into a volume comparable to that of an atomic nucleus, then these space-time fluctuations may well be violent enough to disrupt the entire dynamics of the universe, thereby avoiding the appearance of a singularity and allowing space-time to continue to exist. A second proposal is that gravity might become repulsive rather than attractive at very high densities, because of the appearance of large negative energy or pressure in the universe.

Negative energy and pressure can arise in quantum processes, and behave in such a way as to gravitate repulsively, perhaps causing the universe to 'bounce' at a very high density instead of plunging on at ever-greater acceleration into catastrophic extinction. Finally, there is the possibility that although a singularity might form somewhere, it need not obliterate the whole universe. This would be the case if highly asymmetric motions occurred near the singularity, causing space-time to, roughly speaking, 'twist its way past' the singular barrier, and thereby avoid annihilation.

Although all this is purely conjectural, so little is known about the ultimate limits of gravity and space-time structure that the model of an oscillating cosmos has been at least considered as a serious possibility by a number of scientists. If other cycles of the universe exist, the pressing question arises as to what they are like. Do they resemble ours, with galaxies, stars and intelligent creatures to wonder about them, or could the universe bounce out of each fireball with a totally different structure altogether? According to one point of view, each cycle will be equipped with a new set of physical conditions — perhaps even new laws of physics — in a more or less random fashion, and if this is the case, then cycles like our own will be exceedingly rare.

One of the most profound questions about the nature of the universe we inhabit is why it is the way it is: why the galaxies and stars have the sizes they do, why there are ninety-two naturally occurring elements, why the proton is 1836 times heavier than the electron and not some other number, why the heat radiation from the big bang has the present value of three degrees and not three hundred, and so on. The laws of physics do not seem to determine the values of the physical quantities, or the sizes or numbers of things; nor do they determine the organization of the world. These features are apparently imposed on top of the physical laws with values which seem to have no particular significance. One attempt to explain the bewildering array of features and the apparently arbitrary arrangement of the physical world is to place the universe in the context of a cyclic cosmology, so that the actual numbers and values which we observe, and the arrangement and organization of the universe in our particular cycle, is treated as a purely random selection.

With the beginning of each cycle the universe is supposed to emerge from the fireball with a new set of fundamental values, and the particular numbers we observe now just happen to be the set that turned up this time. It is clear, however, that we could not observe values which differ greatly from the present ones because the existence of life in the universe is sensitive to these numbers. For example, if the electric force of attraction between the electrons and protons in an atom became too strong, then the electron orbits would be dragged inside the nucleus in a very complicated and muddled arrangement which would prevent the formation of stable molecular bonds. If chemistry becomes impossible, then it is hard to see how life could exist. Similarly if the nuclear forces were just a little stronger, then it would be possible for two protons to combine together, in spite of their electric repulsion. If this were the case, one of the protons would soon change to a neutron by emitting a positron and a neutrino, resulting in a deuterium nucleus. This transformation would make helium nucleo-synthesis by hydrogen burning a billion billion times more efficient, with the consequence that all the hydrogen in the universe would have been burned up in the primeval fireball, leaving none for the stars. Without stable stars burning hydrogen steadily for billions of years, life would almost certainly be impossible. Again on a cosmic scale, the global arrangement of matter and energy cannot be arbitrary. If, for example, the primeval heat were very much greater, no planets could exist with liquid water because this background radiation would become comparable with the heat from the sun. In the absence of free water it is doubtful if life could ever form.

If the existence of life depends on certain natural conditions being fulfilled, then we would not expect to observe a universe very different from the one we inhabit: put simply, the world we live in is the world we can live in. This is not an explanation of the natural features around us, only the observation that intelligent creatures could not be here to speculate about it if things were very different. On this view, nearly all the other cycles of the universe would be uninhabited, because the numbers and conditions would not come out right. This consistency between fundamental physics and cosmology on the one hand, and biology and observation by intelligent creatures on the other, is called the anthropic principle, and it implies that our own existence con-strains the structure and evolution of the universe, even on a very large scale.

Some people find the idea of a cyclic universe very appealing. There is still, of course, the question of entropy and the problem of the universe running down, but it turns out that this is sidestepped because of the peculiar nature of gravity. So long as the cyclic motions continue, then the universe cannot reach equilibrium: the cosmic expansion and recontraction continue to 'wind up' the system, and the entropy just goes on increasing.

A recontracting universe, however, is finite in size and, as Newton pointed out long ago, there is an inherent instability which prevents a finite gravitating universe from remaining static: it must always either expand or contract. Cosmic motion must, therefore, continue and the entropy will apparently rise without limit, leading to progressively hotter fireballs and longer and longer cycles. This implies a rather awkward paradox, because if there has been an infinite number of cycles preceding our own, then we would expect the universe to be very much hotter than it is. The heat energy from the primeval fireball is only equal to about all the heat emitted from the stars during just one cycle. Perhaps the paradox can be resolved by supposing that there really is a reprocessing of the cosmos at some sort of singularity in the fireball phase, and this simply changes the value of the entropy and the heat radiation. Unfortunately, in this whole subject area there are few constraints on conjecture, and so little is understood about the issues involved that all these ideas must be regarded as extremely speculative.

We now turn to a still more radical departure from conventional physics and question the very foundation of cosmic degeneration: the second law of thermodynamics. When the law was first discovered in the nineteenth century, the atomic theory of matter was not very well developed. Thermodynamic principles were deduced by experimenting with fluids and heat engines; in all cases, entropy was found to increase with time. By the middle of the century the British physicist James Clerk Maxwell was attempting to understand the atomic basis for the property of heat energy and heat transfer. It was known from studies of chemistry that atoms are very small and in rapid motion, so Maxwell set about examining the physical behaviour that would result from the cumulative motions of very large numbers of atoms. He considered a model of a flask of gas and assumed that the atoms all move according to Newton's laws. Being very small, an atom will move freely for most of the time, until encountering another atom, when they collide and change direction. The whole collection of atoms, which in a real flask would number perhaps a million billion billion, he assumed to be racing around chaotically. When the atoms of the gas collide with the walls of the container, they impart a tiny force; the average effect of vast numbers of these collisions is to produce a considerable pressure against the surface of the flask.

On the basis of this simple model, Maxwell could explain all the usual laws of gases. Heat was seen to be simply the energy of atomic motions. When the gas is heated up, the atoms move faster, a fact which was taken to explain why the pressure of a gas rises when heat is added — the atoms impact more vigorously against the container walls. Temperature is now known to be just a measure of the average atomic speeds, so that temperature also rises when heat is added. Moreover, by averaging over the atomic motions, Maxwell could calculate precise mathematical relationships which exist between quantities such as temperature and pressure and are known to be true for real gases.

Later in the nineteenth century, the Austrian physicist Ludwig Boltzmann set about finding an atomic theory of entropy in an effort to account for the second law of thermodynamics. Boltzmann realized that the growth of disorder in a gas was intimately related to the collisions between the atoms, so he analysed mathematically the effect of collisions in a model of a gas confined inside a rigid, impermeable container. The result was one of the great achievements of mathematical physics. He discovered a quantity that he called H, defined mathematically in terms of the atomic positions and motions and which, under the effect of interatomic collisions, always increases in magnitude. Clearly H is the atomic counterpart of thermodynamic entropy, thus opening up the way for a microscopic explanation of the enigmatic second law.

The way in which a gas progresses spontaneously from an ordered to a chaotic state is easily visualized. Imagine, for example, some perfume, placed in a bottle in one corner of a room, and the stopper removed. At that moment the perfume is in a very ordered condition, being confined to the bottle. Gradually, however, the molecules of perfume diffuse out of the bottle into the surrounding air, and eventually permeate the whole room. The perfume has then completely evaporated and is in a totally disordered condition. Moreover this is the equilibrium condition, because we would not expect any further change: maximum entropy corresponds to thermodynamic equilibrium.

We think of the change which the perfume has suffered as irreversible: there seems to be no way to get the perfume back in the bottle without some drastic interference with the contents of the room. The reason for the irreversible change lies in the chaotic molecular motions. The molecules of air surrounding the bottle are continually rushing about, knocking the perfume molecules randomly in every direction. It is easy to appreciate why, under the impact of this chaotic bombardment, the perfume eventually gets spread throughout the room. It is rather like a shuffling process, with each set of collisions acting as a reshuffle; just as shuffling a pack of cards is a deliberate procedure for disintegrating the orderly organization of the suits, so the molecular collisions destroy the order of the perfume vapour. The same sort of reasoning may be applied to all increases in entropy, including the diffusion of the drops of dye through a volume of water discussed in chapter 6, a process easily explained by the impact of water molecules. The flow of heat from a hot body to a cold body — the original statement of the second law of thermodynamics — can be visualized as the progressive communication of the vigorous atomic motions from the hot body to the less energetic and slower moving atoms of the cold body, through the action of billions of individual impacts.

No sooner had Boltzmann discovered his famous H theorem of irreversible change under the effect of random collisions than there appeared a devastating and far-reaching objection which caused puzzlement and controversy over the century of debate which followed. The basic objection is as simple as it is paradoxical. The laws of motion which both Maxwell and Boltzmann applied to their model gases relied heavily on the laws of Newtonian mechanics to describe the molecular motions. These laws do not distinguish between past and future, or one direction of time and another; they are equally valid both ways. How was it then possible for Boltzmann, using molecular motions which were individually reversible, to prove that a collection of molecules moved irreversibly? Every pattern of collisions, every reshuffling of the molecular configurations must, on Newtonian principles, be reversible. Why then do real systems only evolve one way in time? Why is it that perfume molecules do not find their way back into perfume bottles spontaneously?

The nature of the paradox can be understood more easily by a simple thought experiment. If attention is focused on a particular atom moving on a straight path in a space between other atoms, it will eventually be seen to meet a neighbouring atom which obstructs its path, and the resulting collision causes the atoms to rebound off each other along new paths. A closer look reveals that the atoms are not hard lumps, but they exert forces outside their boundaries; the two atoms therefore do not really interpenetrate or touch in the usual sense, and in any case they are very insubstantial. Instead their paths curve gradually away from each other as they approach, and their direction of motion is altered without actual contact.

Now imagine that two microscopic demons come along with cricket bats and position themselves along the trajectories of the two deflected atoms. At a prearranged moment they both strike the atoms back in the direction from which they have come, reversing their motions exactly. The result is that the two atoms collide once more, but in the reverse direction, and travel backwards along the curved trajectories which they took during the original impact, to end up in their original situation. If the demons arrive in force in the room full of perfumed air, and administer a few billion billion simultaneous swipes, all of the perfume molecules must bounce backwards, in reversed sequence, through all the billions of individual collisions which had dispersed them from the vicinity of the bottle, for if every atomic motion is reversed, the air and perfume gases must reverse their behaviour *in toto*. Thus the perfume ends up back in the bottle. Why, then, do we always encounter things changing one way in time, when their reverses are also possible?

The resolution of the paradox comes from a consideration of the reshuffling analogy. If a real pack of cards is placed in suit order and then shuffled at random, we would not expect it to end up in suit order, or in some other highly ordered arrangement, such as numerical order. Instead, we would expect the shuffling process to destroy the orderly arrangement and produce a chaotic sequence, in accordance with the general principle of increase in entropy. A moment's thought, however, reveals that the probability of shuffling into, rather than from, suit order is not quite zero. A pack of five consecutive cards, say, if shuffled for a few minutes, will almost inevitably end up at some moment in numerical sequence. As the number of cards is increased, so is the time required before continuous shuffling produces an orderly sequence. For a whole pack of cards one could easily shuffle for a lifetime without producing the required suit order, but eventually this arrangement would occur and indeed, if the shuffling continues, any arrangement which one likes to name will eventually occur infinitely many times, so long as the shuffling process is completely random. For most of the time the pack would be very disordered, with no special overall arrangement. Occasionally small fluctuations would occur to produce three or four cards in numerical sequence, but the arrangement would soon disappear again. Larger fluctuations would be much more rare, and a highly remote chance arrangement, such as complete suit order, would be astronomically rare — though not impossible. Very rare fluctuations we regard as miracles, and certainly the shuffling of a pack of cards into perfect suit order would be regarded as miraculous, though in fact it is merely exceedingly improbable.

The essential features of the card-shuffling experiment are that all sequences recur again and again after enormous durations; and the highly ordered sequences are overwhelmingly more rare than the less ordered ones. We could regard the disordered condition of the pack which occurs nearly all the time as being the equilibrium situation because, unless we were to watch very closely, we might well think that the card sequences would never be ordered again. A more careful examination, however, would reveal many small fluctuations, causing minor orderliness to appear, as well as some very rare highly ordered arrangements.

If we apply this analysis to the molecules of a gas, identifying entropy with disorder, and the gas molecules with the cards, it is clear that there is a small but finite probability that the entropy of the gas can decrease, and the second law of thermodynamics be violated or reversed, given enough time. With a million billion billion molecules, however, the chances of this happening are overwhelmingly less than with a pack of fifty-two cards. Even if we waited for the entire lifetime of the universe, we would have a negligible chance of seeing the perfume retreat into the bottle. Nevertheless it would happen after long enough — so long, in fact, that the duration could not be written out even by covering the whole Earth in noughts and measuring time in millennia. Miracles can happen in physics, but they are more rare than we could ever conceive.

In spite of this, we can see minor fluctuations of the spontaneous appearance of order actually at work in a gas. An interesting phenomenon called Brownian motion enables the chance alignments of a few molecular motions to be observed through a microscope. If a small piece of dust is placed in a gas it may happen that a chance arrangement of molecular motions in its vicinity causes a slightly unequal bombardment of the different faces of the dust particle's surface. The effect is to cause the particle to jump erratically and zig-zag about in the gas.

But the effect decreases sharply with the numbers of molecules involved (i.e. the size of the particle). We would not expect a brick to jump about under molecular bombardment, even though the combined energy of impact of the air molecules around the brick is more than enough to hurl it across a room. It is simply too improbable that a chance organization of molecules would just happen to cause the molecules on one side of the brick to retreat from it in unison for a moment, while the other side continued to receive bombardment.

The fact that all systems will eventually return to orderly states again and again resolves the paradox surrounding Boltzmann's theorem. There is complete time symmetry in thermodynamics if only we wait long enough. We are still left with the problem of why we always observe things changing in the same direction in time; for example, why perfume always evaporates away while the reverse is never seen. This problem is dealt with by asking how the perfume got into the bottle in the first place. It did not get there by some miraculous fluctuation from equilibrium, instead somebody put it there. That is, the orderly arrangement which we begin with is created in some way by outside interference. In a truly isolated system, perfume could only get in a bottle by one of those overwhelmingly unlikely fluctuations.

The origin of the outside interference can be traced back to cosmology. As we cannot get outside the universe, for an explanation of the initial orderliness we must consider the creation of the universe. In chapter 6 we saw how the present cosmic organization was achieved by the 'winding up' process caused by the cosmological expansion in the primeval phase. It is this cosmic motion which is the ultimate source of 'interference' producing all the order and structural arrangement we now observe, and whose decay will mark the collapse of the cosmos.

The atomic basis of the entropy law does suggest a number of possible ways to avoid cosmic disintegration. Let us first dispose of an abortive idea which was actually suggested by Boltzmann himself. As discussed above, it is possible for an isolated system to undergo spontaneous, self-organizing fluctuations on very rare occasions. Could it be, Boltzmann speculated, that the order in the universe which we observe is just the result of one of these unimaginably rare miracles from a more enduring chaotic state? Such an explanation supposes that the universe is infinitely old, and for the overwhelming majority of the time exists in a state of thermodynamic equilibrium, with a uniform temperature and no structured arrangement or macroscopic organization of matter and energy.

The time required for random rearrangements to produce the presently observed cosmic order is almost inconceivably long; it could not be written out as a number on a sheet of paper as big as the whole observable universe. Nevertheless Boltzmann supposed that eventually it would happen that all the heat, light and matter spread throughout space would spontaneously converge to form hot stars. The universe we now see is regarded as simply that gigantic fluctuation unwinding itself. The reason that we are privileged to witness such a rare occurrence is precisely because we need the thermodynamic disequilibrium thereby produced in order to exist — the anthropic principle again. But that is not all; when the present organization has run down, and the cosmos has returned to its more probable equilibrium state of chaos, it will not really be the end of all activity, because after a further wait of enormous duration, another random rearrangement will occur to create another ordered universe, and so on, *ad infinitum.*

Contained in this bizarre reasoning is the expectation that after a colossal number of different universes were produced this way at random, the time would eventually come when the next fluctuation would produce an almost identical copy of the universe that we see now, complete with the sun, Earth, Empire State Building and the reader! Of course, before a world indistinguishable from our own had been recreated, an almost limitless number of 'near-misses' would first occur, some without the Empire State Building, even more without Africa, and many many more without the Earth at all. The reason for this is that fluctuations which produce conditions only roughly the same as now, whilst staggeringly rare, are nevertheless exceedingly more frequent than more accurate copies. For every additional little speck of dust to be reconstituted correctly, billions upon billions of already unbelievably rare fluctuations would have occurred. Nevertheless however horrendously large the numbers involved, we are assured, on the basis of elementary probability and physics, to be reincarnated an infinity of times.

When Boltzmann stated these remarkable conclusions, scientists believed that the universe was globally static and unlimited in age. It is now known that there is cosmological expansion and a big bang. If the primeval fireball is taken to be the creation of the universe, there has simply been no time for miraculous fluctuations to occur. Quite apart from this, there is a very real objection to the explanation of world order in terms of a chance arrangement. Elementary probability shows that it is overwhelmingly more likely that only one galaxy would be produced this way rather than two, or that two is the total rather than ten, say. Consequently every time we increase the power of our telescopes, Boltzmann's theory would predict that more galaxies would almost certainly not be seen.

Nobody now believes that the world order was achieved at random, and the status of the recurrences in an expanding universe, which also allows matter to disappear for good down black holes, is not at all clear. It is more probable for a large enough group of atoms to fluctuate, purely by random collective motions, into a black hole, than into, say, a star cluster. Once inside the event horizon, all that is returned to the outside world is the evaporation radiation discovered by Hawking.

One of the central assumptions behind the second law of thermodynamics, and the existence of 'miraculous' recurrences of ordered states, is the randomness of the atomic motions. It is through random reshuffling that order disintegrates into chaos, disequilibrium decays into equilibrium, and organized structure is destroyed. It is the randomness which also ensures that once equilibrium and chaos have been established, they will be perpetuated almost indefinitely. It was also this randomness which led Boltzmann to predict that microscopic rearrangements will eventually reconstitute the universe, but ensures that this will not happen for an 'almost infinite' amount of time.

The randomness of microscopic motions is the basis of the second law and hence of cosmic disintegration. Is it correct? In everyday life, things often appear to be without form or arrangement when viewed in one way, but on closer inspection are seen to possess 'hidden order'. A coded message is one example discussed on page 107: a seemingly random jumble of letters, to the initiated it becomes an intelligent signal with a high information content and low entropy. A hologram is another example: what appears at a casual glance to be a structureless glass plate is reorganized into a detailed picture when laser beams are reflected from it.

When information is folded up in something else, it can be extremely difficult to see. The physicist David Bohn has discussed an experiment in which blobs of dye are placed in treacle (they could be arranged to contain a simple message). The treacle is then stirred up a few times with a rigidly mounted mechanical spoon, which draws the blobs out in thin threads, winding them about in an apparently haphazard fashion, so that soon the whole material appears a uniform colour. In this condition we cannot see the information content of the dye, but it is still there, folded up in the treacle, for if the spoon is counter-rotated, the wispy threads will be compressed and drawn back into the blob shapes from which they originated.

It is impossible for us to be sure that there is no folded up order or information in the universe. We cannot say whether or not the universe began at the big bang with random microscopic motions, or whether there is a hidden arrangement between atoms — a cooperative move-ment of all the tiny particles and waves that is too complicated for us to notice. If such a conspiracy were correct, and all the atoms in the universe were moving in a prearranged pattern to a common end, then cosmic collapse need not occur.

Some years ago the astronomer Thomas Gold, whose fertile imagina-tion helped invent the steady-state theory, proposed that just such an atomic conspiracy was afoot. If the microscopic motions are not random, then the second law of thermodynamics can be violated, not after the usual enormous durations, but at any time. We do not have to wait for an incredibly rare chance fluctuation to occur, because the reshuffling is no longer random, but organized. Order can appear out of chaos right away, simply because the atomic motions have been set up to contrive a collective, cooperative, self-organizing pattern of be-haviour. To many people Gold's universe appears to be nothing short of miraculous, although in fact he suggests nothing which contradicts the laws of physics.

Gold supposes that we live in a big-bang universe which eventually will recontract, organized in such a way at the microscopic level that at the outset of the recontracting phase, the above-mentioned 'miracles' start to take place. When the galaxies begin to approach one another rather than recede, the second law of thermodynamics is reversed. Instead of order giving way to chaos, disordered equilibrium states begin to order themselves and give rise to structured arrangements. For example, heat and light spread out in the cold depths of space would start to flow of their own accord into the stars. Heat would travel from cold objects into hot ones, so that cold objects would get colder and hot ones hotter. The stars would appear as little black dots in the sky, because instead of radiating heat and light, they would be busily soaking it up from their colder environments. Inside the stars this supply of heat and light would migrate slowly to the cores, combining cooperatively with other heat and light on the way, and on reaching the central regions the combined heat and light would set about converting helium back into hydrogen again.

On a planet such as the Earth, things would be very strange indeed. Instead of melting in warm water, blocks of ice would grow larger and emit heat, which would boil the remaining water away. People, instead of growing older, would grow younger, as their body metabolisms were reversed, and their cells gave up energy which would travel by a circuitous pre-arranged route, back into the sun. Every year the mountains would become a little smoother as rivers ran uphill from the sea, were dispersed up the hillside, depositing microscopic particles of dust on the jagged rock faces, and then rose in rain droplets to the clouds. Fallen buildings would rearrange themselves into ordered states, as all the atoms in the bricks collectively imparted upward motions to carry the various materials into their proper places.

This whole scenario seems at first sight to be an extreme flight of scientific fancy, but what is being described here is actually no more remarkable than what we are now observing around us. Indeed, it is what we do observe, but described in reversed-time language. What Gold proposes is that, in a sense, time is reversed during the cosmic recontraction. Strictly speaking, time cannot reverse, because it is not moving: it is really just a measure of change and movement. The choice of words is only a linguistic convenience; what actually happens is that all physical processes undergo reversal in comparison with the original time order. As these processes include the human brain, it is clear that an observer in the recontracting phase of the universe would not notice anything unusual happening. He would be thinking 'backwards' as well as seeing 'backwards'. Indeed he would regard us — rather than himself — as inhabiting the recontracting phase, and consider that it was our processes that were running 'backwards' in time. What we would call the big-bang creation of the universe, he would call the end — the final collapse; and what we call the end, he regards as the beginning. Whether or not we think of this time-symmetric arrangement as averting cosmic catastrophe is really a matter of taste. The lifetime of the universe is still finite, but there is no end — only two beginnings!

Needless to say, most scientists do not really expect this peculiar symmetry to exist, although some eminent cosmologists and astronomers have supported the idea actively. Some of them have questioned whether we would notice anything about the universe now which suggests that it is likely to reverse itself at some future time. One consequence of reversed-time inhabitants in our future is that they could send us messages. The trouble is that their information is our entropy (and vice versa), and so we could not really communicate properly with each other. Any message we receive, we should regard as being our message sent to them — reception becomes transmission — and this of course raises all sorts of paradoxes about free will.

Not only can messages cross between the two halves, but so can starlight. As far as we are concerned, their atoms absorb energy when excited, but our atoms emit it. In their half of the universe, radio waves converge on to transmitters and boost the power supply, in ours the power source is drained as energy flows out of the transmitter and away into space. What happens to this energy when it reaches the time-reversed phase? Is it absorbed, or enhanced? These are difficult questions, and at least one experiment has been performed to test out the ideas involved. The underlying reasoning behind the experiment is, roughly speaking, that if electromagnetism gets reversed in the far future, the effect of this on the power drain from a radio transmitter might be detectable now. This could be interpreted in another way as the reception of time-reversed radio waves from the future. Either way the effect should show up in a transmitter beamed into outer space. The experiment was performed by the American astronomer R. B. Partridge in 1973, but produced negative results.

Some of the deep problems of consistency in a time-reversing universe are alleviated by preventing coherent signals from travelling between the two temporal halves. This would be the case in a cyclic universe which separated the two time phases by a dense fireball stage. In this model the universe expands and collapses, with all processes continuing in the same time direction, entropy increasing and so on, then bounces out into another cycle of expansion and recontraction, but emerges from the dividing fireball with the direction of all the processes reversed in time in comparison with the first cycle. One could conjecture that with each new cycle there would be a new time direction.

A time-reversing two-cycle model raises an intriguing new possibility. What we regard as the end of the next (time-reversed) cycle, is regarded by observers of that cycle to be the beginning. If this beginning happened to be identical to the time-reverse of our own big bang, then the two events could be identified. In other words, instead of time continuing indefinitely, or until a singularity is encountered, we now conjecture that it is closed into a loop. If time is 'circular' then the universe is forced to get itself back into its original condition once again. In such a world there is no beginning or end, although time itself is finite in extent.

One casualty of the circular time universe is free will, for if our future is also our past, then we cannot change the world around us in an arbitrary fashion. Cause and effect become inextricably interwoven, and only self-consistent patterns of activity are allowed. Nevertheless because of the complexity of the world, and the scrambling which occurs during the fireball phases, it is doubtful if we would ever notice such lack of free will.

Science is a fast-moving subject, and the scientific conception of the cosmos has changed radically over the last few centuries. It may well change again. New laws of physics no doubt await our discovery, new concepts and ideas that could remould the entire intellectual framework on which our present judgments about creation, evolution and cosmic collapse are based. The role of man as an intellectual observer and as an active force for restructuring the world through technology could easily shift in perspective in the coming centuries.

What, then, is our present perspective? Very few scientists are prepared to accept the bizarre proposition of cosmic time-reversal. The steady-state theory, with its compelling feature of endless evolution, has crumbled under the pressure of astronomical observation. The cyclic world of death and rebirth is still just a speculative outgrowth of our ignorance about the nature of spacetime singularities. The unpalatable truth appears to be that the inexorable disintegration of the universe as we know it seems assured, the organization which sustains all ordered activity, from men to galaxies, is slowly but inevitably running down, and may even be overtaken by total gravitational collapse into oblivion.

Index

Index

A selection of books published by Penguin is listed on the following pages.

For a complete list of books available from Penguin in the United States, write to Dept. DG, Penguin Books, 299 Murray Hill Parkway, East Rutherford, New Jersey 07073.

Nigel Calder

THE WEATHER MACHINE
How Our Weather Works and Why It Is Changing

Something has been happening to the weather of late! Indeed, recent lost harvests, famine, and drought in the tropics clearly indicate a change in the world's climate—generally a change for the worse. In reporting on current efforts to understand why our weather—a powerful machine of air, water, and ice that is kept in continual motion—should shift gears now, Nigel Calder takes us to the outposts of meteorological science around the world. Here, in plain language, are the latest ideas about how storms work, how oceans generate spells of peculiar weather, and the way volcanoes, changes in the sun, and variations in the earth's orbit can all alter the climate.

VIOLENT UNIVERSE
An Eyewitness Account of the New Astronomy

Unimaginable violence in the far reaches of space, solar storms, the bombardment of earth by neutrinos, the strange whispers picked up by radio telescopes, the big-bang and steady-state theories of cosmology, the birthdays and possible doomsdays of the earth, the sun, other stars, the galaxy, and the mighty universe itself—these are the elements of astronomy today. This succinct, superbly written book is a miracle of compression and a thrilling vade mecum for man's efforts to draw a new and more vivid picture of the universe we inhabit.

Nigel Calder

THE RESTLESS EARTH
A Report on the New Geology

In the late 1960s a group of young earth scientists advanced a bold new theory of the earth which has since revolutionized their field and given us a new story of the earth's history. In this thorough and remarkable book, the result of research and filming in sixteen countries in preparation for a ninety-minute television special, Nigel Calder tells the story, based on the theory of plate tectonics. Earthquakes, volcanoes, and mountain ranges are all connected to a single, comprehensive process—the movement of huge plates that are said to make up the earth's outer shell. Calder explores all the phases and studies of this theory, which for the first time has enabled man to tell not only *what* has happened to his planet but also *how* it happened. In this book, we can, as Calder puts it, "rediscover the earth."

SPACESHIPS OF THE MIND

"The human world, past and future, is shaped by constant pressure from the imagination and ambition of individuals who have 'big ideas.'" It is Nigel Calder's belief that the "big ideas" of today revolve around the colonization of space. In this beautifully illustrated, easily understandable book, Calder reports on the findings and predictions of scientists who see life in space as possible, desirable, and probably inevitable. Talking to pioneer scientists such as Theodore Taylor, Freeman Dyson, Gerard O'Neill, John Todd, James Lovelock, and many others who are now pathfinders for the generations to come, Calder provides us with a fascinating and eloquent survey of the thinking being done around the world about mankind's future on earth and in space. The ideas introduced range from self-perpetuating space factories and spheres to harness the sun's energies to plans to populate the Milky Way and new ways to breed plants and humans.

Nigel Calder

THE KEY TO THE UNIVERSE
A Report on the New Physics

Grappling with the most challenging questions in the universe, to-day's scientists are coming up with answers that only a short time ago would have seemed bizarre, even impossible. Now "quarks" are beginning to be seen as the principal constituents of creation. Success has crowned the frantic search for "naked charm." The "big bang" at last is heard, studied, understood. Even "black holes," bottomless pits of gravity scattered through the cosmos, are coming into focus on the basis of rapidly accumulating evidence from X-ray satellites and radio telescopes. The goal of all this activity is the detection of a law that will account for the tiniest subatomic particles as well as the farthest edges of infinity. Guiding us through secret laboratories where giant machines send probing rays into the depths of space, Nigel Calder has written a book free of technical jargon and alive with the spirit of personal discovery. *The Key to the Universe* leaves us with a dizzying sense of awe for the new horizons of knowledge we face. "Nothing purely terrestrial can approach in excitement the awesome, accelerating drama of cosmology—the study of the universe. . . . Mr. Calder's fine text and diagrams go as far as possible in conveying what all this means to those of us who cannot read the mathematical language"—*Wall Street Journal*. "Nigel Calder is a brilliant explicator, able to make the abstruse absorbing"—*Boston Globe*.

Bob Glover and Jack Shepherd

THE RUNNER'S HANDBOOK
A Complete Fitness Guide for Men and Women on the Run

Here is the indispensable guide, with the (simple) secrets of success, for all runners and would-be runners. Bob Glover's Run-Easy Method adapts to beginners of all ages but will also benefit those at intermediate and more advanced levels. A veteran marathoner, Glover includes advice on competing in races up to and beyond the full 26.2-mile marathon distance, and he clarifies the sometimes confusing training methods and diets. He and Jack Shepherd discuss the fine points of running style, stretching exercises and weight training, selecting shoes and other equipment, preparing for weather and road conditions, and avoiding injury when you can and coping with it when you can't (Glover claims firsthand knowledge of almost every injury that can strike a runner!). They take a quick look at the new field of running and meditation and a longer look at the effects of running on the heart and lungs—information and advice garnered from many of the country's top running doctors. A guide to running spaces in more than twenty-five major American cities is also included.

David Pelham

THE PENGUIN BOOK OF KITES

The kite is now enjoying a world revival that has partly to do with its functional beauty, partly with its paradoxical quality of providing exercise *and* relaxation to both mind and body. This book is a comprehensive and thoroughly illustrated introduction to kites and kiting, covering in detail their history, their construction, and their flying. It contrasts the highly decorative models of the East with the more functional and aerodynamically efficient Western types. Over one hundred detailed and tested kite patterns are included, with all the information required to build kites.

Dr. Frank Ryan

SWIMMING SKILLS
Freestyle, Butterfly, Backstroke, Breaststroke

With swimming more popular now than ever before, Dr. Frank Ryan brings his acclaimed expertise in sports technique to the four competitive strokes: freestyle, backstroke, breaststroke, and the strenuous and spectacular butterfly stroke. The emphasis is on those methods of physical and mental conditioning that not only make world champions but also make the rest of us go through the water a little faster. Dr. Ryan details the mechanics of achieving form, power, speed, and endurance. His book, illustrated with many photographs and diagrams, unites the latest and most innovative theories with the experience and concern of the successful coach.

WEIGHT TRAINING

Weight training, as opposed to weight lifting, is an invaluable aid in preparing for almost every sport. The goal of weight training is to develop coordinated power—the ability of a muscle, group of muscles, or the body itself to go farther or longer, run faster or harder, jump higher or wider. Stressing the need for safety and protection from injuries, acclaimed sports expert Dr. Frank Ryan covers each step in the process of physical development and coordination through exercise with weights and shows how this process can lead to athletic excellence.

Edited by Stewart Brand
SPACE COLONIES

Here, from the people who brought us *The Whole Earth Catalog*, is a fascinating compilation of material on space colonies, some of it new and some selected from *The CoEvolution Quarterly*. Included are items on the history of the idea of space colonies, which began at Princeton in 1969; material by and about Gerard O'Neill, originator of the idea; comments by Ken Kesey, Lewis Mumford, Paul Ehrlich, Richard Brautigan, Carl Sagan, Buckminster Fuller, and many more; reviews of related books; information on space sailing; and pictures and drawings.

Garrett Hardin
EXPLORING NEW ETHICS FOR SURVIVAL
The Voyage of the Spaceship *Beagle*

This unusual and important book combines an ingenious appraisal of what man must do in order to survive on earth with the imaginary story of a spaceship's fantastic journey. Garrett Hardin sees the source of the current ecological crisis in the excessive demands that too many individuals make on limited resources. His unique approach covers population control, pollution control, agricultural reforms, and problems of private property as it shows what far-reaching changes we must bring about in politics, economics, and ethics. Weaving in and out of these ideas is the story of the spaceship *Beagle* and of the incredible worlds its crew encounters during an exciting voyage.

William W. Warner

BEAUTIFUL SWIMMERS
Watermen, Crabs and the Chesapeake Bay

Written in the tradition of Rachel Carson's *Edge of the Sea,* this
book is not only a complete natural history of the pugnacious,
succulent Atlantic blue crab; it is also a colorful report on the
Chesapeake Bay (which provides more crabs for human consumption than any other body of water in the world) and on the frank-
talking watermen who make their living in the crab's pursuit.
Chronicling the seasons of the crabber's year (from autumn of one
year to the uproarious Labor Day Crab Derby of the next) and
superbly illustrated with drawings by Consuelo Hanks, *Beautiful
Swimmers* is sure to delight general readers and naturalists alike.
Beautiful Swimmers won the 1977 Pulitzer Prize.

Lewis Thomas

THE LIVES OF A CELL
Notes of a Biology Watcher

This book, winner of the National Book Award, is subtitled *Notes
of a Biology Watcher*—yet it takes us far beyond the usual limits of
biological science and into a vast and wondrous world of hidden
relationships. Computers, germs, language, music, death, insects,
and medicine are just some of the topics touched on in this bold
and subtle vision of humankind and the world around us. Indeed,
the complex interdependence of all things is the book's provocative
theme. Lewis Thomas writes: "Once you have become permanently
startled, as I am, by the realization that we are a social species, you
tend to keep an eye out for pieces of evidence that this is, by and
large, a good thing for us."

John Boyd

THE LAST STARSHIP FROM EARTH

Mathematicians must not write poetry—above all, they must not marry poets, decrees the state. But Haldane IV, mathematician, and Helix, poet, are in love. They are also puzzled, for they have been studying the long-hidden poetry of Fairweather I, acknowledged as the greatest mathematician since Albert Einstein. As they explore further, the danger for them grows; the state has eyes and ears everywhere. Will they find, before it is too late, the real meaning of the following words by Fairweather I? "That he who loses wins the race, / That parallel lines all meet in space." "Terrific . . . it belongs on the same shelf with *1984* and *Brave New World*"—Robert A. Heinlein.

THE POLLINATORS OF EDEN

The coldly beautiful Dr. Freda Caron has waited too long for her fiancé, Paul Theaston, to return from Flora, the flower planet. Determined to learn what has happened, she begins a study of plants from Flora, and slowly she is warmed by her communion with them. Eventually, she makes the trip from Earth to Flora for further research and to see Paul. What she finds is the secret of the flower planet, but in her initiation she too becomes a pollinator of Eden.

THE RAKEHELLS OF HEAVEN

In the future there will be colonial imperialism—in space! Two space scouts, John Adams and Kevin O'Hara, are sent to explore a distant world called Harlech. The Interplanetary Colonial Authority prohibits human colonization and control of those planets whose inhabitants closely resemble *Homo sapiens,* as the Harlechians do. Thus, relations with their women are strictly forbidden. But such rules were not made for Red O'Hara. From the Adams-O'Hara Probe, only John Adams returns. . . .

Anthony Chandor with John Graham and Robin Williamson

THE PENGUIN DICTIONARY OF COMPUTERS
Second Edition

This is a glossary of some three thousand words, phrases, and acronyms used in connection with computers. It has been designed to assist both technical readers and the increasing number of nonspecialists whose work is to some extent affected by a computer. The entries are interspersed with seventy general articles that cover, more fully, the major computer topics and such business processes as "budgetary control" and "systems analysis," which are more and more being handled by computers.

E. B. Uvarov, D. R. Chapman, and Alan Isaacs

THE PENGUIN DICTIONARY OF SCIENCE
Fourth Edition

This latest edition of *The Penguin Dictionary of Science* has been completely revised and now gives all numerical information in SI units, which are fully defined. Many new words, like *fluidics, holography, mascons, polywater, pulsars,* and the key words in computer terminology are explained simply and accurately. Apart from this new material, the reader will find reliable definitions and clear explanations of the basic terms used in astronomy, chemistry, mathematics, and physics, with a smattering of the words used in biochemistry, biophysics, and molecular biology. This volume provides an up-to-date guide to the numerous scientific and technical words that are increasingly coming into everyday life.

Also:
THE NEW PENGUIN DICTIONARY OF ELECTRONICS
THE PENGUIN DICTIONARY OF BIOLOGY
THE PENGUIN DICTIONARY OF PHYSICS